The HONORABLE SCOUNDRELS

THE SERIES

SOPHIE BARNES

THE HONORABLE SCOUNDRELS

Copyright © 2017 by Sophie Barnes

All rights reserved. Except for use in any review, the reproduction or utilization of this work in whole or in part in any form by any electronic, mechanical or other means, now known or hereinafter invented, including xerography, photocopying and recording, or in any information storage or retrieval system, is forbidden without the written permission of the publisher.

This is a work of fiction. Names, characters, places and incidents are either the product of the author's imagination or are used fictitiously, and any resemblance to actual persons, living or dead, business establishments, events or locales is entirely coincidental.

Printed in the USA.

Cover Design and Interior Format
© THE KILLION GROUP, INC.

ALSO BY SOPHIE BARNES

NOVELS
Christmas At Thorncliff Manor
A Most Unlikely Duke
His Scandalous Kiss
The Earl's Complete Surrender
Lady Sarah's Sinful Desires
The Danger in Tempting an Earl
The Scandal in Kissing an Heir
The Trouble with Being a Duke
The Secret Life of Lady Lucinda
There's Something About Lady Mary
Lady Alexandra's Excellent Adventure
How Miss Rutherford Got Her Groove Back

NOVELLAS
The Governess Who Captured His Heart
The Earl Who Loved Her
The Duke Who Came To Town
Mistletoe Magic (from Five Golden Rings: A Christmas Collection)

THE GOVERNESS WHO CAPTURED HIS HEART

CHAPTER ONE

LOWERING THE LETTER SHE'D BEEN reading, Louise Potter held the expensive sheet of paper between her fingers and glanced at both of her sisters in turn. "I have been accepted for the position. Lady Channing would like me to start immediately."

"That is what you wish to do, is it not?" Josephine asked. At six and twenty, she was two years older than Louise and six years older than their youngest sister, Eve.

"It certainly is a welcome opportunity." With the townhouse serving as their only inheritance, and Josephine working hard to make ends meet for all of them, Louise wanted to find a way to help her older sister. As a result, she now had the chance of becoming a governess to three young children. "My only regret is I shall miss Christmas with the two of you."

"Perhaps the countess will allow you to see us on that particular day?" Eve suggested.

Louise bit her lip. Her employment would require a major move, which was something she hadn't yet mentioned to either of her sisters. "I'm afraid not. If I'm lucky, I shall be able to come to Town during the spring and part of the summer while the Season is underway. Otherwise, most of my time will be spent near Whitehaven."

Her sisters stared at her. "I forget where that is," Eve finally said.

"I believe it is in the north," Josephine told her.

Louise nodded. "It is indeed."

Eve's mouth dropped open. "But then we shall never see you again!"

"As I mentioned, I might return to Town once Parliament opens and the Radcliffe family chooses to relocate to their London home." She paused to consider their unhappy faces. "Unless I decline the offer and remain here. I can do so if you are loath to see me go."

"No." Josephine quickly smiled, though the effort did appear slightly strenuous. "You have been given the chance to accept respectable employment with a highly regarded aristocratic family. Neither of us will stand in your way."

"Are you certain?" Louise was beginning to doubt her own resolve.

Travelling north had seemed like a grand adventure until she'd told her sisters about it. They'd never been apart before, and since their father's death, they'd been especially dependent upon each other, not only to get through the grief, but also to find a way forward in the following whirlwind of chaos.

Louise's grandfather had been the third son of an earl. As such, he'd gone into law and had eventually, upon his death, left his thriving practice to his son. But he had not been as skilled a barrister as his father, nor did he have a head for the business. After he lost a string of cases, clients had chosen to seek counsel elsewhere. As time had progressed and the funds had dwindled, the larger houses had been sold and the meeker residence where Louise and her sisters now lived had been purchased instead. But even this house would be lost to Louise and her sisters unless a decent income could be secured. Especially since their uncle, the current Earl of Priorsbridge, had neglected to take on his responsibility as their guardian.

"This is a wonderful opportunity for you," Josephine said. Meeting Louise's gaze, she did not need to say the money her work would produce could ease their concerns. Instead, she asked a practical question. "When do you intend to leave?"

"Tomorrow." Knowing how surprising this comment was, Louise hastened to say, "The countess has offered conveyance if I do. It seems her uncle, Lord Alistair, will be travelling up then as well, so it has been suggested we go together for practical reasons."

"I suppose doing so would provide you with a better carriage for such a long journey," Josephine said. "But is it wise for you to travel alone with a man whom you've never met before?"

Louise made a face. "At my age?" She shook her head. "You know as well as I that I am almost as firmly on the shelf as you are. And since I am not a young lady with marriageable prospects but rather a soon to-be-governess, I dare say no one will think much about it. Not to mention this uncle must be at least fifty years old considering the countess's age."

"How can you possibly know her age?" Eve asked. "It doesn't seem like the sort of thing she would share in her letter to you."

"Quite right," Louise told her, "but her eldest son is eleven, so I can make an intelligent guess."

"I suppose that is true," Josephine murmured. "Which means you're probably right about Lord Alistair. Besides, I doubt the countess would suggest his escort unless she was sure you'd be safe in his presence."

Louise agreed. "It is settled then?"

"I believe so." Josephine said.

Her remark propelled Louise to hug both her sisters. She then hurried on through to her room and pulled her valise out from under the bed. It was time for her to start packing.

☙

Enjoying a last minute brandy in his study, Alistair Clay Hedgewick, considered his niece's request to bring her new governess with him to Whitehaven. He groaned at the prospect of it– of having to spend a week with a middle-aged spinster instead of alone in his own company as he'd been expecting. Dreading it, he took another sip of his drink. It was a bit early in the day to be imbibing, but under the circumstances he felt he needed the fortification before setting out in another half hour.

He glanced toward the clock on the fireplace mantle. An hour had passed since he'd sent his carriage to collect her, so she should be arriving at any moment. A knock sounded at the door, and

Alistair called for his butler to enter.

"My lord," Mr. Fox said while maids and footmen scurried around behind him, gathering last minute items in need of packing. "Miss Potter has arrived. Would you like me to show her in?"

Alistair considered the question. He could hardly say no, could he? It was tempting since doing so would allow him that extra half hour of peace before embarking on a journey that would force him to stay on his best behavior. Taking his shoes off and relaxing his feet would not be possible. Nor would sleeping, since he had no desire to snore in her presence. In fact, he was giving up a great deal of comfort for a woman he'd never met and did not care about.

"Very well," he sighed, before downing the rest of his drink and rising. He might as well meet his travelling companion, he reasoned, since it was the polite thing to do. Like it or not, he always strove to do what was right and play the part of the well-mannered gentleman, no matter how impractical or aggravating it could be. His behavior, however, reflected not only on him but on his entire family, and being called to task by his brother was something he always tried to avoid.

Mr. Fox returned. "Miss Potter," he said, before stepping aside so a slim woman, wearing a grey gown and a matching pelisse, could enter. On her head, she wore a straw bonnet beneath which he was able to spy a golden display of neatly combed hair. But what shocked him the most was her face, because it did not belong to the middle-aged, rotund matron he'd envisioned, but rather to the angelic youthfulness of a woman in her prime.

More than that, she was the perfect picture of beauty, her delicate features lending an elegance even the highest ranking ladies of society lacked. Her eyes, he noted, were a bright glow of hazel while her lips, parting now with undeniable surprise, were the sort men dreamed of in their wickedest fantasies.

Aware he was staring, he gathered his wits, schooled his features, and stepped toward her. "Miss Potter, it is a pleasure to make your acquaintance."

She gaped at him. "Are you Lord Alistair?"

"The one and only."

She shook her head. "You can't be." Glancing around as if seeking another gentleman, she gradually returned her gaze to him when none was to be found. "You…you…" Waving her hands as if hoping to fashion the necessary words, she finally blurted, "You are twenty years younger than you ought to be!"

☾

Clamping her mouth shut, Louise stared at the man who stood before her. He was not the older gentleman she'd anticipated. Instead he was young, about a head taller than she, and solidly built, judging from his stance. His face, constructed from angular planes, contained a pair of serious eyes, a patrician nose, and a mouth set in a firm line. Whether or not the last feature was capable of smiling had yet to be determined.

"You are not who I expected either, Miss Potter," he said, boldly allowing himself to assess her.

She didn't like the nervous quickening of her pulse or how her insides squirmed with discomfort. Determined to fight it, she raised her chin and squared her shoulders. "How do you mean?"

He drew a breath and appeared to consider. "I assumed you to be in your forties and in possession of a plump figure. All the governesses I have ever seen have been like that. Apparently, that opinion is misguided. You do not fit the image I have of governesses at all."

"I do not know if I should be flattered or insulted," Louise confessed.

His eyes widened with a distinct look of surprise. "How can you think my comment was anything but a compliment?"

"Because you appear to be judging me solely on my appearance."

"Naturally." His tone was dry. He paused as if wondering what to say next, then asked, "What else would you have me judge you on?"

She stared at him. What a typical male thing to ask. It was no different than the sort of comments she'd gotten from her father as a young girl. As well-meaning as he'd been, she'd resented the insinuation that she would do well in life because she was pretty. Which prompted her to say, "My mental faculties for a start."

His lips twitched as if he found her statement amusing, which made her want to hit him right there in the middle of his own study. But then he spoke. "While I may be more capable of judging you on such a fine attribute now, after we've had a brief exchange of words, I certainly wasn't at the time when I made my remark."

Acknowledging her mistake, she gave a tight smile. "Forgive me, my lord. It was not my intention to sound ungrateful."

"And yet you managed to do so anyway," he murmured, making her want to hit him all over again.

The man was not only arrogant but infuriating, and she was meant to spend several days with him in a carriage? She would rather enjoy the company of rodents and was contemplating saying so – or something equivalent but less rude – when the butler returned. "Your carriage is ready, my lord."

"Thank you, Mr. Fox," Lord Alistair said. He cast a contemplative glance at Louise before telling the butler, "I'd like you to ask one of the housemaids to join us."

Louise almost sighed with relief.

The butler dipped his head. "Understood." He then turned on his heel and strode from the room.

Considering Lord Alistair, Louise wondered if he might be dreading their journey as much as she was. But he gave her no reason to suppose such a thing. Instead, his expression remained inscrutable as he gestured toward the door. "After you, Miss Potter," he said. "I believe we had best be on our way."

☾

Alistair knew the sort of woman she was. He was familiar with her type – the type of woman who wanted to be admired for her brain rather than her beauty. The countess was the same way, but unlike Miss Potter, Abigail had good reason to demand such admiration since she'd written several renowned books on the principals of mathematics.

Miss Potter, on the other hand, had yet to prove herself worthy. For as he'd suggested, looks was all he'd really had to assess her by so far. It was much too soon to determine whether or not she was simply a pretty face or if there was actually a sharp mind behind those hazel eyes of hers. Considering her stalwart manner, he suspected there might be more to her than he imagined.

At any rate, she would probably prove to be better company than the sort of woman he'd been expecting, even if he still wouldn't be able to take off his shoes or sleep in her presence. One thing was certain, she would be easy on the eyes even if she elected not to speak with him for the duration of their journey. A possibility, judging from her determination to admire the view from the window.

They'd left London without exchanging another word. A muttered, "Thank you," was all he'd received upon helping her into the landau. Then nothing for the next half hour. And since Bridget, the maid who'd been chosen to act as chaperone, had nodded asleep almost instantly, Alistair could not rely on her for conversation either.

Which brought them to this point.

Discreetly, he considered Miss Potter's profile, which was not so easy to do because of her bonnet. With her face turned away from him as it was, the brim concealed most of her face and all of her hair. A shame, since he would have liked to study those golden tresses more closely.

"It will be at least five hours before we arrive at the first posting inn," he told her.

Starting as if surprised to hear him speak, she turned away from the window, those hazel eyes of hers meeting his from beneath her long lashes. "I suspected as much," she said.

Ignoring her rigid tone, he relaxed against the squabs and stretched out his legs. "Feel free to make yourself comfortable. You can take off your bonnet, if you like. Nobody would fault you for doing so."

She seemed to consider this suggestion which had been equal parts selfish and considerate. Forcing a blank expression, he held his breath in anticipation of what she might do. Her eyes slid toward the spot on the bench where he'd placed his own hat and gloves. A frown puckered her forehead, and he instantly knew what was going on in her head. She wanted to take off her bonnet, perhaps even her gloves, but she worried doing so would remove a shield – break down a necessary barrier between them – and perhaps… No. He would not allow his thoughts to wander in that direction. Still, he found himself praying she would surrender to comfort and sate his damnable curiosity.

After a moment, she returned her gaze to the window. Her hands remained in her lap, and Alistair felt a peculiar pang of disappointment. Not that he would allow it to bother him. She was only a woman after all – perhaps the most delectable one he'd ever seen – but a woman nonetheless.

She was not worth thinking about for any

extensive length of time.

He had other, more important, matters to consider. Perhaps he ought to set his mind to them instead of wondering about Miss Potter's hair. Reminding himself she was nothing more than an inconvenient obligation, he prepared to reach for his satchel and pull out his newspaper, when a movement at the corner of his eye caught his attention.

Glancing toward her, he noted her hands had risen to the bow at her chin where her fingers now carefully tugged at the ends, loosening it with a slow pull that made Alistair's mouth go dry.

Never in his life would he have presumed a bow might be untied so sensually or that he would ever consider the act of doing so arousing. But he did, damn it. His entire body responded, forcing him to cross his legs and straighten in his seat. Then she carefully plucked the bonnet off her head, and as she did so, it took every bit of willpower he possessed to stop himself from staring. Because her hair was indeed as glorious as he had imagined it– more so even – for it wasn't blonde alone, but streaked with silky strands of honey, gleaming in response to the light coming in through the window.

His only regret was how it was tied back in a tight knot at the nape of her neck. Because now that he'd seen it, he wanted to know its length and how it might look spilling over her shoulders. And once he knew this, he'd probably want something else – something far more dangerous than simply taking a look at her hair.

"Feel free to remove your gloves as well, if you

like," he said as he bent to retrieve his newspaper.

He would not look at her any more – not directly at least – lest she worry about being trapped for a week with a man she'd be wise to steer clear of. Honestly, he would have to have a word with Abigail once he saw her. Neglecting to inform him of Miss Potter's young age had been a careless omission on her part. It had also resulted in a twenty minute delay while Bridget packed a bag and prepared herself for departure.

"Thank you," Miss Potter said – the first words she'd spoken to him since climbing into the carriage. She made no effort to do as he suggested, but she did, much to his surprise, continue talking. "I am sorry if I seemed defensive earlier. It was not my intention."

Drawn by the hushed sound of her voice, Alistair allowed his eyes to meet hers. A mistake, since he found himself thoroughly transfixed by their color. To say they were hazel was far too simple. They were a brilliant shade of green at the center, surrounded by warm tones of toffee. Years of practice allowed him to maintain his serious demeanor and not reveal the physical torment which he was starting to suffer. Only two hours in her presence and his gentlemanly ways were being severely tested. It did not bode well for the remainder of their journey.

"Then what was your intention, Miss Potter?"

Her lips parted on the precipice of speech, but then she appeared to force back whatever remark she'd been meaning to make, paused for a second, and finally said, "Beauty can be a blessing as well as a curse. It has always been assumed I would get by on my looks — that men would flock to my door after taking one glimpse and then promptly offer me marriage."

"Most women would be glad if they were so fortunate."

"Perhaps," she conceded. "But in my case, circumstance got in the way. I found myself in a situation where a pretty face would not suffice. Fortunately, my mother, bless her heart, always strove to prepare my sisters and me for such a possibility. She was a practical woman. So while our father insisted there was no need for anything more than basic lessons, Mama demanded proficiency in mathematics, science, literature and French. And because our father doted on her, he allowed it, affording us all an education we can now use to our best advantage."

He took a moment to consider this forthright statement. "You speak of both parents in the past tense." Noting the way her eyes shifted, he quietly said, "I take it they are no longer with you?"

She gave a tight nod. "We lost Mama four years ago. Papa passed last summer."

Which explained her dull attire. "I am sorry to hear it."

A weak smile was her only response, and then, as if seeking a different topic, she quickly asked, "How is it you are as young as you are? Lady Channing referred to you as her uncle, so I rather assumed you were going to be a bit older."

"Yes. You did make that quite clear the moment we met."

Blushing, she glanced at him timidly from beneath her lashes. It impacted him in the strangest of ways. "Forgive me. It was terribly rude of me to respond as I did. I'm afraid surprise got the better of me."

She wasn't the only one, he reflected. "The fact is, my father was thirty years old when my brother, the current Duke of Langley, was born. His mother died in childbirth, and our father remarried, to a woman who bore him no children. After her death, our father married his third wife. By then he was in his fifty-seventh year, while his wife, my mother, was a widow twenty-five years his junior. Hence, there are twenty-eight years between my brother and me since I was born a year after the wedding. Indeed I am closer in age to my niece, Lady Channing, who is only three years younger than I."

"How strange," Miss Potter murmured. "I cannot imagine what that might be like. You're practically an only child."

He couldn't deny it. "The duke has been more of a parent to me than a brother. I was only ten when Papa died."

What he would not say was how much the death had affected him. His father had doted on him, perhaps because he'd been the spare he'd been trying to have for two full decades. There was also the possibility his father had tried to avoid the mistakes he felt he'd made when raising his brother. From what Alistair gathered, little love had been given to the current Duke of Langley. Everything had been about duty and discipline. So when Papa died and Langley stepped in and took his place, Alistair's carefree childhood had come to a grinding halt.

"I am sorry to hear it," Miss Potter said, capturing his attention. "No child should have to lose their parent at such a young age."

Appreciating the sympathy but disliking the mood their discussion had led to, he nodded, then turned his attention back to the newspaper he'd brought along for the ride. Opening it, he set his mind to finding a new investment opportunity – something that would save him from bending to Langley's will.

*

Hoping she managed to do so discreetly, Louise considered Lord Alistair while he read the crisp newspaper he held. His brow was knit in serious contemplation, his eyes skimming the pages with intense interest. Turning a page with a rustle, he leaned slightly forward as if studying part of the text in greater detail.

Being a relatively large man, he seemed to fill the carriage with his presence. The space had felt even smaller when he'd been looking at her. Thankfully, he'd stopped doing so now, allowing the fluttery feel in her belly to settle into something much calmer and more relaxed. His dark perusal invariably made her tighten up inside. It bothered her to no end that she couldn't discern what he was thinking. To do so was impossible when he kept the inner workings of his mind carefully masked behind layers of strict severity. What shocked her most, perhaps, was her reaction to this, for it made her want to shake some emotion out of him. Of course, doing so would likely result in the termination of her employment before it even began.

As she watched him, a dark lock of hair fell across his brow. It made him appear more carefree somehow, even if his expression did no such thing. Flexing her fingers, she fought the urge to reach out and force the errant hair back into place. To do so would be scandalous – completely and utterly shocking.

With this in mind, she drew the blanket he'd given her at the onset of their journey tighter across her lap. As concerned as she'd been about travelling with him after their initial meeting, she had begun to warm to the idea of sharing his company.

For one thing, it was a chance in a lifetime, because being confined to a small space with the best looking man in England was not the sort of thing that was likely to happen ever again. For another, she would not be alone with him. Even if the maid who'd joined them slept the entire way to Whitehaven, her presence ensured propriety would be maintained.

So why worry? Rather, Louise decided she might as well spend the next few days admiring Lord Alistair's perfect figure, the breadth of his shoulders, and how perfectly his well-tailored clothes hugged him in all the right places. This was a rare treat she'd been given, and she'd be a fool not to take advantage.

So she sat back and let her gaze wander up the length of his legs and across his thighs. He turned another page, and she studied the movement, admiring the size of his hands. They were so much larger than hers, though elegant in their own right as they carefully held the newspaper.

Sliding her gaze upward, she took in the leanness of his chest. Many men would have a belly protruding when sitting down, but he did not. Rather, his jacket sat completely flat against his torso, which rather intrigued her. Continuing up over his chest, she reached his shoulders and then the side of his neck where a few fine tufts of hair curled right beneath his earlobe.

"You're staring at me," he murmured.

Louise's heart slammed against her chest and her gaze shot toward his. He was studying her with those dark eyes that revealed nothing of what he was thinking, but they did produce a rush of heat that instantly made her think of flinging herself from the carriage if only to escape her own embarrassment.

CHAPTER TWO

HE'D CAUGHT HER. THE THRILL of it could not be denied. Nor could the wicked sensations rolling through him as he allowed himself to consider the purpose behind her intense scrutiny. And it had been intense. He'd sensed it long before he'd accused her.

"I, er…" She fumbled with her words, her eyes darting about, looking everywhere but at him.

"Yes?" He couldn't help himself. Her discomfort was far too amusing for him to relent.

Puffing out a breath, she waved her hands as if they might conjure the necessary excuse. Eventually, she surprised him by saying, "Very well, you caught me."

Staring at her, he had no choice but to admire her honesty when most women would have denied it to perdition. "Very well?" He was obviously at a loss for words.

She raised both eyebrows and stared him down, incredible female. "I never had a Season," she said as if that explained everything.

Confounded, he folded the newspaper, set it aside on the bench, and gave her his full attention.

"How does that factor in?"

A shrug was her first response. But then she added, "Most of the men I have known have either been family or indistinct. You are neither."

He could feel a persistent tug at the corners of his mouth. Surrendering to it, he smiled, aware she was staring once more. "That would make me distinctive, Miss Potter."

"Yes, well." She waved her hand as if trying to brush his comment aside. "There it is."

"Hmm." He wasn't about to let her get off so easily. "Would you care to elaborate?"

"I beg your pardon?" Her horrified expression made him smile even more.

Heaven help him, he was being awful, enjoying himself at her expense. "In what ways do you find me distinctive?" he asked.

For a long second, she simply sat there looking back at him as if she failed to comprehend the question. She pressed her lips together, and he watched her eyes harden with resolve. When she spoke again, it took every bit of restraint he possessed not to howl with laughter. "In case you're not aware, you aren't exactly hideous. In fact, I might even say you are pleasing to look at."

"And so, considering my un-hideousness, you found yourself staring."

"Of course," she said, surprising him once again with her frankness. "The realization was so astonishing, I could hardly help myself."

He did laugh then, long and hard and with an abandon he hadn't allowed in years. It made Bridget stir enough for him to choke back the rest of the sound before continuing in a whisper. "Good lord, Miss Potter. I'm beginning to see why my niece chose to hire you. That tongue of yours is certain to set her children straight."

"Why thank you, my lord. I *will* take *that* as a compliment." And with that remark, she leaned back in her corner of the carriage and closed her eyes.

The deep inhalations that followed a few minutes later confirmed she'd fallen asleep. What shocked Alistair most about this realization was the disappointment he felt at having to forego further conversation with her at present. Last night, when Abigail's letter had arrived informing him that he was to bring Miss Potter with him, he could not have been more displeased. Now, he anticipated her waking up again so they could resume their repartee.

Which made him wonder if there might be something wrong with him, since he really ought to be grateful for the reprieve she offered by choosing to sleep. It gave him the time he needed to focus on finding a way out from underneath Langley's boot. It also meant he did not have to make an effort to entertain her as he'd been loath to do before setting out. But with each passing mile, he found himself glancing over at her with increasing frequency. Discovering she was pretty to look at was one thing. Learning she was a capable sparring partner was quite another.

☾

Enjoying a pleasant dream in which she danced at a glittering ball, Louise did not appreciate being shaken awake. "Go away," she murmured, trying to retreat from the hand squeezing her shoulder.

"I'm afraid I cannot do so."

The low baritone made her eyes snap open to find Lord Alistair's face within inches of her own. "What?" Her voice was a squeak. She shifted in her seat, and he finally leaned back, though not without allowing her to inhale his scent. A rich smell of musk and bergamot wafted past her defenses, assaulting her with their delicious aroma. The effect it had on her was one she would rather not consider at the moment, lest she do something highly regrettable, like lean toward him and inhale more deeply.

Thankfully, she wasn't given the chance to do so as he moved back to his own seat, snatched up her bonnet, and handed it to her. "We've arrived at the first posting inn." He glanced at Bridget who promptly sneezed. Lord Alistair frowned. "I hope you're not getting ill."

"No, my lord." Bridget sniffled a little. "I am perfectly well."

His frown deepened, but rather than question the maid any further, he said. "Very well then. If you'll both accompany me inside, someone will show you to your rooms so you can freshen up before supper. You'll be with the other servants, Bridget, but close enough to Miss Potter to offer assistance, should she need it."

The decisive manner in which he spoke was sobering. It reminded Louise that there was a purpose to this journey and that it did not involve her losing her head over a duke's brother, no matter how sinfully handsome the duke's brother happened to be. So she gave him a nod, waited for him to exit the carriage, then allowed him to help her down first. She was far too practical to care about the way in which his fingers curled around her hand or the fact that he offered her his arm once she and Bridget were both on the ground. To do so would be silly, daft, and completely senseless. And yet a part of her – that feminine part yearning for romance – could not quite help but bask in the whole experience.

The basking came to a swift halt, however, when her bag was carried in and Lord Alistair handed her and Bridget over to a servant, who promptly marched them upstairs and down a narrow corridor to their respective bedrooms. Once alone, Louise set down her bonnet, then took a moment to appreciate the crisp linens dressing the bed and the water waiting for her on the washstand. A stack of clean towels sat beside it, drawing her closer. Splashing cool water onto her hands, she washed her face, savoring the soothing effect it had on her skin.

Crossing to the window, she glanced out, expecting to find a view of the English countryside. Instead, a courtyard where the arriving carriages were being parked filled her vision. Lord Alistair's landau was there as well, but it wasn't the carriage that caught her attention so much as the man who appeared to be helping the grooms with the horses. In spite of the cold, Lord Alistair had taken off his jacket and rolled up his shirt sleeves. He was unhitching one of the horses. The impatient animal whinnied, tossing its head until Lord Alistair grabbed hold of the reins and led it swiftly away from the carriage and toward the stables. A few minutes passed before he returned. Moving toward the next horse, he reached up and stroked its muzzle, then led it away as well.

Remaining by the window, Louise puzzled over this curious effort on Lord Alistair's part. As far as she knew, aristocrats never lowered themselves to doing common chores. And since he did have a coachman, she found his action intriguing. One thing was certain – he was gradually proving to be something more than she'd first thought him capable of being. And as she watched him return to the courtyard with a sure stride and address his coachman, she couldn't help but appreciate the line he seemed to walk between employer and friend, for although his stance suggested authority, his mannerisms made it clear that was able to enjoy an easy discussion with the driver. Her father had not had this skill, she reflected. He'd always kept the servants at a distance, and whenever he'd addressed them, it had been in a stern and overbearing tone.

She was still considering this when Lord Alistair suddenly turned and, as if sensing her, looked up. Their eyes met for a fraction of a second before she spun away, removing herself from view. Which was silly, really. Why should she care if he spotted her at the window?

Because he knows you were looking at him.

Just as she'd done in the carriage. She lowered her face to the palms of her hands. Lord help her, she had to stop letting this man whom she scarcely knew fill up her head. Nothing good could possibly come of it.

When Miss Potter arrived in the private dining room he'd secured for them, Alistair did his best to aim for casual politeness. Which was no easy task after catching her by the window earlier. She'd been staring at him again – something he would do well to ignore. She was, he reminded himself, going to be in Abigail's employ. If this alone, coupled with Bridget's presence, was not enough to deter him from making advances, Miss Potter's innocence was. And she *was* an innocent. He knew it as well as he knew his own name, and he would be damned if he was going to take advantage of that.

Rising to greet her, he paused to reflect on the fact that she was alone. "Will Bridget not be joining us?"

"I recommended she stay in her room and rest. That sneeze in the carriage was only the first. Looks like she's caught a serious chill."

"That doesn't bode well." He moved to pull out her chair, but as she stepped in front of him, he drew a breath and instantly froze in response to the sweet aroma of jasmine clinging to her hair or her skin or wherever it was that it clung. It was like elixir to his senses, suffusing him with a sudden desire to press his nose against her and inhale more deeply. And with that notion, he felt himself stir with sudden arousal. It was worse than it had been in the carriage, forcing him to clamp his jaw shut and grip the chair while he waited for her to lower herself to the seat.

Pausing, he wondered how best to return to

his own chair without drawing attention to the inconvenient reaction he was having to her. "Are those sheep?" he asked, pointing toward the window.

She turned to look, allowing him the chance he needed to circumvent the table and sit down across from her. "It's a bit dark to tell, but yes," she said. "I believe they are."

Nodding, he breathed a sigh of relief. "I thought so." He lowered his gaze to the piece of paper comprising the menu. "Are you hungry?"

"For sheep?"

When he glanced back up, her eyes were sparkling with mischief. She was teasing him, and he found he rather liked it. "I'm sure we can have one of them brought in on a platter," he offered in an equally nonchalant tone.

"Thank you, but I think I'll have the roasted chicken and mashed potatoes instead."

"A commendable choice. I'll have the same," he said. "And to drink?"

This question stumped her, judging from her baffled appearance. "I don't really know. Perhaps you can recommend something?"

"Let's enjoy some red wine then."

Agreeing with his decision, she waited for him to place the order, then leaned forward and asked, "Do you always help your servants with their tasks?"

Taken aback by the question, Alistair met her curious gaze. "I must confess that I find your question surprising."

She tilted her head. "Why?"

"Because of what it implies."

Blushing, she averted her gaze, and for a second he was sure she would shirk from the topic, but then she said, "You know I was watching you, my lord. Denying it seems rather silly."

"I suppose it does." He didn't think such a factor would deter most young ladies from pretending they'd been admiring the scenery instead. There was no doubt in his mind they would rather lie than admit to spying on him. But not Miss Potter. She was different in ways he not only liked but admired. "In answer to your question, I don't enjoy idleness. If I can lend a hand, I do. Especially when it comes to my horses."

Hesitantly, she raised her gaze to his once more. "I find that commendable."

He wasn't sure why that pleased him as much as it did, but he felt his chest puff out a bit in response. "Thank you, Miss Potter."

The wine arrived and he filled their glasses, then clinked his with hers and took a sip. Watching as she set the rim to her lips, he held his breath while she drank. The tendons in her throat flexed to accommodate the liquid. It was a mesmerizing sight from which he could scarcely look away. And yet he did precisely that before she became aware of *his* perusal for a change. He would have to get his growing desire for her under control somehow. Especially since he'd only met her that morning. It really didn't do for him react so strongly, least of all when he would spend seven more days in her company. If his attraction toward her continued to grow at a constant rate, he'd turn into a lust-crazed lothario before they reached Whitehaven, and then where would they be?

So he forced himself to think of something to talk about — something to take his mind off her silky hair, her dazzling eyes, and her kissable lips. Christ, he was even beginning to find her grey, long-sleeved dress with its high collar alluring. It made him wonder what she might look like beneath.

Feeling himself respond to her closeness once more, he took another sip of his wine. "Have you always wanted to be a governess?" he asked.

She gave him a peculiar look. "I don't think it's the sort of position any woman aspires toward. It certainly wasn't for me."

"So you would rather do something else?"

Her eyes widened a fraction, and she hastily said, "You mustn't misunderstand me, my lord. I am extremely happy your niece deemed me worthy of being in her employ, and I do look forward to teaching her children. But it is also a job I've been forced to take out of necessity, not one I dreamt of having when I was a girl."

"What did you dream of then?" He knew they would delve into personal territory if she answered his question, but he could not help himself from asking it. She intrigued him in ways no one had ever intrigued him before, perhaps because it surprised him that a woman in possession of Miss Potter's beauty and grace had not yet married. He would have to inquire about her reasons for that as well if he wanted to sate his curiosity completely.

A soft smile teased her lips in a way that lent a nostalgic element to her expression. "Of traveling the world and exploring new and wonderful places. I dreamt of writing a book and getting it published and even of studying literature at university."

"You are aware that women do not attend university?"

Nodding, she said, "These were my dreams, and in my dreams, anything was possible, even that."

"What sort of book did you think of writing?" He chose to focus on the least impossible dream.

"An adventure novel in which a young woman travels the world exploring new and wonderful places."

He grinned, as did she. "You would live out the life denied you by writing about it."

"In a sense."

The food arrived, and he waited until the serving girl had left them alone once more before saying, "If you'd married, you might have had the chance to travel abroad. I have no doubt your husband would have accommodated such a wish."

"Perhaps." A distinct touch of sadness clung to her voice. "But after Mama passed, marriage became impossible."

"Why?" He simply had to know.

But rather than answer, she shook her head and focused her attention on cutting her food. "Might we talk about something else? I find this subject incredibly depressing."

And personal.

She didn't have to say he'd dug too deep. That much was implied in the way she spoke and the stiffness of her comportment. "Of course." He tried to hide his disappointment beneath a casual tone. "I could tell you about Whitehaven instead so you know what to expect. Geoffrey, Henry, and Jack are wonderful children, but they are boys, so getting into mischief is an inevitability for them."

"I hope I can be the disciplinarian they need me to be," she said as she stuck a piece of chicken in her mouth. "So they won't run completely wild."

"I doubt that will happen," he said. "You stood up to me without any trouble, proving you have an exemplary backbone. Considering your looks – and this is a compliment lest you think otherwise – they will probably be smitten the moment you walk in the door."

Her blush turned her whole face a lovely shade of pink, and although he sensed she found it uncomfortable, he didn't regret his comment one bit. On the contrary, he enjoyed how easily she responded to his flattery.

"This may surprise you, but I find your remark about my backbone more pleasing than the one about my looks. It pertains to my character, and that is something I can take some credit for, while the other was merely a lucky coincidence."

Chuckling, he ate his mashed potatoes and chicken while pondering how rare this woman was that she simply refused to be admired for her beauty. Her explanation made perfect sense, although it wasn't something he'd ever considered before she'd pointed it out.

With this in mind, he chose to focus more on her intellectual capabilities, but before he could do so, she asked, "Is it terribly grand, the Channing estate?"

"It is large, to be sure, and it is also quite ancient. But Lady Channing has given the building a comfortable touch, so I'm sure you will feel at home there."

"Do you think she and I will get along?"

"Certainly." He could tell by her careful phrasing and the softness with which she spoke that she was nervous. "You needn't worry. She and her husband are good people – kind people – the sort who will do what they can to make you feel welcome."

Expelling a breath, Miss Potter nodded. "Thank you for putting my mind at ease. It has been a great many years since I've last ventured into high society."

That comment gave him pause. Why would a soon-to-be-governess – a member of the working class – ever have mingled with the peerage? Unless… "Are you gentry?"

She went completely still, her fork hovering between her plate and her mouth. Then she finished the action of eating, followed her bite of chicken with a swallow of wine, and afforded him with the most pointed look he'd ever received. "Does it matter?"

"I'd say so." For one thing, it made her more untouchable if she were, and for another, "You should be seeking a husband, not going off to work."

That hardened her expression. "My lord, I am four and twenty, so I dare say the time for finding a husband has passed. And as far as working is concerned, it is necessary, not shameful."

"But—"

"My path has been determined. Finding fault with it will serve no purpose at this point, so please stop trying to do so."

"I am merely attempting to understand you," he said, but the dubious look on her face suggested she didn't believe him. Which prompted him to say, "Even you must admit how unusual it is for a young lady of good breeding to take on such a position." In fact, he believed it might be unheard of, but chose not to say so as this was clearly a prickly subject for her.

"Perhaps," she conceded, "but one does what one must, my lord. Seeking employment as a governess in a respectable household is, in my opinion, better than the alternative."

"Which would be?"

"None of your business."

And on that note she clamped her mouth shut, bowed her head, and gave all her attention to her meal.

Alistair dropped his gaze to his own plate, then set his knife and fork aside. He'd pressed her until she'd put up a wall, and he'd lost his appetite. "You're right," he said, and he meant it. "You asked me twice already to leave the matter alone and I refused. Please forgive me for being so insensitive. My only intention was to try and understand you."

Blowing out a deep breath, she looked up, her eyes – filled with tortured pain and regret – touched his heart in a way nothing else ever had. "Why?" Before he could answer, she said, "You and I have only just met, and while circumstance has forced us to share each other's company on our way to Whitehaven, our acquaintance will come to an end upon our arrival there. My position demands it, since governesses do not socialize with their employers or their employers' friends and family. Instead, they take their meals alone and keep to themselves whenever they're not busy caring for the children."

"I know." He did not like it, but he was well aware that once their journey was over, he would only catch rare glimpses of Miss Potter during his stay. And then he would return home and not see her at all until his next visit. "So you see no point in getting to know each other better."

"As diverting as I find our conversation since it does make the passage of time more bearable, the subject you wish to discuss is one that will force me to open up in ways I've no desire to do with someone who doesn't care about me."

"You make me sound like an unfeeling cad."

She gave him a sharp look. "You know what I mean."

Regrettably, he did. Her past was a painful one, and to speak of it would make her feel vulnerable. She did not want to take such a risk with him – a man she could not even call a friend yet – one of higher rank who might find reason to judge her.

Deciding in that moment to avoid any further prying, he turned their conversation back to something safer and asked her about her favorite authors. This led to an entertaining debate – one which made him regret the moment when she asked about the time and said she ought to retire. Knowing she had a point, however, since they would set out early the following morning, he escorted her out of the dining room and through to the stairs.

"After you," he said, since the stairwell was much too narrow to let them walk side by side. So he followed her up, unable to ignore the gentle sway of her hips while she walked or the wild imaginings such a perusal provoked. All he had to do was reach out and she would be there. His fingers itched at the idea of doing precisely that – of allowing himself to feel the body she hid beneath layers of unflattering wool.

By the time they reached her room, his blood was pumping fast through his veins. She opened the door, allowing him a glimpse of her bed – the bed where she would soon be lying – and he felt himself tremble in response to this particular fantasy as lust took control of his body. It took every ounce of self-control he possessed not to push her inside, follow her through, and shut the door firmly behind them.

Instead, he stepped back, drew a deep breath, and bid her goodnight. He then turned on his heel and strode away, wondering how the bloody hell he was going to survive seven days in her company when he was barely able to get through one.

CHAPTER THREE

UNFORTUNATELY, WHEN LOUISE WENT IN search of Bridget the following morning, she found the poor maid huddled beneath her bed sheets and trembling with fever. "Is it already time to leave?" Bridget asked, punctuating her question with a wet cough.

She looked worse now than she had the previous evening. After saying good night to Lord Alistair, Louise had left her room and gone to check on the maid. Her face had been flushed but she'd assured Louise that a good night's rest was all she required, but she'd clearly been mistaken about that.

"We're supposed to depart in half an hour," Louise said, handing Bridget a handkerchief.

Blowing her nose, Bridget nodded. "I'll be right down."

Louise frowned. She really shouldn't suggest this, but demanding a woman with influenza endure a week-long carriage ride when she'd be far better off in bed prompted her to say, "I think you ought to remain here." She also had no desire to catch the affliction and pass it on to the Channings.

"Oh no, Miss. I can't do that." Bridget tried to sit but promptly collapsed onto the mattress with a groan. "You'll have no chaperone. It wouldn't be proper."

Louise was keenly aware of the fact. "I am well aware, but you are not in any condition to travel and we cannot delay our journey. Lady Channing expects our arrival." She hesitated, perturbed by the only logical option yet quite intent on being practical. "And Lord Alistair *is* a gentleman."

"Yes, but for you to be alone with him in the carriage is inadvisable."

"I'll be fine," Louise said, hoping to dispel not only the maid's concerns but her own as well. "You obviously can't travel in this condition, and we cannot wait for you to recover. All things considered, it will be best for you to remain here until you are fully recuperated." She had no idea how Lord Alistair would respond to her making such a decision, but it seemed like the reasonable thing to suggest.

As it turned out, he fully agreed. So they left the inn after he ensured enough funds were left to support Bridget's continued stay and her subsequent return to London.

Two hours passed. Although they spoke amicably of their various interests, Louise regretted the comment she'd made the previous evening. In an effort to respect her wishes, Lord Alistair had refrained from asking personal questions and had shared nothing special about himself, either. And while she knew she ought to appreciate this, she now felt as though a ravine had been wedged between them. It strained the atmosphere and turned it into a stilted awkwardness that grated on her nerves.

"I think I made a mistake," she finally said, when the fourth hour rolled around, and they'd exhausted their opinions on fashion, their thoughts on art, and their views on the British landscape and agricultural industry.

He frowned. "How so?"

She drew a deep breath. "I've ruined what promised to be an enjoyable journey and turned it into something from which I'm sure you now wish to escape."

A gruff sound made her wonder if he agreed, but then he said, "Nothing could be further from the truth. The fact is, I like you. More than I imagined I would. And if you will set your preconceived ideas aside for a minute, I would like to say that I never turn my back on my friends. No matter what."

"I wasn't implying you would." She was suddenly horrified by the possibility that she might have insulted him.

"Yes, you did. I know I didn't comment at the time, but I intend to do so now since you've opened the topic." Leaning forward, he braced his elbows on his knees while peering into her face. His eyes held hers so confidently, she was prevented from looking away. Instead, a tiny thrill of something unknown ignited inside her, the intensity of it tightening her belly and prompting her heart to beat faster. "You may be taking on the role of governess, but you will be doing so in an unconventional household. Mark my word when I say you will become fast friends with the countess, and I myself would never in a million years be able to ignore you."

Swallowing this assurance, Louise dug her fingers into the bench on which she sat. For reasons she could not begin to imagine, he'd made her skin prick with awareness, her insides quiver with a strange sort of anticipation, and her mouth go completely dry. And all he'd implied was that he'd be her friend. But the way in which he'd said it while subjecting her to a most intense stare left her feeling a bit out of breath.

"It is kind of you to say so, but—"

"Kindness has little to do with it, Miss Potter." He must have perceived the puzzlement she felt since he chose to clarify. "I am a man and you are an extremely attractive woman. Ignoring you would be out of the question."

Her heart made a funny leap and heat surged inside her. She'd known he found her pretty – beautiful even – for he'd told her so plainly enough. What she hadn't considered was a possible attraction – the sort that wasn't based on looks alone but on need and desire. She felt it now as he held her gaze. It hummed through her body, tickling her senses, heightening her awareness, and forcing a longing upon her she'd never felt before.

"I…"

Words failed her as the reality of her situation came barreling toward her. She was alone in a carriage with a handsome and virile man who'd all but expressed his desire for her while making her acutely aware of her own. She should be afraid – very, very afraid – and yet she found that she wasn't. Quite the opposite, really.

Which was why his next comment felt like a bucket of ice water dumped on her head. "You needn't worry however. I will remain on my best behavior. Nothing will happen between us. You're perfectly safe."

As relieved as she ought to have been to hear it, disappointment brought her swiftly back to reality – the reality in which a man like him was not supposed to have designs on a woman like her. One in which he could have, if she'd belonged to the middle or lower classes. But now that he knew she didn't, he'd be sure to keep himself in check and avoid succumbing to any form of temptation.

"Thank you," she muttered. "I cannot tell you how grateful I am to hear you say that."

He tilted his head, studied her a moment, and then, "I believe I may have upset you."

"Upset me? Not at all, my lord. You merely caught me by surprise, that is all."

"Are you certain?"

"Quite."

This comment resulted in a long moment of silence. Eventually, he reached inside his satchel and retrieved the newspaper he'd purchased at the inn before their departure. An hour passed while the carriage rolled onward. Louise occasionally glanced across at Lord Alistair, whose expression appeared to be set in stone as he flipped from page to page and studied the text. Bored with watching the scenery, she considered reading the book she'd brought with her.

Instead, she found herself saying, "The news must be serious, judging from your expression."

THE GOVERNESS WHO CAPTURED HIS HEART 39

He turned his attention toward her, straightened himself, and lowered the paper. "Important, is more like it," he said, leaning back in his seat.

"Would you care to discuss it?" she asked. Perhaps if they could focus on whatever it was he'd been reading, she'd be able to forget the feelings he'd stirred up inside her or how attractive she actually found him. Such things could only lead to ruin and a fate far worse than the loneliness awaiting her at Whitehaven.

He blinked. The edge of his mouth twitched, and then his eyes narrowed on her with intent. "Certainly. But only if you are willing to tell me why you've chosen to seek employment."

Her breath caught. "You wish to blackmail me?"

"Not at all. But my interest in this newspaper is no less personal than your desire to become a governess, so what I propose is an exchange."

It sounded fair and reasonable. "Very well," she said, denying the fear she had of letting him in, of sharing her innermost thoughts, and of being vulnerable. "Shall I go first or will you?"

☙

Seeing anxiety mark her features, Alistair felt compelled to earn her trust and put her at ease. "Allow me," he said. He was actually glad she'd asked him to open up, for it would allow him to focus on something besides the knowledge that she was as attracted to him as he was to her. Up until an hour ago, he hadn't been certain. Her discreet glances and interest in him could have been passed off as nothing more than normal curiosity. But then he'd watched her pupils dilate while her lips parted. He'd heard her tremulous inhalations of breath and seen the rosy hue sweeping across her face. And he'd instinctively known their desire was mutual.

Fearing he might act rashly in spite of his assurances to the contrary, he'd grabbed his newspaper and tried to block her out of his mind, which had been damnably hard to do since she was right there on the opposite bench. The print he'd tried to read had blurred before his eyes, and no matter how many times he attempted to focus, the only thing he could see was her, parting her lips, welcoming his advances, and giving him leave to do things no respectable gentlewoman would allow.

"My lord?"

"Hmm?"

"Are you all right?"

Collecting himself, he nodded, even though he wasn't the least bit all right. His pulse was racing, his blood was ablaze, and his lungs were struggling to take air in and push it back out. Discomfort did not begin to describe the predicament he was presently in, and crossing his legs did little to help. So he forced himself to speak in the hope that doing so would somehow calm his ardor. "I need to find a new source of income, so I'm looking for possible investment opportunities."

"Are you having financial trouble?" Stunned by her frankness, he stared at her, to which she responded with a hasty apology. "I should not have asked that. How rude of me."

"Well..." In for a penny, in for a pound. "I

wouldn't exactly call it trouble. It's more of a snag really."

Her brow creased with distinct curiosity. "How so?"

Sighing, he passed his hand over his face before saying, "My brother has been supplying me with a yearly stipend since I reached my majority twelve years ago. He is now threatening to stop doing so unless I marry Lady Channing's sister-in-law, Lady Gwendolyn."

Miss Potter's eyes widened. "Really?" When he nodded, she knit her brow before saying, "Well, I suppose it's not too unreasonable of him to make such a request."

"I know it isn't, especially since I'm more than his brother. I'm also his heir."

"What?"

"Langley has no sons and probably never will. He's pinning his hope for the title's succession on me, though I could do without him selecting my bride. Truth is, I've been relying on his support for far too long." When her frown deepened, he felt compelled to say, "I haven't been completely idle. There are tenants at my country estate who bring in a yearly income, but it's not much. My brother's generosity has enabled me to maintain the standard of living to which I have always been accustomed, but perhaps… Perhaps I need to consider cutting some costs and living more frugally. In any case, a good investment would be helpful, hence my interest in the newspaper."

He hadn't meant to say quite that much. It revealed a part of himself he hadn't been proud of lately. But rather than pass judgment, she said,

"Perhaps I can help. If you hand me one of the sections, I'll go through it. Maybe I'll notice something you missed."

Appreciating the offer, he thanked her.

"But first," she said, averting her gaze, "I need to be as honest with you as you've been with me." He steeled himself for what she would say, then felt his heart twist when she quietly murmured, "My sisters and I are barely scraping by. I sought to become a governess so I can help them financially, so we don't lose our home, and so my youngest sister, Eve, might have the Season Josephine and I were denied."

Knowing this was a touchy subject for her, he tried to think of a way to ask the questions her comment evoked. There wasn't really a delicate way in which to do so, however, so he softened his tone and said, "I must have misunderstood you earlier. I assumed you had ties to the aristocracy, but—"

"My great-grandfather was the Earl of Priorsbridge," she said. "My grandfather was his third son. He went into law and opened a firm that my father inherited upon his death. Unfortunately, Papa was not as skilled a barrister as Grandpapa, but at least he made an effort until Mama passed away. Her death changed everything. Papa started drinking; he neglected his clients, lost a lot of cases, and was finally forced to give up the business. We were forced to move to a more affordable part of town. Whatever money was set aside for my sisters and me was spent. So were the rest of Papa's savings." She struggled to draw breath, then averted her gaze and took a moment to compose herself. "All we have left now is the townhouse, and while we know we could sell it and move into something even cheaper, we're hoping to do what we can to avoid such an outcome."

Alistair stared at her in amazement. It had occurred to him that she might tell him her family had fallen on hard times, and she had no choice but to find work, but he hadn't expected her situation to be quite so dire. It explained her reluctance to speak of it. "I'm so sorry," he said. "I cannot begin to imagine how difficult life must have been for you in recent years. All things considered, I'm surprised you've done as well as you have. It could have been worse."

"I know." She forced a smile. "Our mother's insistence to educate us has been a blessing. Josephine managed to find work as an accountant, an unusual position for a woman, but one which thankfully brings in a decent wage."

"But it isn't enough."

She shook her head. "Not if we're to keep the townhouse and give Eve a proper Season. The expense will be enormous, but it will be her best chance of finding a husband and securing her future."

He decided not to mention that doing so without the proper connections would be a challenge. A thought struck him. He might be able to help in some small way. But did he really want to involve himself in someone else's troubles when he had plenty of his own? Looking into her watery eyes, he knew the answer immediately. "If you like, I'll put in a word with Lady Channing. I'm sure she'd be happy to assist with Eve at one of the dances and introduce her to some of her friends. I'll also dance with her myself, if you like. My attention toward her may encourage others to take notice."

The smile that appeared upon her face was priceless. "You would do all of that?"

When he nodded, she flung herself forward and wound her arms around his neck in a tight embrace. The gesture was so shocking, so startling, it made him immobile. And before he could gather his wits, she'd withdrawn to her seat. "I'm so sorry. I can scarcely think what came over me. I'm so extraordinarily happy I could sing!"

Touched by her joyous response, he grinned right back at her. He did not think of what it had felt like to have her pressed up against him, if only for a moment. To do so right now would tarnish the mood. So he made a deliberate effort to push his desire for her aside and to focus on her moment of happiness and the pleasure it brought him, knowing he was the cause of it.

☾

For the next three days, Louise took pleasure in Lord Alistair's company. The weather grew increasingly cold the further north they travelled, and he began making sure she had hot bricks to warm her feet every morning when they set out. She told him about her childhood, and he told her about his. Conversation flowed freely between them, and she began to wonder if she might have made a mistake by opening up to him. Because the more they talked and got to know each other, the more she liked the man he was proving to be.

Which meant she would miss him once this ride was over, and they would be separated by duty. So she tried not to think about that. There would be plenty of time to do so later in the loneliness that would shape the rest of her life.

But in the meantime…

"Do you ever wonder what your life would have been like if you hadn't been born into the aristocracy?" she asked on Saturday morning after leaving the latest posting inn.

Glancing at the ceiling, he sat for a moment in silence before saying, "All the time." Lowering his gaze, he smiled across at where she sat. "There are days when I wish my life was simpler."

"Some might argue that there is nothing simple about having to work for a living – of having to worry about putting food on the table."

"You're right. Truth is, I can't really imagine what it might be like to have to struggle in order to get by. But that doesn't stop me from occasionally wondering if the harvest isn't richer in another field, if there isn't something to be said for being able to go where you please, live as you wish, without the pressure of continuing the lineage hanging over your head."

"At least you are a man. You've been granted several years more than any woman in which to make the right match and settle down. And considering your position, it cannot possibly have come as a surprise to you that doing so would eventually be required."

He pushed out a breath. "You're right of course. The trouble is, I've been avoiding it."

"And now, with your brother's demands, you

feel as though you've lost any possible say in the matter."

Nodding, he crossed his arms and held her gaze. "How is it that you can so easily understand me when the people I've known my whole life fail to do so?"

Smiling, she asked, "Did you confide in them as you have done in me?"

He shook his head. "No. Mama and Langley are not the sort of people with whom one has an open conversation."

"Perhaps that's the problem. In order to know someone well, one has to share one's thoughts and aspirations, one's hopes and one's fears."

"And what are your hopes and fears, Miss Potter?"

The question was casually posed, yet Louise couldn't help but sense its importance. To answer would tangle their lives up even more than they already were. It would deepen their bond and make parting all the more difficult in the end. So she considered changing the subject, then said, "Right now, I hope to make a good impression on Lady Channing and to be a successful governess so I can help my sisters. My fear is I'll fail."

"Why would you do that?"

She shrugged. "I have no experience with being a governess, so it is likely that Lady Channing will find me wanting, or that I won't know how to enforce the discipline her children require, or that the other servants won't like me. Any number of things can go wrong."

"I don't think worrying about it will help."

"You're right." She drew a deep breath and

expelled it. "But what of you, my lord? What are your hopes and fears?"

His expression tightened, and his eyes grew slightly darker. "My hope is to find a way to avoid doing as my brother demands. My fear is I will be married by Christmas to a woman with whom I have nothing in common."

"Perhaps all you need is to get to know her better." When he gave her a dubious look she said, "Look at the two of us. We were strangers five days ago and now here we are enjoying each other's company remarkably well."

"Perhaps I should marry you then?"

She grinned in response to his teasing tone, even as she felt herself tighten up inside. "You know as well as I that doing so would be impossible."

"Because I'm the heir to a dukedom and you're a governess?"

"Yes."

He scoffed. "You're still an earl's great-granddaughter."

"As if anyone is going to care about that."

When he failed to answer, she knew she'd made her point. The blue blood that had run in her grandfather's veins had been thoroughly diluted during the recent generations. He and her father had both married into the middle class, and all of this was without considering her father's downward spiral. He'd failed to provide for his daughters, failed to continue his father's legacy, and had finally drunk himself to death. The blemish he'd left on his family was an undeniable one. And although Louise had never resented him for it before, she did so now.

Because meeting Lord Alistair had changed things. It had made her wonder what it might be like to be the suitable match for a man like him. And as time wore on inside the carriage, a new fear began to grip her – one apart from her duty toward her sisters and the possibility of failure – namely that she might have started liking him far too much for her own good.

She was certainly feeling things for him – things no young woman had any business feeling for a man so high above her station. And yet, with every glance he sent her way, her pulse quickened, and with every word he spoke, she sensed a yearning. It was built on fluff and fantasy of course, but that didn't make it feel any less real.

"Perhaps you're right," he murmured, scattering her thoughts, "but that doesn't make me want you any less."

Stunned by his comment, she gaped at him. Surely she must have misheard. But the way in which he was watching her now suggested she hadn't, because there was something so utterly wicked about his expression, it made her pulse leap and her skin heat with awareness. "What?" She tried to focus.

"I suppose I shall have to restrain myself, however, since marrying you would be so incredibly impossible."

Staring at him, she did her best to make sense of what he was saying. "Surely you jest?"

He raised an eyebrow. "Do I?"

Befuddled by this strange turn in their conversation and feeling as though she might slide to the floor in a sinful mess of unfulfilled need, she averted her gaze and looked out the window. Still, she could feel his presence so keenly her heart rate failed to slow. Instead, his voice echoed inside her head. *That doesn't make me want you any less. I shall have to restrain myself.*

Good lord!

No one had ever told her something like that before, yet the words had come from the handsomest man she'd ever laid eyes on – a man who now made her wonder about certain things, like what might happen between them if he lost control. Would he kiss her with abandon? She dared not look at him as she imagined what that might be like. Delicious, no doubt, if her racing heart was any indication.

"It looks as though it's starting to snow," he remarked a while later, startling her from the inappropriate ponderings she was having.

It was all his fault. If he hadn't said anything...

She sighed. Who was she trying to fool? Her attraction to him had been there from the moment they'd met, but his admission made it so much more acute. "Yes," she said as she watched the white flakes drift toward the ground. "And the light is beginning to dim." Because stating the obvious was so much easier than having to think of an interesting subject to discuss when her mind and body still lingered on his lust-driven declaration.

A sharp turn of the carriage served as a welcome distraction. It jostled her sideways. A bump in the road made the entire conveyance lurch. And then a sharp crack filled the air and the whole thing tilted to the sound of whinnying horses.

"Hold on," Lord Alistair warned. He leapt across to her seat and pushed her into the corner, protecting her with his body while the carriage dipped even further. It eventually righted itself and drew to a jarring halt.

"What happened?" she asked as he leaned back slightly. His hand was on her shoulder, his thighs pressed up against hers, and if she did not speak of practicalities, she would likely do something reckless like close the distance between them and kiss him.

"I think we may have lost a wheel." The comment seemed to sober him for he suddenly removed himself completely from her person, opened the door, and climbed out, leaving her alone in a crooked carriage to wonder about how her life had gone so awry.

Hearing voices, she made her own way outside into the chilly late afternoon. Beneath her feet, the gathering snow provided a soft tread while she walked toward the spot where Lord Alistair stood in conversation with the coachman.

"The inn's about a mile up ahead," the coachman was saying. "With the wheel broken, a quick repair is out of the question. One of us is going to have to go and get help."

Lord Alistair nodded. "Let's move the carriage to the side of the road if we can. I'll take Miss Potter to the inn on horseback so she can get out of the cold." He went to assist the coachman, while Louise watched in amazement.

Lord Alistair was a capable man, his strength evident in his ability to push the carriage forward while the coachman directed the horses. And rather than pant or groan from the exertion, he quickly went to help unhitch one of the horses, collect her bag, and come to help her up. "All you have to do is swing your leg over the side," he said when he placed his hands on her waist.

Before she could think too much about what it felt like to have him touch her like that, she was in the air. Her right leg went over the horse's back as he'd advised, so she sat astride in a way most people would frown at.

As if reading her mind, Lord Alistair met her eyes through the falling snow. "I apologize for not having a sidesaddle." Before she could answer, he glanced down at her exposed legs and grinned. "Then again, perhaps I'm not sorry at all."

Handing her the blanket from the carriage so she could wrap it around her shoulders, he pulled the horse into a walk and started toward their destination. "Will you not ride with me?" she asked after a while. She'd warred with her conscience about suggesting he do so. But having him closer would help keep her warm, even if it wasn't the wisest course of action. Especially not after the comment he'd made about her legs. Still, seeing him trudge through the snow while she sat like a queen filled her with guilt.

He muttered something imperceptible before saying, "I don't think I should."

"Because you claim to want me or—"

"Precisely."

He said nothing further, and neither did she. But that didn't make her any less aware of the tension that seemed to have formed between them. It was palpable, like a ball of dry hay waiting for a spark to set it on fire.

☾

By the time they arrived at the inn, Alistair's clothes were permeated by frost. He could feel it all the way to his bones, his feet so cold they'd practically gone numb. Helping Miss Potter down from the horse, he felt her shudder and knew she wasn't faring much better. A hot bath would help, but before such a wonderfully soothing experience could be his, he would have to return to the carriage with a couple of men and a spare wheel.

But as they entered the inn and he became aware of how overcrowded it was and that several patrons were deep in their cups, he was forced to reconsider. Leaving Miss Potter alone here would not be the right thing to do.

So he led her over to the counter and addressed the elderly man who stood there. "Are you the innkeeper?" he asked.

"Aye," the man responded.

Explaining his situation, Alistair asked if the man could spare a couple of grooms and if he had an extra wheel available too, offering decent compensation for both.

"I've two strong lads out back. I'll ask them to go help your coachman bring the carriage here."

"We'll also need two bedrooms and a spot in the loft for my coachman to rest."

The innkeeper raised both eyebrows. "As you can see, we're practically filled to capacity."

"Practically?"

Nodding, the innkeeper glanced at Miss Potter.

"I've one room left. You might consider sharing."

Appalled the man would suggest such a thing, Alistair shook his head. "That's out of the question." Miss Potter was an innocent young woman, who needed to be protected from the likes of him. "What about the hayloft?"

"There's no more space up there. I'm afraid your coachman will have to sleep in the carriage. We can provide some blankets for him so he can be comfortable."

Which still left Alistair without a bed unless he agreed to do as the innkeeper had initially suggested. Glancing at Miss Potter, he chastised himself for even considering such an inappropriate course. Especially when she was standing there, hugging herself in an effort to get warm. "Show us up, please." He would decide what to do with himself later, once she'd been made comfortable.

The room turned out to be of the smaller variety, with the bed propped up against the wall and a chair in one corner. Setting Miss Potter's bag on the floor, Alistair turned to the innkeeper. "I don't suppose there's room enough for a tub to be brought in?"

"It's been done before," the innkeeper said. "I'll have it brought up as soon as possible."

"And if we could please have some food as well, that would be splendid."

The innkeeper nodded. "The beef stew is good. Will you want to eat it downstairs or up here?"

Thinking of the drunken men in the taproom, Alistair told the innkeeper to bring it up. He waited until he was gone before turning toward Miss Potter. "I apologize for the way this evening is going."

"It's not your fault." She considered the room, observing its small size before meeting his gaze once more. "I'm happy to share this room with you, if you like."

The tension that had been gripping him with increasing force since the moment he'd met her began to take its toll. "Thank you," he said, clenching his jaw. "But it would not be proper."

"I am well aware of that, Lord Alistair. Especially after what you have told me."

He dipped his head and moved toward the door. "Then I shall leave you to rest. The bath will be up soon, along with the food. I hope—"

"But with no room in the hayloft and your coachman sleeping in the carriage, what will you do?"

"I don't know." It was the truth. But when it was clear his comment did not agree with her, he hastened to say, "I'm sure I'll figure something out."

"Really?"

He made a curt nod. "Yes."

She crossed her arms and gave him a stern look. "I wasn't offering you the bed, you know. But the chair over there does not look too uncomfortable, and I dare say it will be better than one of the wooden ones in the taproom. Not to mention the noise down there is unlikely to give you much peace."

"As true as that may be and as generous as you are being, I still don't think it is wise for me to remain here."

"Why? Because you plan to pounce on me when

I least expect it?"

That suggestion certainly stirred his blood. "Of course not," he managed to say while visions of ravishing her swamped his brain.

"Then let's be practical about this, shall we? You are definitely as cold, tired, and hungry as I. The fact you're a man does not diminish your need for warmth, rest, or sustenance."

"I suppose that's true, though many would disagree."

"Well, they're not here right now. It's only you and I, and I say you ought to have a comfortable spot for the night. What's your opinion on the matter, practically speaking?"

"Well…"

A knock at the door served as a welcome distraction. Opening it, he found a servant holding a tray with food. Three more men stood behind him, two of them holding a brass tub, while the third carried a pail of water. Alistair waved them inside, maneuvering about so they could set everything down in the decreasing space.

"That does look rather tempting," Miss Potter said, as soon as the servants had finished filling the tub. It had taken several trips up and down the stairs, but they'd eventually gotten it done. Turning toward her, Alistair found her staring down at the tub. Waves of steam rose from the hot water. Hands on hips, she glanced at where he stood. "Will you go first or shall I?"

The question, posed with a genuine look of concern in her eyes, almost knocked him off his feet. Clenching his fists, he dug his nails against the palms of his hands and focused on that discomfort, hoping it might alleviate another. "You will *not* be bathing in my presence, and I shall *not* be bathing in yours," he clipped.

"Of course not!" She stared at him. "Heavens, I wasn't suggesting something that scandalous. It goes without saying that we would step outside to allow the other the privacy they require."

His limbs felt as though they were going to break beneath the strain of his carefully held control. "Then by all means, proceed. I shall return in fifteen minutes." And with that, he stepped outside the room, shutting the door behind him while wondering if it was possible to survive seven days of constant arousal, or if it was destined to kill him. Because it sure as hell felt as though it would.

☾

Sinking into the soothing water, Louise took a moment to think of her situation. If she encouraged him, she'd no doubt in her mind that Lord Alistair's resolve would waver, and the two of them would enjoy a passionate night together. But as tempting as that was and as attractive as she found him, she could not allow such a thing to happen. Doing so would put everything at risk, because nobody on God's green earth would want to employ a fallen woman as their governess. And while she was fairly confident Lord Alistair would refrain from mentioning any kisses they happened to share to his niece, Louise could not take the chance of her finding out. Her sisters relied on her too heavily for that.

So she picked up the soap and proceeded to

wash. Her friendship with Lord Alistair would be short lived, but it would provide her with wonderful memories to look back on. Not because of the desire he felt for her, but because of how well they'd gotten to know each other, the confidences they'd shared, and the lengthy discussions they'd had.

Every word they'd spoken had strengthened the bond between them in a way she'd initially feared. She'd been wrong to do so, however, because getting to know Lord Alistair properly wasn't something she could regret. In another place and another life, they would likely have made the perfect match. But they were here, in England, their actions dictated by social protocol. Soon they would arrive at Whitehaven where he would meet the woman whom he was supposed to marry. She was going to be a governess, and their lives, so intertwined in this moment, would move apart once more.

With this in mind, she finished her bath and stepped out of the tub, drying herself with the towel. She would count her blessings and the chance she'd had to know a remarkable man – a man who wasn't too proud to help his servants, a man who put aside his own wants and needs in favor of doing what was right, a man determined to do his duty whether that meant adhering to his brother's demands or finding a way to provide for himself without relying on others.

Managing to throw her dress over her head two seconds before he returned to knock on the door, Louise hastily tied the ribbons in place while she called for him to enter. He strode in with a grim expression hardening his features. The door closed behind him, and he stopped to take her in. She held her breath, unsure of what he might be thinking, then watched as his gaze slid sideways toward the bed where her undergarments were strewn about. Being in a hurry to finish up, she hadn't put them back on again, though she wished she'd at least tidied them away.

When he considered her next, it was with flames dancing in his eyes. His throat worked and he dropped his gaze to allow for a slow and studious perusal of her entire body. Her belly tightened against a surge of heat, her skin tingling in anticipation of what he might do. Pointing toward the bed, he closed his eyes on a tortured breath. "Please put those things away."

His request propelled her into action. Hastening forward she snatched up her stays, her stockings, and her chemise and stuffed them into her bag. She then hurried toward the door, grabbing her boots while she went, which forced her to move right past him, her arm brushing his as she did so.

The sharp inhale of breath he took sent shivers racing up her spine, and then she felt his hand upon her wrist, clutching her tight and halting her progress. "Will you save me from my insanity, Miss Potter?"

Swallowing in the face of his resistance, she lifted her chin toward his anguished expression. "I cannot."

His jaw seemed to harden against her words, but he bowed his head in submission. "Of course not. I don't know what I was thinking to ask." And without speaking another word, he turned on his heel, flung open the door, and stormed out.

☾

Spending the night on a wooden bench in the taproom wasn't Alistair's idea of fun, but it had been necessary. After exiting Miss Potter's room so she could bathe, he'd gone for a brisk walk in the snow and had imagined himself capable of joining her for supper. Until he'd seen her standing there with her hair unpinned, the tips dripping wet, and her bare feet peeking out from beneath the hem of her dress.

He'd averted his gaze only to find himself staring at her undergarments lying on the bed, which meant she'd been utterly naked beneath the grey wool she'd been wearing. This thought had, in the space of one second, led to others. He'd imagined pulling the gown up over her head and taking a thorough look at her, of flinging her onto the bed and delving between her thighs in ways that topped his most erotic fantasies.

But when he'd asked for permission to do exactly that, she'd denied him. And rightfully so. In fact, he was glad of it, because what sort of woman would she be if she had allowed him to have his way with her like that? Christ, he was being a selfish scoundrel. She was an innocent woman whom his niece had asked him to escort to her home. The only problem was he'd been expecting a middle-aged spinster, not a goddess.

Groaning in response to the constant discomfort that plagued him, Alistair went to speak with his coachman. He would ensure the carriage was ready for departure before fetching Miss Potter. The anticipation of seeing her again made his muscles flex. Never in his life had he wanted a woman as much as he wanted her.

He'd mentioned marriage on impulse – as a lark, really – not as something he thought she might agree to. Her shocked response followed by her insistence that such a thing would not be possible had not banished the idea from his head, however. Instead, it had cemented itself in a way that demanded his attention. And if he did indeed marry her, then he could have her as often as he pleased and…There was more to it than that. He genuinely enjoyed conversing with her.

An idea struck him. His brother insisted he'd cut him off unless he married the woman who waited for him at Whitehaven. But would Langley really follow through on such a threat if Alistair married Miss Potter instead? And would he care? Was lust enough to make him take such a risk? He could still try to make some investments. He could even sell his country estate if doing so would help him provide for a wife.

Unsure of how far he was willing to go in order to sate his needs, Alistair did what had to be done in order to get ready for the rest of the journey. When Miss Potter came to find him half an hour later, he greeted her with politeness, then handed her up into the carriage and closed the door. She looked out of the window at him and frowned. "Will you not be riding in here with me?"

"Not today," he said, then went to join his coachman on the driver's block before she tried to convince him to keep her company instead.

Alone in the carriage, Louise tried to pass the time with her book. When doing so lost her interest, she gave her attention to the snow-covered landscape. Once this lost its appeal as well, she tried to distract herself with a game of solitaire. By the time luncheon finally arrived, she had to admit this day was turning out to be the longest of her life. It was only made worse by the realization that Lord Alistair wouldn't be joining her for a meal. Instead, he left her to eat the ham and cheese she'd been served at the inn where they'd stopped, while he remained at the bar, conversing with other travelers.

Vexed, she did her best to remind herself that she was the one who'd denied him, and that if his passions ran as high as he'd suggested, she ought to be grateful to him for adding distance between them. But it was to no avail. The truth was she missed him, and as unwise as spending time in his company might be, she could not ignore the yearning of her heart.

So once she was finished eating, she exited the inn and waited for him to join her outside. "My lord," she said, drawing his attention, "I've purchased the local gazette. Perhaps you would care to read it with me?"

Stopping next to the carriage door, he stared at her. "To do so wouldn't be wise." He then extended his hand, offering to help her up.

She remained where she was. "My name is Louise, by the way. In case you were wondering." And on that note, she climbed up into the carriage without accepting his help.

C

Louise.

It was a beautiful name – one that suited her much better than Miss Potter. Still, it was personal and intimate, and after the incident between them the previous evening, it made him wonder about her motive in sharing it with him. One thing was certain, she'd been quite enraged when she'd done so, and while such high emotion ought to have dampened his lust for her, it seemed to have done the opposite. Which was why he found himself telling his coachman that he would ride inside the carriage for the rest of the day, upon which he flung the door open and climbed in after the maddening woman who drove him to want things he'd no business wanting.

Seated in the far corner, she stared at him as he slammed the door and took his seat. He then pinned her with the hardest glare he could manage and asked, "What are you trying to do?"

Her lips parted and she quietly shook her head. "I honestly don't know. All of this..." she waved her hand between them, "is terribly confusing."

"Well, it isn't for me. In fact, my carnal appetite for you is so acute I can scarcely sleep at night or think straight during the day." He watched her draw in a shuddering breath which only made matters worse. Aggravated, he felt a perverse need to destabilize her, to make her world feel as chaotic as his did right now. "Do you have any idea how uncomfortable it is to be in a state of unfulfilled arousal for several days in a row?" Her eyes widened and she shook her head. "I know it was wrong of me to proposition you last night, I know I must get you to Whitehaven without tossing up your skirts and having you right here in this carriage, but God help me, I'm only a man, so if you keep using your feminine wiles on me — as innocent as you think it may be — I won't be able to answer for the consequences. Do you understand?"

"I…" She gave a quick nod. "Yes. I understand. I didn't realize that was what I was doing. I've no experience with using feminine wiles, you see."

Blowing out a tortured breath, he leaned his head back against the squabs as the carriage rolled into motion, jostling him. "Well, you're quite adept at it, I must say."

She was quiet for a second, then asked, "In what way?"

Groaning, he rolled his head to the side so he could look across at her. "You're doing it right now by asking that question."

"Oh." Another pause, a twitch of her nose, and a furrowing of her brow, and then, "Ohhhhh…"

The penny had finally dropped.

CHAPTER FOUR

"I'M SORRY," LOUISE SAID, FOR she could think of nothing else to say under the circumstances. One thing was certain, and that was her state of discomfiture, because the things he'd said – the directness of his declaration – had made her squirm. She'd felt a knot form in her belly. Her skin had grown hot, and a needy, unfamiliar ache had begun to swell within her. Even now, her brain felt fuzzy from all the sensations that had collided and made her want things – wicked things – things she could never have without dire consequences. But, oh, it had been tempting to tell him she felt as he did, that she was as susceptible to the stirring of desire, and that resisting temptation was proving to be an unpleasant chore.

But instinct told her doing so would only open the floodgate, and once that happened, they couldn't go back. So she fought to put an invisible barrier between them and reminded herself that allowing Lord Alistair's advances would be extremely unwise. Her position was at stake, for heaven's sake!

So she sat back and stiffened her spine. "It was

not my intention to cause you discomfort." His nostrils flared while he stared back at her. She pressed her fingers into the seat beneath her, steadying her resolve even as her body trembled. "Thank you for being a gentleman. A lesser man would have succumbed to weakness."

"Yes…well…" He turned his head away as if deliberately blocking her from his view. "You may thank me when you arrive at our destination with your innocence intact. Until then, I would advise you to treat me as you would a prowling lion – with caution and trepidation."

Sobered by this comment, Louise said nothing in return. She'd had no romantic plans for her future when she'd resolved to become a governess. On the contrary, she'd been quite prepared to sacrifice matrimony and children and passion in favor of doing what was right for her youngest sister. It had been an easy decision to make. She'd had no male acquaintances. Her heart had been free, and she'd known her moment of eligibility had passed. Seeking employment had been the logical step forward for her, and yet now, sitting in this carriage with a man she'd gotten to know so well in such short time – a man who managed to challenge her beliefs while stirring her up inside – she couldn't help but wish things could be different.

"I didn't like you at all to begin with," she found herself saying, when the silence between them became too uncomfortable to bear. Speaking to the passing landscape, she sensed a shift in the air around her and knew without looking that he had turned toward her.

"That's quite all right," he said. "I didn't like you either."

Smiling in response to his sarcasm, she pressed the palm of her hand to the cool windowpane and watched as it left a steamy mark upon the glass. "You were arrogant and stern, without a hint of kindness about you. But then our journey began, we starting talking, and I shared things with you I've never shared with anyone else. Not even my own sisters." He said nothing, but she knew he was paying attention. "Over the course of only six days, I've allowed you to access my most private thoughts, forging a bond that must soon be broken." She felt her heart clench as she forced out those words. "You ought to know, when that moment comes, it will be the most difficult thing I have ever had to endure. Because God help me, I…"

I've fallen in love with you.

That part remained lodged in her throat. She could not say it – could not be quite so daring – could not take the risk when she doubted he felt the same way. So instead, she forced back the threatening tears, drew a deep breath, and tamped down all her emotions. "I have never admired a man as much as I admire you, Lord Alistair."

"I think we can dispense with the lord part," he murmured.

Chuckling, she nodded before adding, "You have proven yourself to be charming, kind, righteous, and courageous. You've listened to everything I had to say with interest, and you have overcome temptation." She turned to look at him, to meet his turbulent gaze. "I have been so lucky to spend this carriage ride in your company, and I shall always look back on these days we shared with fondness."

"Louise…" His voice was a raw rasp of emotion. It went straight to her heart, forcing her to look away once more before he could see she was crying.

"I wish you all the happiness in the world, Alistair. You deserve it."

"You speak as though we are parting ways forever when we arrive at Whitehaven."

"Because that is what we shall do," she said. "I am a governess – no more than a servant – while you are a duke's heir. Your days at Whitehaven will be spent courting Lady Gwendolyn. And frankly, I won't be able to watch that."

"Why not?" The gruffness of his voice denoted the importance of his question.

Knowing she'd said too much, she shook her head. "It doesn't signify."

"It does to me." His hand found hers, and when she tried to pull away, he held on tight. "I know you desire me as much as I desire you. It's in your eyes whenever you glance my way, which is why it's been so damnably hard for me to stay the proper course. But if there is more than that – if you feel a deeper connection to me, tell me and—"

"And what?" She could feel herself crumbling as they spoke, and she didn't like it one bit. Damn him for forcing the truth upon her like this, for trying to make her share what was in her heart when it wouldn't make an ounce of difference. "You will marry me instead of Lady Gwendolyn?

You will risk your brother's wrath? Your position in Society? Financial security?"

"I will inherit my brother's title one day, and the fortune that comes with it."

"And until then? Will you look forward to your brother's demise because of how it will benefit you?"

Releasing her hand, he sat back with a look of horror upon his face. "Of course not."

She nodded. "You do not know what it is to be poor or to be exiled from your social class. If you choose that path, you will come to resent me as much as I will come to resent you for denying me the chance to help Eve. And what will we have then besides bitterness and regret?" When he said nothing, she knew she'd opened his eyes to a world that waited beyond the passion he felt right now – a world in which he would have to live out the rest of his days. "Marrying Lady Gwendolyn is the right thing for you to do. She's a marquess's daughter – an earl's sister – and she will make a good match for a man of your rank."

"So then, this is really it?" He sounded as though he didn't want to believe it, and yet she could see by his stark expression he already did.

"I'm afraid so."

☾

The remainder of their journey passed with stilted bits of mundane conversation. By the time they arrived at the final posting inn, Louise escaped upstairs to the room where she would spend the night and elected to take her supper alone. Alistair made no effort to stop her. If she felt as raw inside as he did, she would need some time alone to prepare for the following day's arrival at Whitehaven.

So much had been left unsaid between them. He'd seen it in her eyes, the misery there enough to shatter his heart. Taking a moment to search the depths of his soul that evening, he contemplated a life without Louise in it. Was such an existence worth having?

No.

She was the only woman he would ever consider marrying. Not because of her beauty or because of how desperately he wanted her in his bed, but because he'd fallen in love with her – completely, madly, irrevocably – and no other woman would do. Which meant he would have to fight for the right to make her his, firstly by ridding himself of the problem his brother had created when he'd picked Gwendolyn as his bride.

So he set out at dawn after penning a note to Louise and hiring a horse from the inn. Riding fast through the bitter cold, his breath like steam from a boiling kettle, he reached Whitehaven by ten.

"My lord!"

One of the grooms ran to greet him, grabbing the horse's reins while he swung himself down from the saddle. Thanking the lad, Alistair climbed the steps to the front door and opened it sharply.

"Lord Alistair," the butler exclaimed, hastening toward him. "We weren't expecting you quite this early. My apologies for not being there to greet you." He looked past him for a second before asking. "Is Miss Potter not with you?"

"She will arrive later. I chose to ride ahead." He removed his hat and pulled off his gloves, handing the items to the butler. "Has the family risen yet?"

"Indeed." The butler gestured in the direction of the dining room. "They are having breakfast as we speak."

Alistair didn't wait for the man to show him the way, striding forward briskly until he reached his destination. Halting for a moment, he drew a deep breath, steadying his resolve before opening the door wide and striding through it. Four pairs of eyes turned to stare at him.

"Alistair!" Abigail was the first to convey her surprise. She prepared to rise, but he motioned for her to stay seated. "Is Miss Potter with you? I'm so eager to meet her."

"She will arrive later," he said.

A bit of silence followed that revelation, and then Lord Channing gestured toward a vacant chair. "Do come and join us, Alistair. I'm sure you must be eager for some refreshment after your journey."

It was tempting to accept, but the anxiousness coursing through him would not make sitting still at the table a pleasant experience. "Thank you, but I would prefer to wait in the library." Addressing Gwendolyn, he added, "If you would please join me there when you're ready, I'd be much obliged."

Gwendolyn's eyes widened. "Of course," she murmured.

Silence followed for an awkward moment. Alistair met his brother's grave expression with one of his own and then quit the room, closing the door behind him.

※

Pacing back and forth in the library, Alistair waited for what seemed like an insufferable length of time, even though the clock said no more than fifteen minutes had passed by the time Gwendolyn arrived.

"I trust you are well," she said, before taking a seat on the sofa.

He remained by the fireplace. "Quite. And you?"

"I wish the weather were warmer, but aside from that, I have no complaints."

Nodding, Alistair wondered how best to broach the subject he wished to discuss with her, and then decided directness might serve him best in this instance. "Regarding my brother's insistence we marry…" he began.

A tiny crease appeared upon her brow. "He says it will be the perfect match."

"Is that what you believe?"

Her silence unnerved him, forcing him to cross the floor. He paused, then turned and strode back, flexing his fingers while doing his best not to yell with frustration. Drawing a fortifying breath, he pinned her with his gaze. "Gwendolyn?"

She bit her lip and looked away. "Yes."

His heart plummeted all the way to his toes. This would not be as simple as walking away. And yet, there was something in her expression and posture that gave him pause. "Then allow me to ask you a different question. Will marrying me make you happy?"

She raised her head so sharply he took a step back. Her eyes met his, and he felt his heart pause on a thread of hope. "I mean no offense when I tell you this, but I have no desire to be your wife."

That thread of hope began to expand. "You don't?"

"No. I'm in love with someone else – an untitled gentleman, as a matter of fact. Channing wants to see me happy, so he approves of the match."

"Does Langley know about this?"

She shook her head. "We thought it best for me to break the news to you directly before informing your brother."

The thrill Alistair felt in response to those words was so acute he could scarcely credit it. He stared at Gwendolyn, at the woman who'd represented a dreaded fate until she herself had saved him from it. "I don't know what to say."

"I hope you're not too disappointed or angry."

"No. Of course not." His heart was humming with joy. "I am none of those things. On the contrary, I am grateful to you, and so incredibly pleased on both our behalves."

☾

By the time she arrived at the manor that would now be her home, the enthusiasm Louise had felt when she'd set out from London had completely vanished. Still, she did her best to smile as she greeted her employers.

"You're younger than I expected," Lady Channing said when Louise met her in the parlor after settling in. "Prettier too."

A petite woman with dark brown hair, big eyes, and a wide smile, Lady Channing was proving herself to be as kind as Louise had judged her to be by the tone of her letters. She'd even given Louise a choice between two bedchambers, informing her which one faced east, in case she favored the morning light.

"Did I not mention my age in our correspondence?" She could have sworn she had.

"You wrote that life has been difficult for you in recent years, that you were well past the age of marriageability, and that you anticipated a quiet and peaceful life in the country." Lady Channing dipped her chin and quirked her lips. "It seemed like something a middle-aged woman might say."

"Forgive me. It was not my intention to deceive you in any way."

"Perhaps not, but I can assure you I would not have suggested you travel alone with Lord Alistair if I'd known your age. At least, I would have insisted upon a chaperone."

"Thank you, my lady. I fear I am to blame for this misunderstanding. You may rest assured however that Lord Alistair did ask a maid to accompany us, but she became ill the first night and was unable to continue onward with us."

"It is a relief to know that he made an effort to protect your reputation." Lady Channing gave Louise a sharp look. "I trust he treated you well?"

"Yes. He was the perfect gentleman."

Expelling a breath, Lady Channing nodded. "I didn't expect him to be anything less, but when he arrived before you, looking as though he'd escaped hell to get here, I couldn't help but wonder. Especially after seeing you for myself."

"I can assure you that you have no cause for concern," Louise told her. "If anything, I believe he was eager to arrive here so he could speak with Lady Gwendolyn."

"Yes." Lady Channing gave Louise a pensive look. "They will make quite a match, don't you think?"

Recalling the other woman she'd met upon her arrival, Louise gave a curt nod. "Without a doubt."

"Hmm…" Lady Channing rose, as did Louise. "Papa only wants what is best for his brother."

"Of course." Louise couldn't help but wonder why Lady Channing was sharing all of these details with her. She was a servant, nothing more. Being a confidant was not in her job description. Uncomfortable with it, she tried to keep her responses as short as possible. Speaking of Alistair and the woman he would eventually marry was not something she wanted to continue doing. So when they entered the hallway, she chose to say, "Perhaps I should go and spend some time with the children."

"You arrived this afternoon, Miss Potter. Nobody expects you to start work until tomorrow." Linking her arm with Louise's, she drew her toward the back of the house where French doors overlooked a snow-covered lawn sloping down toward a lake. "And as you can see, the children are otherwise occupied at the moment."

Louise watched as the three boys skated across

the lake. Allowing her gaze to wander, she studied the men who stood to one side, their heads bowed in what appeared to be serious discussion. Lord Alistair and his brother, Langley. "I see," she said, before turning away. Squaring her shoulders, she faced the countess. "In that case, perhaps you'll allow me to go and rest. This past week has been rather trying, and I should like to recover from it by tomorrow."

The countess took a moment to answer, her eyes resting on Louise's in quiet contemplation. Eventually, she smiled. "Of course. Supper is at eight, if you would like to join us."

Surprised, Louise couldn't help but say, "As grateful as I am for the offer, I am a servant, my lady. Sitting at your table would hardly be appropriate."

"Perhaps not," the countess agreed, upon which Louise took her leave and headed up the service stairs to her chamber.

☾

"I have spoken with Gwendolyn, Langley, and she is no more thrilled about the idea of marrying me than I am with the idea of marrying her," Alistair told his brother. His conversation with her had managed to expel the pain that gripped his heart.

His heart.

He'd never wasted much time considering that particular organ. But then Miss Potter – Louise – had swept into his life and stirred a fiery passion. He'd wanted her desperately, struggling each day to do what his conscience demanded, even going so far as to suggest marriage for the sole purpose of getting his hands on her.

Until she'd delivered her emotional speech in the carriage.

I have never admired a man as much as I admire you.

He'd felt as though pain was pouring out of her, and it had not only caused his own heart to break but had made him realize what he felt for her was more than lust and passion. It went deeper, the roots of it digging into the depths of his soul. And when he'd suggested marriage again, and she'd given him every reason why such a thing was impossible, he'd felt as though life had finally lost its meaning.

Hating the weight of lost hope, he'd suffered the rest of that day's journey in a disheartened state. When they'd arrived at the posting inn, he'd given Louise her privacy, retreating to his own room in order to contemplate his fate. By morning, his depression had turned to fury, and he'd left the inn with one clear intention in mind – to have an honest talk with Gwendolyn and then to confront his brother.

The first part had gone surprisingly well, and he was now ready to argue with Langley in whatever way was necessary in order for things to play out to everyone's advantage.

"Really?" Langley asked. He was looking out over the lake where his grandchildren skated.

"Did it ever occur to you that we might want to marry other people?"

That comment seemed to grab his brother's attention. He turned his hard blue eyes on him and frowned. "Have you formed an attachment, Alistair?"

Swallowing, Alistair crossed his arms. His eyes settled on a nearby tree. "Not precisely," he said, since the woman he wanted had so adamantly refused him.

His brother snorted. "I didn't think so, though I was hoping you might have. Forcing your hand was never my intention."

"Really?" Alistair looked at him with incredulity. "Insisting I marry or forego my stipend was not an attempt to do so?"

Langley's frown deepened. "What I hoped was that it would give you some incentive to do as I've been asking you to do since you turned thirty. You've had three years in which to find a wife. Surely that's enough."

"Perhaps, but I was reluctant to settle down with someone I felt nothing for."

Sighing, Langley shifted his weight so he faced Alistair more fully. The hair that had once been a dark shade of brown was now threaded with grey, but that did not distract from his power. "I know this is going to be difficult for you to believe, all things considered, but I'm doing this for you, because it is what I believe to be in your best interest."

"You're right," Alistair murmured, "I do find that difficult to believe. You're only trying to secure the title. You had no sons of your own, so you want me to give it a shot whether I want to or not."

Smiling, Langley stared straight into Alistair's eyes and shook his head. "You've judged me harshly if that is what you really think."

"Am I wrong?"

Allowing his gaze to slide away from Alistair's, Langley looked out across the lake. "Your mother and I are both in our fifties. You have no other siblings and no close family besides my daughter and her husband and children. Which means the day will come when you will be faced with a lonely existence. If you live to be as old as I, you'll have seventeen years to get through on your own. Your niece has her own family to occupy her time, so while I'm sure she will always welcome you for the occasional visit, you cannot rely on her to give your life meaning."

"It would never occur to me to do so."

"And I doubt your friends will have much time for you either," Langley continued as if he hadn't spoken. "As far as I know, they're all members of the aristocracy and faced with their own responsibilities. From what I hear, Gratford and Townsend are already setting up their nurseries, while Everton has recently gotten himself engaged. Before you know it, you'll be the only bachelor left, and what then?"

Rankled, Alistair gave a shrug. "I'm sure I'll find a mistress with whom to divert myself," he said, for the pure sake of being argumentative.

Langley blew out a breath and stuck his hands in his coat pockets. "The point is, I want you to be surrounded by love and laughter, to know what it's like to hold your children in your arms and feel their kisses upon your cheek. And I will take comfort in knowing that you will be happy."

"Then let me pick the woman of my choosing."

Scoffing, Langley slanted a look in Alistair's direction. "Does such a mythical creature exist?"

It was Alistair's turn to surprise his brother. "Yes. I believe she does, and if happiness is what you want for me, then you'll give me your support."

꩜

Avoiding Alistair required more skill than Louise would ever have imagined. She'd thought the house big enough to prevent their paths from crossing, but somehow, whenever she passed through a hallway, he'd materialize before her, forcing her to turn on her heel and hasten away in the opposite direction before he could say something gut-wrenching, like, "How do you do?"

Four days passed like this, and twice she had to say she'd promised to show the children something before hurrying from the room right after he entered. After that, she'd remained upstairs in her bedchamber unless she was busy with lessons.

"Tomorrow will be Christmas Eve," Lady Channing said when she sought her out one afternoon. "We would like to invite you to join us for supper."

"That's really kind of you, but—"

"You cannot refuse," the countess told her. "I shan't permit it."

"In that case, I will be happy to attend," Louise lied. "Thank you."

She'd then waited for the countess to leave before putting on her coat and boots. A brisk walk in the frosty outdoors was what she needed. But as she made her way along one of the paths, she found the peaceful silence to be the most devastating thing in the world. It left her alone with her sorrow, filling her mind with him—the intensity of his gaze, the dimples at the edge of his mouth, the passion with which he tore down the boundaries between them and opened her eyes to a promise she dared not let him fulfill. She'd fallen in love with a man she could not have, and the pain of it was tearing her apart.

Yet she would now have to sit at the dining room table with him. She would have to smile and laugh and pretend she was enjoying every torturous moment. The thought of it led her back toward the house on heavy feet. She climbed the service stairs and drifted along the corridor. When she reached her bedchamber, she stepped inside and closed the door. She then drew an anguished breath and began removing her coat.

"Chasing you has become a tedious process, Louise."

Startled by Alistair's voice, she spun to her left where she found him reclining in the armchair next to the fireplace. "You can't be in here!" She glanced around at the room as if to ascertain that she hadn't entered the wrong room by mistake. "It isn't proper."

Tilting his head, he allowed his gaze to appraise her. "No it isn't, but apparently it is necessary if I am to speak with you at all."

"I thought we said what there was to say in the carriage," she told him, hoping he'd leave.

Instead, he stretched out his legs as if getting more comfortable. "You might have done so, but

I did not say nearly enough."

Turning away from him, she hung up her coat and then clutched her hands together. "Please leave," she whispered, without daring to look at him further. "If anyone finds you here I'll lose my position."

The sound of seat cushions shifting beneath his weight caught her attention. He was standing. A pause followed and then the muted tread of shoes upon the carpet. Next came the touch of his hands upon her shoulders. "Don't." The word was wrought from her chest on a sob of despair and she felt herself tremble against his touch. "I cannot bear it. I simply cannot."

"Then marry me, Louise." His hands smoothed over her arms, nudging her closer until she felt his solid form against her back. "Tell me you love me as much as I love you and that you will be my wife." Shocked into silence, she tried to make sense of his words. "Come," he whispered gently. "Let's end this state of torment we are in and follow our hearts."

"But…but…" Was this really happening or was it a dream? "What about Gwendolyn? What about your brother's threat?"

"You know I meant to avoid marrying Gwendolyn either way. You also know I meant to do so by finding a way in which to increase my income. And so I have."

"That's…wonderful." She blinked as she stared up into his handsome face.

"There's a new club opening in London," he explained. "I wasn't aware of it until Langley mentioned it to me this afternoon." His throat worked as though he was struggling with what to say. "Turns out all he wanted was for me to be happy."

Frowning, she tried to wrap her head around that. "I don't see how forcing you to marry someone you do not want to marry was going to accomplish such a goal."

"I'll explain it all later. First, you ought to know, before you commit to anything, that I have asked him to remove my stipend. It's time for me to stand on my own two feet, which means life might not be as easy as I would like it to be for a while, but eventually, it ought to improve. I'll still support your sisters. That goes without saying. My affairs aren't as bad as all that."

"Speaking of which…" Moving away from him, she went to pick up yesterday's newspaper. "I found something that might be helpful to you." She handed it over and watched while he read the text to which she pointed.

"Eastern European wine?"

"It's just an idea, but the article says they're much cheaper than the French wines and equally good. The journalist even describes some sweet varieties as tasting like nectar. I just thought it might be worth looking into."

"And so it is," he murmured. "I cannot believe you continued to think of this, that you kept on trying to find a business opportunity for me."

"I just wanted to help."

He stepped toward her. "Because you care about me?"

"I…"

"The truth is in your eyes, Louise. Please tell me

you'll spend the rest of your life with me."

"But…" Oh, how she wanted to say yes. "My father was not well respected. Everyone knows he died a drunk. To attach yourself to me would only harm your reputation. You cannot possibly—"

"My brother knows all of this and has given us his blessing. With his support and our love for each other, we can weather whatever storm comes our way. I'm absolutely certain of it."

Blinking, she tried to gather her thoughts, which was proving to be increasingly difficult now that his hands were smoothing down over her arms. "What about my position? What about—"

"Say yes, Louise. The rest will sort itself out."

And she knew deep in her heart that he was right and that as long as they had each other and his family's approval, they stood a chance of true happiness together. So she allowed her eyes to meet his. "Yes." Joy washed away her pain to leave a smile upon her lips. "I love you, Alistair, and nothing would please me more than being your wife."

"We'll have to see about that," he told her gruffly. And then his mouth descended on hers, unleashing all the pent-up passion he'd been holding back since the moment they'd met in his study.

CHAPTER FIVE

SURRENDERING HEART AND SOUL, LOU-ISE wrapped her arms around Alistair's neck and pressed her chest to his. Lord, it felt wonderful! So did the feel of his hand moving over her back and the press of his lips against hers. If a woman could melt, she believed she would do so at any given moment.

But then his lips parted, and she was no longer in danger of melting but of catching fire.

"Just follow my lead," he murmured.

So she did, tasting and touching as he did. Her hands slid over his shoulders, testing their shape beneath the wool of his jacket. Then down over his back and around his waist. He did the same, though perhaps with more skill and daring. His palm now rested against her breast, and the way he was kissing and touching her… It made heat curl its way through her until she found herself consumed by an inexplicable need. It was like hunger, but not for food – for something different and unfamiliar.

It was unlike anything she'd ever experienced before, and it was wonderful! And when he pressed up harder against her, the urgency building inside her expanded until a desperate plea for more was forced from between her lips. He answered it by trailing kisses along her neck and down over the wide expanse of skin that rose from beneath her neckline. There, with his face nestled against the top of her breasts, he expelled a rough breath and, to her great frustration, went utterly still. "Louise." His murmured words tickled her skin.

"Yes." She raked her fingers through his hair, encouraging him to continue.

But he didn't. Instead, he muttered a curse before pulling back. When his eyes met hers, they bore a strenuous look of hard-won control. His arms, still wound around her, trembled as he leaned back further and finally spoke. "We should wait."

Louise felt her entire body contract with appalled displeasure. "What?"

His jaw clenched, and he was suddenly gripping her harder. "I have refrained from seducing you – from ruining you – for the past two weeks, Louise. It wasn't easy. In fact, considering all the opportunities with which I was presented, it felt bloody impossible at times. And yet somehow I managed to be the gentleman I've been raised to be." Lowering his arms, he took a step back, adding distance. "To ruin that now in a hasty moment of weakness would be a mistake." Swallowing, he closed his eyes briefly before opening them again. "I don't want us to start our life together with a mistake. You deserve better than that."

"Thank you, but I—"

"*We* deserve better than that. Which is why I

insist we wait until after the wedding to consummate our union."

Was he serious? His determined expression suggested he was. "That will be at least three weeks if we marry locally. Longer if we return to London."

"Is that where you wish to get married?" His voice was hoarse. "I suppose you would like for your sisters to attend."

"I honestly haven't really considered it yet, since I'm still getting used to the idea of getting married. But waiting a couple of months seems rather infuriating."

He smiled in response. "It would be a trial for both of us, I suspect." Growing serious once more, he said, "I also refuse to make you mine here beneath my niece's roof. Even if no one found out, it would still feel disrespectful and wrong, which is the opposite of how I want it to be."

"I suppose so," she agreed with some reluctance.

He touched his hand to her face, tipping her chin so she would meet his gaze more directly. "There is the option of procuring a special license. My brother can take care of that for us, if you like. Or we could go to Scotland."

"We could be husband and wife within a few days." As much as she wanted her sisters to be present, the idea of starting her life with this man as soon as possible also felt incredibly right. So she nodded, thoughtfully at first and then with greater assurance. "I would welcome a marriage license for Christmas."

She was back in his arms before she could draw breath again, succumbing to his kisses and his whispered words of thanks. "I will see to it immediately then," he promised when he released her once more. Eyes twinkling, he stepped toward the door and took one last look at her before opening it. "And I will promise you that you will not regret your decision. We'll visit your sisters immediately after the wedding."

☾

Alistair second-guessed his insistence to take the honorable path at least a thousand times in the days that followed. It didn't help that Louise began dressing more like a young lady ought and less like a stuffy old spinster. But as soon as the news of their engagement had spread to the rest of the family, Lady Channing had whisked Louise off to a seamstress after declaring the soon-to-be Lady Alistair ought to be dressed in silk instead of coarse wool. And if Alistair had thought his niece would protest over having to give up her newly acquired governess, he'd been wrong. Not even his brother was as thrilled as Lady Channing was to welcome Louise into the family.

The two had quickly become fast friends, sharing confidences over tea until Alistair felt the need to drag his fiancée off to a private room somewhere so he could have her for himself. Which was probably what Lady Channing suspected him of wanting to do, for the woman stuck to Louise's side like glue, denying him any chance at all of stealing a kiss or two.

Which was probably for the best since a kiss would not be enough at this point. In fact, he was beginning to fear he might grab a pistol and shoot someone by the time his wedding day rolled around. But as he stood in the church that morning, tapping his foot, as if doing so would speed things along, he also felt a surge of great satisfaction. Because now, when he finally took her to bed, it would be the most anticipated moment of his life – a prize unlike any other – and an unforgettable moment to be cherished forever.

Wearing a pink silk gown with a fur-trimmed velvet spencer to match, Louise came toward him at a quicker stride than a bride was expected to use when walking up the aisle. Her smile was wide and exuberant, her eagerness to reach him expanding his heart until he was overcome by anticipation and joy. She was everything he'd been looking for – her presence in his life more valuable than anything else in the world – and she would be his in another few minutes.

The realty of it struck him when she reached his side and placed her hand in his. Her hazel-colored eyes reflected the contents of her heart, the sincerity and love assuring him that marrying her was the best decision of his life. Faintly, in the background, he registered the reverend's voice asking him if he would have Louise to wife, to live together after God's ordinance in the holy estate of matrimony. "Wilt thou love her, comfort her, honor, and keep her in sickness and in health; and, forsaking all other, keep thee only unto her, so long as ye both shall live?"

"I will." His voice was loud and clear, as was hers when she said her vows. Other words were spoken before the reverend finally handed Alistair the ring for him to place on Louise's finger. He did so swiftly, barely waiting for their union to be confirmed before pulling his wife into his arms for a kiss that resulted in loud cheers and clapping from those who'd gathered to watch.

A wedding breakfast, beautifully arranged by Abigail, followed the service. The cake was cut and eaten, and it was finally acceptable for Alistair and Louise to take their leave. "I thought we'd never escape," he said, once they were alone in his carriage.

She leaned into him, surrounding him with her sweet perfume. "It was kind of Abigail to arrange a celebration. To leave any sooner would have been ungrateful on our part."

"You're right, but every second of it still passed with sluggish tediousness." Dipping his head, he kissed his way along her cheek until he was able to whisper in her ear, "I've been anxiously anticipating our wedding night."

A tiny gasp, not of surprise but of pleasure, made him wish he could force the horses into a gallop. Instead, he put his arm around her and pulled her closer, loving the comfort of having her near and the affinity that bound them together.

"Are you nervous?" he asked, when he closed the door to the room at the inn where they'd chosen to spend their wedding night.

She shook her head. "Not really."

"Anxious?"

Again, she shook her head. "On the contrary, I feel inexplicably calm and…ready."

He knew what she meant for he felt the same way, though he couldn't deny the eagerness that made his heart pump a good deal faster. For five long days he'd looked forward to this exact moment —fantasized about how it might be. Now, he moved to where she stood, untied her bonnet and tossed it across the room.

"Alistair!"

"Hmm…" He unbuttoned her pelisse and threw it onto a nearby chair, then took a step forward and drew her into his arms.

She looked up, her eyes more green than brown, and she gave him a tender smile. "I love you, you know."

Pressing a kiss to that gorgeous mouth of hers, he whispered against her lips, "And I love you."

☙

Recognizing the moment when Alistair gave up control, Louise welcomed the urgent touch of his fingers tugging and pulling, unbuttoning and untying until layers of clothing began falling away. Her gown went first, then her stays and chemise, until she was left wearing only her stockings. "You look delicious," he murmured, trailing his fingers over her sides, leaving molten heat in their wake.

Stepping back, he held her gaze, eyelids lowering while he began to untie his cravat. Involuntarily, she licked her lips as more of his skin came into view. "Lord, you tempt me to be improper," he said, discarding the long piece of linen. Shucking his jacket, he tossed it aside and in one swift movement pulled his shirt up over his head. The garment fell to the floor and Louise's mouth went dry.

Never in a million years would she have imagined herself so fortunate as to marry a man like him. He was the embodiment of masculine power and virility. His chest rippled with hard planes and grooves, the muscles of his arms bunching when he flexed his fingers.

"Come here," he murmured, his dark eyes luring her to him, forcing her closer until her breasts grazed his chest. Nostrils flaring, he lowered his mouth to hers, kissing her while he picked her up in his arms and carried her to the bed. There, he laid her down gently before removing his trousers and smalls.

Louise stared. She couldn't seem to do anything else when more of his glorious body came into view. And then he was climbing onto the bed, his hands sliding up her leg and over her thigh. She sighed as he kissed her again.

"Yes."

The pleasure he wrought was divine – touching, tempting, teasing – heightening her pleasure in ways she'd never believed possible. And when he finally nestled between her thighs and she dug her fingertips into his back, he blew out a tortured breath of his own while joining his body with hers.

Another, "Yes," was wrought from his throat, and when he started to move, he set a pace that carried her higher – up to a place where every sensation was sharp and dazzling. Then suddenly, on a rush of euphoria, everything seemed to collide in waves of pure pleasure.

"Amazing," was the only word Louise could

think to describe what had happened between them, when she lay cocooned in Alistair's arms a short while later.

"And to think we get to do this every day for the rest of our lives," he murmured. His hand swept along the curve of her back.

"Every day?"

"Without doubt." Kissing the nape of her neck, he ran his fingers over her side and down across her belly.

"I'll hold you to it." Turning in his arms, she welcomed his kiss with the keen awareness that surrendering was so much sweeter than holding on to control, and that loving this man as he loved her, was the greatest reward in the world.

THE EARL WHO LOVED HER

CHAPTER ONE

THE DAYS WERE GETTING COLDER. Eve could feel it in her bones. Glancing toward the empty fireplace, she addressed her sister, Josephine. "Are you sure you want me to go?"

"Yes." The word was spoken without the slightest hesitation. "Going to Amberly Hall to visit with your friend Margaret is a wonderful opportunity for you, Eve – one you mustn't pass up."

"You didn't mention my going there to Louise before she left," Eve said in reference to their other sister, who was four years older than Eve and two years younger than Josephine. She'd left the day before, after being offered a position as governess in the northern part of the country.

"I worried she would postpone travelling or decide not to go at all if she knew. She didn't like the idea of leaving us alone for Christmas, but she took some solace in knowing we would at least have each other."

"Except now you will be by yourself in this miserable house."

Josephine gave her a sharp look. "We are fortunate to have a house at all. Things could be worse."

Knowing how true that was and how hard Josephine had worked to keep a roof over their heads, Eve apologized for the comment and said, "Perhaps we should let our guardian know about our difficulties."

"No! Absolutely not, Eve. We have managed to get by without relying on any man this past year since Papa died, and we shall continue to do so. Because to take money from a stranger..."

"He is our uncle."

"And yet we have never made his acquaintance." Josephine shook her head. "It wouldn't be right to ask for his help, and I would hate to feel beholden."

"Very well. We will find another way."

"It will be easier now after Louise has found employment."

Eve was well aware. She wished there were more she could do so she could stop feeling guilty about her sisters working while she did nothing besides look pretty. But Josephine wouldn't even let her sweep the floors. Hoping to provide Eve with the season she and Louise had been denied, Josephine insisted Eve should not show any signs of work, which meant her hands had to be kept smooth and unblemished.

Eve picked up her tea and took a sip, wincing in response to the tepid water as it slid down her throat. She drew her shawl tighter around her shoulders. "There is no guarantee my going to Amberly Hall will benefit us in any way."

"No, but it is more likely to do so than your staying here would." Pressing her lips together,

Josephine turned a fierce pair of eyes on her. "Margaret's family is well connected. You are lucky she still remembers you, now our positions are no longer what they once were."

"We've known each other since childhood, Josephine. It would have been cruel of her not to do so."

Josephine sighed. "No, dearest. It would have been expected. But her kindness and consideration—the fact she has invited you to stay with her for the holidays—does speak highly of her character."

"Perhaps I should ask her if you might join me."

"Absolutely not," Josephine said. "To do so would be taking advantage, which is something I refuse to do. Besides, I have my work here. It does not pause for the holidays. So you will go to Amberly alone and enjoy yourself with your friend. I will be perfectly content here, Eve. My only concern is for you travelling alone."

"The distance isn't too great. There are no overnight stays along the way, and I'm sure other travelers will be joining me. So I won't be without company."

"I suppose that is true."

But in spite of the smile Josephine gave her the following day when Eve stepped onto the stagecoach, Eve sensed her sister was doing her best to put on a brave face for her sake. It was the first time they would be apart for more than a day.

Squeezed into a spot by the window with three other passengers beside her on the bench and four more across, Eve caught a final glimpse of Josephine as the carriage lurched into motion.

"Write to me when you get there!" Josephine called.

A quick nod was all Eve could manage before the conveyance turned right, carrying her through a series of streets and out toward the Great Western Road that would take her to Bournemouth. If all went well, she ought to be there by late afternoon, in time to enjoy a cup of tea with Margaret before preparing for dinner.

The carriage charged ahead, stopping every hour to change its team of horses. Sleep proved impossible with every bump in the road jostling her until her bottom got sore. Her comfort did get somewhat better as other passengers arrived at their destinations, allowing for a bit more room inside the cabin.

"Amberly Hall," the coachman finally called, pulling the carriage to a halt at around four o'clock. Darkness was already setting in, encouraged by the thick clouds blocking the sun. Eve climbed down and retrieved her bag from the top of the coach. Gripping it in her hand, she watched the coach lurch into motion once more and disappear down the road.

Right.

She glanced about. Margaret had said she would send a carriage to collect her, but the coach had made good time, so she'd arrived a half hour earlier than expected. With the wind picking up and the light growing dimmer by the second, she elected to start walking toward the lights she could see in the distance. Perhaps she would meet the carriage on her way. One thing was certain, however, and that was the fact she might freeze to death if she stood still for one more second.

Bryce Elliot Harlowe, Earl of Ravenworth, was preparing to enjoy the brandy he'd poured when a knock at the door brought his butler into the library. "My Lord," Radcliff said, "a woman has arrived."

"Does she have a name?" Bryce asked. He glanced across at his favorite chair. Enjoying a peaceful moment of reading by the fire would clearly have to wait.

"Miss Potter. She says she is here to see Mrs. Havisham."

"Then she must have taken a wrong turn somewhere." The Havisham home was six miles in the opposite direction.

"I wish to know if I might offer her the use of your carriage. It is almost dark outside, you see, and it has started to snow. Sending a young woman back out without escort would not sit well with me."

Bryce had to agree. It wouldn't be right to send any woman away again under such circumstances, no matter her age. "Have Peter make the necessary preparations, and in the meantime, please ask Miss Potter to join me." He received few visitors these days and was starting to grow weary of his isolation.

"Very well, my lord." Radcliff left, returning moments later with a woman who stood encased in a long black pelisse. She wore a floppy bonnet which dipped across her forehead, concealing her eyes. Several shawls were wrapped tightly across her shoulders and chest. "May I present Miss Potter?"

The woman attempted a curtsy even as she shivered, which prompted Bryce to step forward quickly and guide her toward the fireplace. Once there, he took a step back and sketched a short bow. "It is a pleasure to make your acquaintance, Miss Potter. I am the Earl of Ravenworth."

She tipped her chin up, her surprise unmistakable. It encompassed her entire face. But what caught his attention the most were her dark blue eyes. They left him completely dazed. Radcliff coughed, pulling Bryce out of his trance and enabling him to gather his wits. He turned toward his butler. "Please arrange for some tea and sandwiches to be brought up and—"

Miss Potter sneezed and then she sneezed again. And a third time.

"Oh dear," she murmured as she took a step closer to the fire.

Oh dear, indeed.

Bryce gave her an assessing look before addressing Radcliff once more. "I believe we should get her out of her wet pelisse and hang it to dry in the kitchen next to the stove. The same goes for her shawls."

"Yes, my lord." Radcliff, being the practical, no-nonsense man he was, crossed to where Miss Potter was standing and held out his hand. "If you'll please give me your outerwear, miss."

Miss Potter hesitated. She glanced at Bryce, who gave her a reassuring nod. "We would hate for you to catch a cold," he said. "Such a thing could very well ruin your Christmas."

That seemed to get her cooperation. Her fingers quickly untied her shawls and peeled them away before going to work on the buttons of her pelisse. This garment came off too, revealing an equally black dress. But not without hinting at a slender yet curvaceous form. Beneath the other layers of clothing, her breasts had been undefined and unremarkable. Now, their rounded curves stood out, drawing Bryce's attention in a way that made him wish she would keep on undressing.

Of course she didn't. But she did take off her bonnet as well, exposing a pile of blonde curls that appeared to have been twisted and pinned down by force. It made him wonder what her hair might look like if it were set free – allowed to fall down over her shoulders and…

He swallowed and turned away, grabbing his glass and tossing back his brandy before swinging around to face Radcliff. "That will be all for now."

The butler hesitated, gave a curt nod, and took his leave without closing the door as he usually did. The gesture was not lost on Bryce, reminding him that Miss Potter, whatever her station, was a young, most likely unmarried, woman. Being alone with her behind closed doors would not be appropriate, even if it meant losing heat from the room.

Sighing, he considered the figure she presented, standing there warming her hands, and he found his attention drawn by the shape of her neck. It curved so delicately, joining with her shoulders before disappearing beneath her gown. A few stray strands of hair curled against it, and for reasons unknown, his fingers itched to draw them back into place.

Wincing, he stepped toward her. "Would you like to sit?" he asked, indicating the armchair closest to the fire.

"Thank you." She turned and lowered herself to the seat, then focused her captivating eyes on him. "I am sorry to intrude upon you like this, my lord."

Bryce's muscles flexed. The way she said, my lord... Damn, but he could too easily imagine her addressing him so in a far more intimate setting, a setting in which fewer clothes would be required.

"You needn't be," he managed to say while he claimed the other chair. His voice sounded rougher than he would have liked.

"It is kind of you to offer your carriage, give me tea and sandwiches, and allow me to warm myself by your fire." She averted her gaze. "You did not have to."

"No. I don't suppose I did," he agreed. "But turning you away would not have been right."

This brought her eyes back to his with aching vulnerability. "Do you always do what is right?"

"I try to. Yes." *Though you might tempt me to toss that principle straight out the window.* It was a good thing she wouldn't be staying long. He'd not had a woman in quite some time, and with Miss Potter's arrival, he was starting to recognize the strain of it.

"That is admirable," she said, and he could see she meant it, which in turn made his chest tighten around his expanding heart.

A maid arrived with a tray, setting it down on a small table before departing the room once more. Bryce watched Miss Potter fill two cups with tea. "Milk and sugar?" she asked.

He shook his head. "No thank you."

She poured a splash of milk into her own, picked up the cup, and set the rim to her lips. Her eyes had initially distracted him from this particular attribute, but he took greater notice now. And as he did so—as he watched that soft piece of flesh press against the delicate china—arousal took hold. Never in his life would he have imagined the simple task of drinking tea could look so bloody erotic, yet Miss Potter, dressed in her modest black gown, managed to make it so.

Crossing his legs, he deliberately strove to hide the effect her arrival was starting to have on him. Clearly, he'd put off procuring a mistress for far too long. Tomorrow, he'd set his mind to it.

First thing in the morning.

In the meantime, however, "I understand from my butler you were trying to reach Amberly Hall?"

"Yes. Mrs. Havisham is a longtime friend of mine. She invited me to visit with her and her husband for the holidays."

"And when you are not in this part of the country, you are in…"

"London," she said, finishing his sentence. "I live there with my older sister."

"What about your parents?"

She gave a small shrug as if to diminish the importance of her next words. "Papa died last year, three years after we lost Mama."

Bryce frowned. "I am sorry to hear it." And he was. He knew all too well how hard it could be to lose a loved one.

"At least my sisters and I have each other."

"So there is more than one?"

"Yes. But Louise no longer lives with us. She has recently accepted the position of governess for the Earl and Countess of Channing's children. In fact, she left for the north of England yesterday."

So Miss Potter was working class. He'd suspected as much, considering her attire, but he hadn't been sure because of her friendship with Mrs. Havisham. He was curious to know what the older sister she'd mentioned did for a living and what she herself planned on doing, but couldn't quite think of how to ask without imposing.

As it turned out, he didn't have to. She revealed the answer by saying, "Josephine, my oldest sister, is an accountant at the Park View hotel in London. Her earnings are enough for all of us to get by on, but since she would like to give me a Season, she..." Miss Potter drew a deep breath. "Forgive me. I don't know why I'm telling you all of this." She made a nervous chuckling sound and reached for a sandwich, filling her mouth with the bread, ham, and cheese.

"That's quite all right. I was interested, so you needn't apologize." But the mention of a Season... Perhaps he'd been wrong about her being working class. "In fact, I must confess you have managed to heighten my curiosity."

"Really?" A few fine breadcrumbs spilled into her lap, and she hastily set about trying to gather them up and discard them on her plate.

"What is your family's background, if you don't mind my asking?"

She went completely still, and he wondered if she might give him a set down for such an imposing question. They were strangers after all. He really had no right to pry. And doing so was doubly wrong in light of what he knew about her deceased parents and working sisters. So much for her impression of him doing the right thing.

"My great grandfather was an earl," she eventually said. "His third son, my grandfather, went into law and opened a successful business. Unfortunately, Papa did not have the same legal acumen, and when Mama died, he gave up on making the effort. Money was lost in an effort to maintain a lifestyle we couldn't afford, assets were sold, and my sisters were denied the Seasons they'd always expected to enjoy, until work became their only option." She dropped her gaze, but not before Bryce was able to notice the sheen of moisture gathering against her lashes. "Josephine and Louise have made so many sacrifices for me. I have to get to Amberly, if only to make the connections I am sure to make with Mrs. Havisham's help."

"Of course." So she was gentry, and if her sisters had anything to say about it, she would remain so, even if they had to join the working class. Understanding the guilt and responsibility she probably felt, he chose to turn their conversation toward a more positive subject. "The annual Christmas dance will be hosted at the assembly hall this Saturday. I'm sure the Havishams will take you."

"Oh." Miss Potter's face brightened. "That would be diverting. I've never attended such an event before." She gave him an uncertain look before asking, "Will you be there too?"

He almost laughed at the absurdity of such a question but managed to maintain his composure. "No. I prefer to keep to myself."

"Why?" She slapped her hand over her mouth, eyes widening with chagrin as she hastily apologized for asking.

"There's nothing wrong with being curious," he told her gently. He himself was finding it difficult not to be when every word she spoke made him eager to find out more about her. Clearly, this self-imposed seclusion of his was beginning to have its toll. "However," he went on, "it is my prerogative to refrain from answering, and I intend to do precisely that." He did not want the only person with whom he enjoyed a bit of conversation for the first time in three years to hate him as much as everyone else did. "We all have our secrets, Miss Potter. You must allow me to keep mine."

*

The gravity with which the earl spoke and the shadows darkening his eyes prompted Eve to wonder what sort of secrets he might be keeping. Her curiosity regarding this man had been gradually increasing since the moment she'd stepped into his library and laid eyes on him.

An angular jaw and well-defined cheekbones provided his face with a rigid structure. It was not as displeasing as it might have been without the soft curve of his mouth and the dark brown warmth of his eyes. His hair, she noted, was almost black, shot through with lighter chocolate-colored tones.

Standing tall, at least a full head above her, he exuded confidence and power, the sort that could send fear shooting through any man who crossed him, and Eve found her heart beating more rapidly than it had upon her arrival. Left alone with him to enjoy her tea and the warmth of the fire, she'd calmed her nerves with talk of her sisters and her situation without once considering how little interest a man like him would have in such matters.

But when she'd glanced at him, he hadn't appeared the least bit bored. Rather, he'd considered her with compassion, then brought up the country dance, which had prompted her to take leave of her senses and ask a most forward question. His response had only made her wonder more about him and why he might choose to avoid a social gathering. As far as she could tell, the house was fairly quiet. Surely his wife would have materialized by now, if he had one.

She bit her lip and glanced around, wondering when the carriage might be ready so she could be on her way once more. However hospitable the earl was proving to be, she was certain he would prefer to return to whatever plans he might have for the evening.

"This fireplace would be perfect for roasting chestnuts," she said, when the silence seemed to drag on for longer than what was comfortable.

Lord Ravenworth's eyes filled with amusement. "Is that what you were thinking about?"

Unwilling to tell him *he'd* been the subject of her musings, she quickly nodded. "The house I grew up in had an equally large fireplace. Roasting chestnuts on it was such a lovely pastime activity on cold winter days."

He chuckled lightly. "You're too young to be getting nostalgic, Miss Potter."

"Perhaps. But the path my life has taken has made it impossible for me not to be."

"You sound as though you have regrets."

Averting her gaze, she stared into the dancing flames. "Not regrets so much as a feeling of overwhelming loss. I miss the comfort of my childhood and the simplicity of my life when both my parents lived. I miss them both terribly, and I miss the bright future my sisters and I looked forward to with innocent anticipation."

A knock sounded at the door, drawing her attention to the butler who had returned. "My lord," he said, addressing his master. "May I have a private word with you?"

Looking over at Ravenworth and noting his deep frown, Eve couldn't stop apprehension from coursing through her. He gave a curt nod and rose to his feet, departing the room and leaving her alone to wonder what might have occurred. Of course, there was the possibility it had nothing to do with her. After all, this was a large household. Any number of things might demand the earl's attention.

But when he returned a short while later and pinned her with his serious eyes, she knew the matter he'd been made aware of had *everything* to do with her. "Forgive me, Miss Potter, but there seems to be a snag in our plan to get you to Amberly Hall tonight."

Lips parting with surprise, she blinked. The significance of his comment began to sink in. "I cannot possibly remain here," she said. "Unless there are other women living under this roof, it would be most—"

"Improper," he said. He held her gaze. "Believe me, I am quite aware of the fact, and to answer your question, I am the only person in residence, besides the servants."

"Then you must agree my staying here is impossible." If anyone were to find out, as Margaret and her husband eventually would, her reputation would be called into question. And while she might be able to convince them that nothing untoward happened while she spent the night in a bachelor's home, they would not in good conscience be able to introduce her to eligible young gentlemen. "If there is a problem with the carriage or one of the horses, I'll be more than happy to walk the distance. You need only point me in the right direction."

"Absolutely not." The adamancy with which he spoke sent a jolt through Eve's body. "No gentleman would ever send a woman out into the freezing night so she can walk six miles to her next destination. It is unconscionable for me to treat you with so little consideration. And what would your sisters say, or your friend, Mrs. Havisham, if something were to happen to you? *I* would be to blame!"

He drew a shuddering breath and raked his fingers through his hair. "My apologies. I did not mean to be so brusque about it, but the fact of the matter is, ice has formed on the road within the past hour. To venture out by carriage, on horseback, or on foot will be hazardous. I'll not risk it. Which means you will remain here as my guest."

"But surely—"

"Your reputation may remain intact if you simply inform your friend that the coach with which you were traveling lost a wheel and was forced to stop at an inn for the night."

"You want me to lie?"

"Either that or risk ruining your chance of enjoying the Season your sisters are working so hard to give you." It was as if he could read her mind. "In the meantime, I will ask my housekeeper to have the maids prepare a spare bedroom for you. You may even have a hot bath brought up if you like. And once you are ready, I would like you to join me for dinner. I find I've been eating alone for far too long."

Without further comment, he left the room while Eve was forced to admit that, as much as she dreaded the possible impact of staying here, she was secretly thrilled with the prospect of spending more time in the Earl of Ravenworth's company.

CHAPTER TWO

AS SOON AS HIS HOUSEKEEPER, Mrs. Dudley, had taken Miss Potter upstairs to the guestroom, Bryce went to the side table and re-filled his glass. He was in the middle of taking a sip when Radcliff returned, making his presence known with a knock on the door. Bryce turned toward him. "Yes?"

"My lord, I apologize if I am about to overstep, but in light of the current situation regarding Miss Potter, I would like to offer a bit of advice in order to…ahem…minimize the impact of her visit." Having previously served in his father's employ, Radcliff had known Bryce his entire life. He'd stood by him when no one else had and took no issue with speaking his mind whenever doing so served his master's best interests.

"You worry I might make certain advances?"

Radcliff's eyes went wide. "Oh no, my lord. I would never suppose such a thing. You are far too gentlemanly to even think of imposing yourself on a young woman."

His butler was right, but that hadn't stopped Bryce from *thinking* of making advances since

Miss Potter's arrival. To say so would not be helpful, however, so he asked instead, "Then what is your concern?"

"If I may be blunt, what you do or do not do will hardly matter once word of her spending the night here without a chaperone gets out. Your reputation—"

"I'm damn well aware of my reputation," Bryce growled.

"Then perhaps you will consider sleeping here in the library?"

"Let us re-visit the part you mentioned about overstepping."

"For your own peace of mind and hers," Radcliff went on as if Bryce hadn't spoken, "it might be best if you pass the night on separate floors of the house. If anyone should inquire about what went on here later, I shall happily testify that everything was proper."

"Nobody will believe you." Bryce knew what people thought of him. To suppose they would not imagine the worst was naïve.

"Nevertheless."

Bryce nodded. "Very well. I shall do what you suggest." *If only to end this discussion.*

Radcliff nodded and took his leave, allowing Bryce to return his attention to his brandy. Crossing the floor, he reclaimed his seat from earlier, leaned back, and glanced at the armchair Miss Potter had vacated a short while ago. With a grimace, he sipped his drink, savoring the rich flavor while a log snapped and sparks crackled in the fireplace.

She was beautiful and she was here, as if sent

by the devil himself in order to tempt him. But he would resist… He curled his hand around the armrest. He would prove to the world he wasn't the monster he'd been accused of being.

And yet, even as he made this vow with conviction, an unbidden image of her undressing began to invade his thoughts. She would bathe before dinner. A tub filled with hot water had been requested. Which meant she would unbutton her unflattering gown to reveal a pair of stays…a chemise… Bryce's mouth went dry. He took another sip of his drink and surrendered to the fantasy of Miss Potter removing these last items of clothing. What harm was there in doing so? It wasn't real, no more than a dream—a sinful wish—a secret hope… Another log snapped in the fire. His breath caught, and his heart rate kick up as arousal assailed him once more.

He had to stop this. It wasn't helping. And yet he could not rid his mind of her sinking into hot water with a sigh of pleasure, of taking the soap and running it over her bare skin, of washing her breasts, her belly, the juncture between her thighs…

The glass in his hand shattered. Bryce muttered a curse. The remains of his brandy stained his trousers while shards of glass littered the carpet. He would have to call a maid to clean it up, though doing so would have to wait until he'd gotten himself under some semblance of control. So he simply retrieved his handkerchief and pressed it to the tiny cut his wicked imaginings of Miss Potter had caused. It was only one night. Surely he would be able to get himself through it without expiring from lust. And then tomorrow, after seeing her safely returned to Amberly Hall, he would set his mind to procuring a mistress. A necessary matter which seemed to be long overdue.

But when he sat down to dinner an hour later with Miss Potter directly to his right, the prospect of bedding another woman went straight out the window. He wanted this one, and he wanted her with a feral resolve that made his entire body ache with need. "How was your bath?" he quietly asked. Apparently, he would submit himself to torture.

"Oh." She'd just taken a bite of the ham they were having. She chewed it, chased it down with a sip of wine, and gave him a smile that tightened all of his muscles. "It was lovely. Exactly what I needed after a long day of traveling."

"And your bedchamber?" He ought to turn his mind to other subjects before he did something rash, like haul her into his lap and kiss her breathless. "Is it to your liking?"

"Indeed, it is so incredibly comfortable and luxurious." A dreamy look overcame her features, and Bryce became transfixed. "The plush carpet is heavenly beneath my feet and the bed..." She actually sighed. "I cannot wait to lie back against its inviting mattress."

Bryce stared. Did she have any idea how alluring she was being right now? Of how erotic she sounded? Of course she didn't. She was an innocent young woman hoping to get herself married to an eligible young bachelor. The last thing she'd want to do was encourage a stranger to take certain liberties with her. "I'm glad you like it," he managed to say, before returning his attention to his food in the hope of finding some distraction.

"I suppose you enjoy reading," she said, after a couple of minutes.

Bryce blinked and met her inquisitive gaze. The blueness made him stop for a second in order to gather his thoughts. "I don't hate it," he finally managed.

She grinned, lifting the unhappy atmosphere filling his home for so long. "Considering the impressive size of your library, I should hope not."

Allowing a slight smile of his own, Bryce held her sparking gaze. "Books have always felt like a sound investment."

"So you're a collector?"

He dipped his head. "I suppose you could say that."

She nodded as if she understood, and perhaps she did. "Have you read them all?"

"No. But I have read the most interesting ones."

His answer seemed to satisfy her. She gave a succinct nod and took another bite of her food before asking, "Do you collect other things besides books?"

"Coins and…" He snorted, wondering what she would think of this next revelation. "Flowers." She stared at him for a second, and it occurred to him he was holding his breath in anticipation of what she might say.

"How intriguing." She sounded pensive. "May I see them after we finish our meal?"

The interest with which she asked the question could not be denied. "Of course." It would mean more time in her company, and however unwise that might be, he could not stop himself from giving in to temptation.

So he led her away from the dining room once they'd finished desert and guided her toward his most private sanctuary. He produced a key from his pocket, opened the door, and waited for her to enter, then followed her into the room where nature was turned into lasting pieces of art.

☾

Standing close to Ravenworth, Eve was acutely aware of his masculine presence. The scent of him alone—of sandalwood and pine—was enough to make her insides shiver. And although she hadn't considered him handsome in the classical sense to begin with, the intensity with which he studied her, the focus with which he addressed each subject of conversation, and the manner in which he carried himself were so attractive, she could not help but be drawn to him in a way she'd never been drawn to any man before.

It was wrong, of course. She was well aware. He was an earl, and she was practically nobody. And then there was the impropriety of the whole situation, of her being in his home without a chaperone and about to spend the night there. She ought to be dreading every moment of it. Instead, she was thrilled with the prospect of having him near and of…trying to understand her curious reaction toward him.

It felt strange—as if her body could not decide if it wished to be hot or cold. Her stomach had started to twist itself into various knots each time he glanced her way, and she could feel the occasional tremor darting across her skin whenever he was close enough to touch.

It was most unsettling really, but it was also something so curious it demanded further exploration, if only to understand it. So she steeled herself and moved a bit nearer to where he was standing. It happened at the exact same moment he took a step toward her. The movement brought her almost shoulder to shoulder with him, and yes, there it was again, that strange lurch in the pit of her belly. A surge of heat rose up her spine, flushing her skin. She hastily added more distance by going toward the display case spanning the length of the wall. Heart pounding, she tried to focus on what it contained while she made every effort to slow her galloping pulse.

"Are those real?" she finally asked, when she realized what she was looking at.

"Yes. Some are from hothouse bouquets, others are wildflowers picked in various parts of the country. I paint them with gold leaf so they can last forever." There was a slight pause, and then, from behind her left shoulder, "I also appreciate the beauty."

Eve's heart ricocheted wildly as Ravenworth's breath brushed over the back of her neck. Her lungs struggled to draw breath, and there was something else, something that hadn't been there before. Unsure of what it might be, Eve remained perfectly still while pretending to show great interest in all of the gilded flowers. But inside, she was in turmoil. Her body began responding more urgently to Ravenworth's nearness. Which was silly, since she'd only met him a few hours earlier, not to mention incredibly embarrassing, when he would never be equally attracted to her.

Sobered by her reflection, she moved away to admire the rest of the room. He'd set up a table—a workspace with flowers carefully stored in transparent glass boxes, a few brass containers, what appeared to be a small oil-powered stove, and various tools. "You should turn these into jewelry," she said, once the table was placed between them and there was less risk of her melting into a needy puddle of inexplicable desire.

Because that was what this was, wasn't it? Her mother had warned Josephine about it years ago, about how it could divest both man and woman of their senses and prompt them to ignore the consequences. It was nature's way of securing a continuation of the species, but it was wrong to allow outside the bounds of marriage. And since she would not marry him, she would have to ignore the effect he'd started having on her. She would stay one night. Surely she could get through it without losing her sanity. After all, she was here to see her friend, not to cavort with an earl.

"I have done so with a few of the pieces." He went to a drawer and pulled out a flat box. Setting it on the table, he opened it to reveal a rose pendant attached to a gold chain. His eyes met hers. "What do you think?"

"It is lovely. Absolutely lovely."

"In that case, it is yours." He held the box toward her.

Eve stared at it before peering back up at him,

her skin tightening across her body in response to the forcefulness of his gaze. She shook her head. "I couldn't possibly." Her heart thudded loudly and she forced herself to retreat all the way to the door. Once there, she swallowed hard while steadying herself against the doorframe. "Thank you for your hospitality this evening, but I find I am rather exhausted. If you'll excuse me, I must…I must…"

Her breath caught, and words became impossible to speak while he simply stood there watching her with a hooded expression. "Good night," she finally managed, upon which she fled. Because to remain there alone with him in that room, overcome by the masculinity he exuded, would be like playing with fire. And if there was one thing she hoped to avoid doing, it was getting burned.

Bryce watched her agitated departure with interest. She'd seemed especially flustered since entering this room and increasingly so, the closer he'd moved to where she'd stood. Sighing, he closed the jewelry box and returned it to the drawer. What the hell had he been thinking to offer her such a gift? The gesture had likely offended her in its impropriety. A man did not give jewelry to a woman unless she was his wife or his mistress. But when he'd seen her reaction to the piece—the appreciation shining in her eyes while she'd stood there admiring it—he'd felt as though it ought to be hanging around her neck instead of being hidden away from the world.

Leaving the room, he headed back to the library, removed his jacket, and kicked off his shoes. Radcliff had a point. He should not be sleeping on the same floor as Miss Potter. It would not be right, nor would it allow him a moment's rest, knowing she was but a few doors away, tucked into the comfortable bed she'd mentioned at supper.

Groaning, he turned down the oil lamps so only a dim glow from the fire remained, then settled himself on the sofa and prepared to get some rest. But sleep was impossible to find when contemplating his houseguest produced a flare of heat in his loins. The clock chimed midnight, and Bryce blew out a breath. Throwing his arm over his eyes, he tried to find a distraction, something with which to cool his ardor.

Seventeen multiplied by eight, divided by four, and subtracted from five hundred and fifty nine...

A creak caught his attention. Pausing to listen, he heard it again. It sounded like it came from the hallway, so he held his breath and glanced at the door. Perhaps it was Radcliff making a final round to ensure no lights had been left burning, though it was rather late for that.

The door eased open, and a figure that definitely did not belong to his butler appeared. Mesmerized, Bryce watched Miss Potter enter the room. She was carrying an oil lamp, ,the glow from it bathing the nightgown she wore in golden light.

Christ!

He squinted through the darkness, aware she was unlikely to notice him, which allowed him to do what no gentleman would ever consider doing, and simply observe.

Carefully, she moved toward the bookcase, bringing her slightly closer. Setting her lamp on a nearby table, she turned up the light a little until...

Bryce clenched his hands and bit back a growl while he watched the opaque white cotton she wore turn translucent. Feeling his chest work against his attempt at keeping his ragged breathing as soft as possible, he watched her rise up onto her toes and pick a book from a higher shelf. The nightgown rose with her, sliding up over her legs. And then, as if that weren't enough, she grabbed the book and turned around, allowing him a blatant view of her perfectly rounded breasts, outlined by the fabric.

Closing his eyes, Bryce began counting backward from one thousand.

He was going to die, plain and simple.

"What happened to him?" some would ask, and others would answer, *"I hear he was consumed by lust."*

A limerick would probably mark his headstone. Something along the lines of:

This randy fellow would not be appeased,
His appetites grew but could not be pleased.
Sadly unsated,
He miscalculated,
The dangerous outcome of being teased.

A quick intake of breath–something much like a gasp–had him opening his eyes to find Miss Potter staring straight at him. He sat up, because pretending he wasn't there was no longer an option.

"Miss Potter," he said, doing his best to sound surprised. Which was bloody difficult when she was standing closer than before. Especially since the light from her lamp washed away her nightgown completely, leaving nothing but soft feminine curves.

"Oh dear," she murmured, her eyes wide and stricken and…something else…

Aware.

He thanked the Lord he remained shrouded in darkness so she wouldn't see his expression too well or the inappropriate effect she was having on him. Because since she was standing, he had to do so too, which meant a certain part of him would become embarrassingly visible if any more light spilled his way.

"What are you doing here?" he tried to ask by way of continuing to pretend he'd awoken to find her there.

"I, er, I could not sleep, so I decided to come down and find a book."

"Very good."

A moment of silence fell between them, and then she asked, "How about you?"

"Hmm?"

"What are you doing here?"

"Trying to sleep," he said. "Radcliff suggested it might be better if you and I did not occupy the same floor at night."

"Oh." She clutched the book she'd selected against her chest. "Then I should leave. This…" She waved her hand in an awkward way. "I'm so sorry to have intruded."

"You needn't worry. I do not plan on mentioning it to anyone, though I would advise you to wear a dressing gown when venturing beyond your bedchamber in the future. That nightgown you're wearing..." He allowed his gaze to travel over the length of her body. "It reveals a lot more than you'd wish to know."

A sharp breath was her only response before she turned on her heel and practically ran. He knew he'd behaved like a cad, but he also believed in honesty. If the woman thought there was nothing wrong with what she'd been wearing, he'd hopefully taught her otherwise. Because if a lesser man had seen her in such a state of dishabille, she would likely have been on her back in a second, with her scandalous nightgown hitched up around her waist.

As it was, Bryce had pushed back the urge to approach her and to seduce her, not because she would have resisted–he was starting to sense she might be more open to such an advance than even she was aware–but because he still liked to think of himself as an honorable man. Even if his thoughts did belong in the gutter.

☾

Panting from the exertion of racing up a long flight of stairs and darting through a hallway, Eve leapt inside the sanctuary of her bedchamber, shutting the door behind her and locking it for good measure.

Good Lord!

Heart pounding, she crossed the floor to the mirror with hesitant steps, paused while she gathered her courage, and then raised the oil lamp so she would see what *he* had seen. A hot shiver raked her skin as she took in the image she presented. It hadn't occurred to her that her nightgown might be see-through, but aided by the light from the lamp, it most certainly was. And the worst part was she was totally and completely, undeniably naked underneath, which meant he had seen… Dear God, Lord Ravenworth had seen… Swallowing, she set the lamp on her nightstand and turned down the light before climbing back into bed.

Her heart still beat a frantic rhythm. So she drew a calming breath and allowed herself to think back on the incident. He'd been in the dark, so she hadn't noticed him until she'd prepared to leave. And although he'd been silhouetted against the shadows, she'd known he'd been without his jacket. That knowledge alone had been enough to make liquid heat pool in the deepest part of her belly.

But then he'd told her what he'd seen and she'd fled. The knowledge had stirred a fire within her, and in that moment, she had been terrified. Which now made her thump her fist against her mattress. The earl was no gentleman to say such things to a woman. He was a scoundrel, and she could not afford to lose the chance she had of securing her future on account of him.

Which meant it was just as well she would leave his home and go to Amberly Hall tomorrow. Her only hope was of Margaret not questioning her explanation about a coach delay on account of the weather. Because if she did, Eve feared she might stand to lose an important friendship. And she was not prepared to do so for a man she'd met that same afternoon.

But when she descended to breakfast the following morning intent on facing her host with resolve, her decision to quit his company was swiftly expelled the moment she entered the dining room and met his gaze.

He stood and moved to pull out her chair. "I fear you must stay here at least one more day," he told her. "It snowed heavily last night. The horses will not be able to make their way through it, never mind a carriage."

"But... No." She shook her head. "I cannot stay here any longer."

"As eager as you are to leave my company, I regret to tell you that you are solidly stuck." He gestured for her to sit, and when she failed to do so, eyeing the empty chair with a wariness that must have showed, he expelled a breath and came toward her. Lowering his voice so the nearby footman wouldn't hear, he whispered, "Please rest assured I will remain on my best behavior. What I told you last night was unforgiveable. I hope you will accept my sincerest apologies."

"It doesn't change what you saw or the fact I know you saw it," she muttered. Try as she might, she could not stop her cheeks from flushing. But she held her head high and kept her spine straight in an effort to maintain some pride.

"No. But if it is any consolation, you may rest assured there was nothing wrong with what I did see. Quite the contrary."

His mischievous smirk and the devilish gleam in his eyes were so unsettling, she balled her hand into a tight fist and punched his upper arm. "You are insufferable," she declared. She marched across to her chair and sat before he had a chance to assist her.

"You hit me!"

He stared at her, but she didn't care. She was much too annoyed to let his dismayed expression affect her. Instead, she busied herself by piling food onto her plate: bacon, eggs, toast, and kippers. Perhaps if she ate, her mood would improve.

"I tried to apologize." He sat back down in his chair.

Grabbing the butter, she sliced off a glob and proceeded to spread it across her toast with tight little movements. "Yes. You did. And then you went and ruined it with the sort of comment for which you apologized seconds earlier." *Ugh!* The man was really getting on her nerves today. Especially the part of him that sent little butterflies fluttering about in her belly.

"Should I insult you instead? Would it be better if I told you I found you displeasing or if I suggested you eat less cake?"

That did it!

She set down her knife and glared at him with as much disdain as she could give a man who'd offered her shelter, a nice warm bed, and some excellent food. "I am beginning to understand why there is no *Lady* Ravenworth," she bit out between clenched teeth. "No woman in her right mind would want to subject herself to..." Her words trailed off as she watched his expression harden.

Without warning, he shoved back from the table and stood. "If you'll excuse me, there's a pressing matter to which I must attend," he told her crisply. "Do make yourself at home, Miss Potter. My servants are at your disposal." And on that note, he turned and strode from the room, leaving Eve with a sour taste in her mouth and a shameful feeling of guilt in her heart.

CHAPTER THREE

SHUTTING THE DOOR BEHIND HIM, Bryce locked it and pushed out a breath. Her words should not have stung. She was a virtual stranger, a woman he'd never laid eyes on before she'd arrived at his house, shivering from cold, yesterday afternoon. And yet, there was no denying the tightness squeezing his chest or the tension constricting his veins. With a few angry words, she'd managed to hurl his past toward him so fast it had hit him with full force, bringing with it the pain and resentment he was certain he'd buried so long ago.

For three years he'd kept mostly to himself, and whenever he'd ventured out, he'd held his head high and ignored the reproachful looks being sent his way. He'd told himself he did not care, that other people's opinions did not matter. Well, apparently Miss Potter's did. And although she couldn't possibly know about the incident that had changed his life for the worse, her comment still grated. *I am beginning to understand why there is no* Lady *Ravenworth.*

Inhaling deeply, he went to his work table where a bit of mistletoe waited. Snatching it up by its stem, he twirled it between his fingers. Somehow, in no more than twelve short hours, Miss Potter had breached his defenses.

What a fool he was to have allowed such a thing to happen. He, of all people, should have known better. But he'd been taken with her from the moment she'd turned her dazzling blue eyes upon him. Little by little, she'd drawn him in, until last night... His mouth went dry once more as he reflected on how tempting she'd been in her nightgown. Her body...

He winced and tossed the piece of mistletoe aside. He'd do well not to think of it. No good would come of doing so since they were destined to part tomorrow. Somehow, he would get her out of his life by then, because not doing so was bound to drive him mad.

Removing his jacket and rolling up his sleeves, he sat. A few hours of working on his flowers ought to distract him from his alluring houseguest. *She has a vicious tongue,* he reminded himself as his mind began to betray his determination to think of anything other than her. *Only because I incensed her.* She'd been right to get angry with him. What he'd told her had been inexcusable. It only confirmed what everyone already had concluded—that he was the worst sort of scoundrel to walk the earth, a man so selfish and cruel not even his own family wished to stand by him.

A gentle knock sounded at the door. Bryce stared at the rose before him, propped up by a cleverly crafted stand. It was almost covered in gold, painted by the brush he held between his fingers. Blinking, he wondered how long he'd been lost in his musings. An hour or two at least, considering his progress.

The knock came again, and Bryce sucked in a breath. It was her. He knew it in the pit of his stomach. And although he wanted to let her in, he also wanted to keep her away. Doing so was best for both of them. Neither could allow themselves to give in to temptation. Not when the stakes were as high as they were, with her intending to make a good match and him more than likely to ruin that for her.

So he didn't respond, waiting instead for the gentle tread of retreating footsteps. Regret welled up inside him, but it was for the best. This way, they could both go on with their lives as if crossing paths with each other was nothing more than a slight inconvenience.

☾

He didn't want to speak with her. That much was clear. While his withdrawal annoyed her, she couldn't blame him for it. Not when she'd behaved so abominably. She felt awful about what she'd said. Her words had clearly struck him with greater force than she'd ever expected. Which made her wonder. Why wasn't he married? Perhaps he had been, and his wife had died? It would certainly explain why her cutting remark had bothered him so.

Intent on offering him an apology, she'd sought him out. But he'd refused to let her into the room where he'd secluded himself, and after knocking a couple of times, she'd granted him the solitude he wished for. Which meant she would have to entertain herself until it was time to eat again. Because surely he would show up for luncheon.

But he didn't. Nor did he put in an appearance for dinner. At which point it became clear he had no intention of seeing her ever again. She would depart the following morning, and she doubted he would be there to see her off. It was as if he'd banished her from his life already, and although she should not care, she did—a lot more than she'd like to.

After retiring that evening, she remained in her bedchamber. She would not venture downstairs in hope of encountering him in the library. No. She would respect his wishes and allow the distance he wished for to sink between them. And then she would leave, intent on enjoying Christmas with Margaret and her family, in a home that would not contain a man with a serious frown and eyes as black as the darkest night.

She would forget him and go on to live a happy life with a suitable gentleman of her choosing. Or so she told herself even though, somewhere deep down inside, a little voice whispered no other man would ever affect her as Ravenworth did. The feelings he stirred in her were like little whirlwinds, spinning out of control.

Staring up at the ceiling, she pictured his face, the intensity of his gaze, and the tight lines bracketing his mouth. He was not a man prone to amusement, the severity of his features suggesting he'd had his fair share of troubles. But whenever she caught him observing her, she came alive in ways she'd never imagined she might. It was intoxicating and frightening in equal measure, and since she'd no experience with such things, she hadn't a clue how to deal with it besides doing what she could to preserve her reputation and leave the source of these strange new sensations.

Which was why, when Radcliff informed her of a fallen tree the following morning, she determined it would not be enough to keep her in Ravenworth's home for one more second. Not after eating breakfast alone and being told his lordship had said she was welcome to play the piano or stroll through the gallery or pass her time with some painting. *He*, however, would not be joining her.

So she'd returned upstairs and packed the few things she'd removed from her bag. Looking out of her bedchamber window, she considered the thick snow blanketing the ground. Travelling through it on foot was going to be tiresome but not impossible. And since it was daylight, she was confident she'd find her way to Amberly Hall, even if she had to climb over a fallen tree in order to do so.

With her mind made up, she penned a note of thanks to Ravenworth, put on her pelisse, and wrapped her shawls around her. Tying her bonnet into place, she slipped on her gloves, took one last look at the room, and carefully entered the hallway. Pausing there, she listened for any approaching footsteps. All was silent. She expelled a sigh of relief and made her way toward the stairs. She stopped there again, her heart leaping a little when Radcliff crossed the foyer below. He didn't look up, however. Nor did the footman who followed him through to the hallway.

Eve clenched her fists, steadying her resolve. She wasn't a prisoner, but if they caught her trying to leave, they would name all sorts of reasons why she ought to postpone her departure. And that was something she couldn't allow. Not with her future hanging in the balance and her sisters expecting her to get introduced to a few potential suitors. Certainly not when she feared her heart might have opened too much to a man whom she barely knew, a man who would never want to make her a permanent part of his life. His rank was too elevated compared with hers to allow for such a possibility. And she was a fool to even consider it.

So she tiptoed down the stairs, hurried across the floor, and eased the front door open. Stepping out into the chilly air, she closed the door gently behind her. Then she took a deep breath and strode out into the snow.

☾

Awakened by a loud pounding sound, Bryce groaned in response to the pain slicing its way through his skull and rolled onto his side. "Go. Away." Unless a catastrophe had occurred, he'd no desire to rise. Whoever dared to disturb him after he'd made it clear he wished to be left alone was going to be dismissed.

"My lord?"

Bloody hell!

He climbed from the bed and flung his robe over his shoulders, tied it shut, and marched across to the door. Pulling it open, he glared at Radcliff. "Someone had better have died," he growled.

Seemingly unfazed by his angry outburst, Radcliff spoke with swift precision. "Miss Potter has gone."

His comment put Bryce back on his heels. "Gone?" He scratched his head. "So the snow and ice have melted, and the road is once again passable?"

"No, my lord."

Bryce stared at his butler. "What exactly are you telling me?"

"To be blunt, she slipped out, leaving behind a note for you in her bedchamber." Producing said note, Radcliff handed it over.

A swift touch of dread sliced through Bryce's body. He unfolded the paper and read, his heart thumping faster and faster with each passing word. She was grateful for his hospitality and apologized for not seeming more appreciative. *I am sorry for what I said. It was unkind and unjust. You are a good man, and I have been fortunate to know you.* And yet she was gone, out into the freezing cold in her black pelisse and threadbare shawls.

"When did she leave?" he asked. An image of her trembling body from two days earlier snuck its way to the front of his mind.

"An hour ago, I should think."

Bryce winced and muttered a curse. Her note crumpled in the palm of his hand. "Tell Jenkins to come and help me dress."

"I am already here." His valet materialized from around the corner of the doorway.

"Good." Bryce spun away from his servants and

went to wash his face, only dimly aware Jenkins followed him into the room and proceeded to lay out clean clothes. His mind was on Miss Potter. What the devil was she thinking to go out into such weather alone without any idea of where she was heading? She'd likely get lost again and…

His gut clenched in response to all of the awful outcomes he could imagine. "Let us make haste," he told his valet. With an hour's head start, there was no telling how far she'd gone or how easily he would be able to find her.

*

Gritting her teeth, Eve tried to stand again, only to fall back when splintering pain shot through her ankle. She'd most likely twisted it after losing her balance and falling over. So now she sat, waist deep in the freezing snow and too far away for anyone to hear her calling for help. She'd already tried to do so repeatedly, until her voice had gone hoarse and only a weak little sound emerged.

Wrapping her arms around herself, she fought the shivers shaking her shoulders. If she could only find a fallen tree branch to offer support, she'd be able to make her way forward again. But there were no branches in sight, only a wide smooth surface of unforgiving whiteness.

Teeth chattering, she pushed herself up once more, whimpering in response to the pain as tears started to burn the back of her eyes. Staying here and freezing to death was not an option. She tried to step forward, but collapsed with a suffering groan. *Oh God*! What an idiot she'd been to leave the comfortable warmth of Ravenworth's home. Why hadn't she listened when she'd been told the roads were impassable?

Because staying there with him had felt impossible. She'd needed to get away. And now she was hurt and stranded, and it was beginning to rain. The first icy droplets fell on her head with a slow drip, drip. Seconds later, what might have been nothing more than a bit of additional dampness had turned into a steady downpour of sleet. Eve's throat began to close, and the first hot tears slid down her cheeks. She would die here, cold and alone and without fulfilling her duty.

Sobbing while water soaked through her clothes, she forced herself to stand once more, but taking one single step would have been difficult on a warm sunny day. In deep snow, it was impossible. Equally impossible was the chance of anyone rescuing her any time soon. Which was why she was startled to hear a voice shouting what sounded as though it might be her name.

She paused to listen and had begun to think she must have imagined it when she suddenly heard it again. It was louder this time. "Miss Potter!"

She twisted around, looking between the trees in the direction from which it had come. "Over here," she called as loudly as she could manage.

A few seconds passed, and then a figure emerged, striding forward with hunched shoulders and a deliberate stride. Ravenworth. He hadn't sent a footman or some other servant out to look for her. He'd come to find her himself. She was mortified by the prospect of having to face him after the trouble her leaving had caused, but she was too grateful to care about any of it at the moment. Instead she waved her hand to make sure he'd seen her.

It wasn't until he was almost before her that she could see his face and the furious expression he wore. "You…" Whatever he meant to say was snuffed out by a misty puff of air. He bent down beside her, studying her appearance. His eyes met hers in an unyielding stare, forcing her to shrink back a little. "Are you hurt?" he asked.

Nodding, she told him about her ankle and how much it pained her to move.

His nostrils flared, and then he reached out, sliding his arms beneath her and picking her up. "We'll discuss your stupidity later." He turned and headed back toward the house. "For now, the most important thing is to get you dried off before you catch your death."

Knowing nothing she said would erase her error in judgment, Eve held her tongue and settled against him. He might be angry with her, but that did not diminish how safe she felt in his arms. His strength seeped through her. It lifted her spirits and offered a welcome sanctuary where the wet and the cold were swiftly forgotten. All she could think of was him, the firmness of his chest and the way water clung to his hair. His jaw, set in a strict line, was rough with day-old bristles, affording him with a rugged look that made her heart beat even faster.

Dipping his chin, he glanced down at her. His eyes narrowed. "What is it?" he asked in a tone of undeniable irritation.

Smiling, she nestled her head against his shoulder. "Nothing," she murmured. "I think I rather like you, that's all."

He said nothing by way of response, but she felt his chest vibrate with a guttural sound to match his unkempt appearance. Pressing her cheek to the place where his heart resided, she could feel the vital organ drumming a wild tattoo. It warmed her to no end, because it suggested that in spite of his stern expression and the clipped tone with which he'd spoken, he would eventually forgive her for doing what she had done, even if he did mean to chastise her first.

☾

Pushing his feet through the snow, Bryce marveled at how Miss Potter had managed to walk as far as she had. It certainly proved how determined she'd been to leave his home in favor of Amberly Hall. But when he'd finally happened upon her, the gratitude lighting her eyes had made his heart swell with something surpassing the attraction he had toward her. Relief had been one emotion, brought on by the fact he'd actually found her. Anger had also been prevalent, inspired by the fear of what might have happened if he hadn't. But there had been thankfulness too, the kind that made him realize he cared a great deal about her well-being.

And then she'd smilingly told him she liked him, and he'd been lost lost in the feel of her trembling form pressed up against him and lost in the startling awareness he would never again let her go. It shocked him to think of it, all things considered. The irrationality of it could not be denied. And yet, the idea of losing her, of worrying where she might be in the world and of what might be happening to her…

He shook his head. He didn't even know her given name. To imagine building a future with her made no sense whatsoever. Except it made perfect sense. And although he might not know much about her, he knew her character.

She was fiercely determined, loyal toward her sisters, intent on doing her duty, and daring too. Embarrassed as she had been when she'd realized he'd seen her naked, she hadn't crumbled in a fit of hysterics, but faced him and given him a proper set down to boot. Which meant she wasn't a coward but rather…a perfect match.

Setting his jaw, he pushed back the thrill that threatened to give him hope, and focused on getting her home instead. She liked him. That was surely a good beginning. Whether she would continue to like him later when she discovered what he'd been accused of was a different matter. He would not think of that now. But he would take advantage of their situation. While the weather remained what it was, she was his guest. Which presented him with a wide variety of possibilities, most notably the chance of endearing himself to her even further.

☾

Awoken by whispering voices, Eve kept her eyes closed and strained to listen. It sounded as though they were far away and muffled. A door creaked open. The gentle tread of approaching footsteps brought someone closer, shifting the air around her. Peeking beneath her lashes, she spied a man's jacket and opened her eyes more fully to find the earl standing over her bed with a grave expression. It softened as he watched her come more fully awake.

"I hope I didn't disturb you," he said.

His voice was gentler than usual and his eyes... Eve caught her breath. "You look worried."

Grimacing, he pulled up a chair and sat down beside her. "A willful woman determined to brave the elements at her own peril is presently in my care. What reason do I have to worry?"

"I'm sorry," she said, not shying away from the turbulent look in his gaze. "I just...I was sure you wanted me gone, and I also feared what might happen the longer I stayed. But it was foolish of me to attempt to reach Amberly Hall in this weather. Especially after being told doing so would be dangerous."

"At least you're owning up to your mistake."

She winced. "I believe I've been punished with an ankle that hurts like the devil."

Tilting his head, he raised his eyebrows as if to say, "You've only yourself to blame." But he didn't. Instead, he told her something completely different. "I treated you unfairly yesterday. Avoiding your company was inexcusably rude and inconsiderate. So I'm not surprised you believed you were unwelcome here. For that, I am truly sorry, Miss Potter."

"Eve." She didn't know why she felt compelled to share her name with him, but since he'd saved her from the elements and was showing nothing but kindness when what she truly deserved was for him to be vexed with her, it seemed incredibly right.

His eyes widened, the pupils dilating while tiny flecks of gold popped into view. "Eve." He spoke her name on a whisper of breath, and with such reverence, she almost melted right then and there. "What a lovely name. It suits you tremendously."

Smiling up at him, she didn't quite know what to say besides, "Thank you." But she could sense something had shifted between them, as if they'd crossed a wide expanse to meet in the middle. It felt incredibly good and right, better than anything else ever had.

His eyes drifted down the length of her duvet-covered body before returning to her face. "Your foot will require a few days' rest. If you need help with anything, simply ring the bell-pull here." He gestured toward the velvet rope hanging beside her bed. "Day or night, it doesn't matter, Eve."

"I'd hate to bother anyone."

"No arguing," he told her sternly. "You are not to leave this bed without assistance. Is that clear?"

"You've shaved," she said, not answering his question.

A look of disorientation overcame him. "What?"

Settling back against the plump pillows, her eyes grew heavy. Her eyelids began to close. "You were so," she yawned, "rugged earlier."

A pause before asking, "You liked it?"

"Mmm hmmm." She was drifting away.

"Promise me you'll call for help if you need it,"

he said.

"I promise."

Sound faded into the distance as sleep overwhelmed her, though she did imagine the barest hint of a kiss being pressed against her brow. A dream, most likely. That's what it was. And she welcomed it with pleasure.

CHAPTER FOUR

❦

BRYCE KNEW WHAT HIS BUTLER was going to say before he opened his mouth. "My lord," Radcliff began in that dry affected tone of his. "Regarding Miss Potter…"

Eve.

Bryce hadn't been able to get her name out of his head since she'd mentioned it to him the previous day.

"Yes, Radcliff, I am aware of the impropriety of her prolonged stay here, but what would you have me do? I cannot throw her out, nor am I able to transport her to Amberly Hall. So what choice do I have but to ensure she is comfortable and well cared for while she is here?"

"None whatsoever," was Radcliff's shocking reply.

Bryce stared at him. "I beg your pardon?"

The older man raised his bushy eyebrows, took a step forward, and closed the door to Bryce's study behind him. "If I may speak plainly, my lord?"

"Of course." Bryce leaned back in his chair. He was more than a little curious to hear what his butler was going to say.

"When Miss Potter first arrived," Radcliff began, "I was very much opposed to the idea of her remaining here, even though there was no alternative, given the road conditions."

"Your point?"

"Well, the thing of it is..." Radcliff drew a deep breath. "After *the incident*, your lordship has stopped all attempts at courtship, so I was thinking, hoping actually, with Miss Potter spending several nights here in your home without chaperone, you might consider making an offer. Of marriage, that is."

It was something Bryce had been thinking over, though he did not say so. He was far too intrigued by the fact Radcliff appeared to be blushing. "I have not compromised her," he murmured.

"No one will know that."

Wincing, Bryce met his butler's eyes directly. "You're right there. Everyone will think the worst."

"Then perhaps—"

"Miss Potter deserves a choice. She did not stay here of her own free will. On the contrary, she made a valiant effort to leave. So I intend to help her do so once the roads become passable. If it comes to it, I expect you and the rest of the servants to say she was never alone in my company." Yesterday, he'd decided not to let her go. Today, with a clearer mind, he'd acknowledged that doing so was his only option. For one thing, he wouldn't keep her by force, and for another, she had to be given the freedom to make her own decision.

Radcliff nodded. "You have my full support,

my lord, though I do wish you would reconsider. Seems to me the two of you would get on well as husband and wife."

"Not when she finds out about what I did."

Radcliff snorted. "You did nothing wrong."

"Nobody has ever believed that. Not even my own family." His shoulders grew tense so Bryce made an effort to relax them.

"Yet another reason for me not to like them."

Bryce smiled. He appreciated the loyalty. "But you like Miss Potter?"

"I do. Which is why I think it might be best if you were to tell her what happened yourself."

"It won't change her purpose in coming here. What she wants is to go out and make good connections. I am not a good connection, Radcliff. Which is why I intend to have her brought to the Havisham home at the first opportunity. Her friend can take her dancing at the assembly hall and introduce her to gentlemen more eligible than I."

Radcliff sighed. "Very well, my lord, but as your butler and longtime employee, I think it is my duty to tell you when you are being an idiot."

The comment was so swiftly delivered and with Radcliff's typically affected tone, it took a moment for Bryce to comprehend that the man had insulted him, at which point he had departed the room, leaving Bryce alone to reflect upon their conversation. It was tempting to do what Radcliff suggested—to convince Miss Potter that, under the circumstances, she really did not have other options but to marry him. It would certainly put an end to his craving for her since she would finally be his. But it would also be inexcusably selfish. And because he cared about her, he wanted to give her the chance to fulfill her dreams – to reach for the future she'd come here hoping to gain.

Drumming his fingers upon his desk, he resolved to go and check on her. The maid he'd assigned to her care had told him she was awake an hour ago, which meant she must have finished her breakfast by now. He stood and paused. If he truly wanted to protect her virtue, he'd keep his distance until she was able to get on her feet and meet him downstairs. But that could take days, by which time the roads would likely have cleared, and she'd be well on her way to her next destination.

To hell with it.

She was already in his home. His sitting by her bedside was hardly going to make matters any worse. So he went to the stairs, taking them two at a time in his sudden haste to see her. No woman had ever consumed him as much as she did.

Reaching her door, he stopped for a second to gather his composure. It wouldn't do for him to look like an eager young lad succumbing to love. Yet that was how he felt. His heart pounded and his body trembled while his stomach turned itself inside out. *Love?* It couldn't possibly be. He did not know her well enough. And yet the idea of her lying in there, hurt and in pain, was enough to make his soul ache. So he drew a breath and knocked on the door as calmly as he could manage, intent on hearing her tell him how she was feeling.

"Come in," came the soft response.

He carefully opened the door and stepped inside without closing it again. Whatever the world might think, he would do what was right and proper, keeping his conscience intact even if his heart did break as he feared it might do the moment Eve left.

She was propped up against a thick pile of pillows, her face turned toward him so he could observe her eyes. They were unbelievably clear today and infused with warmth. His heart stuttered a little at the possibility it might be due to his coming to see her.

If only…

"I was beginning to think you might have forgotten about me," she said, when he was close enough to study her features. Her bottom lip dipped subtly in the middle, and her nose was not as straight as one might think when looking at her for the first time.

He gave her a teasing glance and pulled up a chair. "A woman who'd rather sprain her ankle than remain underneath my roof?" He sat. "I couldn't possibly do that."

Crossing her arms, she presented him with a bit of a pout, "I did not choose to fall and hurt myself."

"No. I don't suppose you did." He grew once again serious while he studied her beautiful face. "But you ought to have considered the possibility of such a thing happening, or worse." His throat worked while he thought of what might have happened if he had not found her when he had.

"You're right," she whispered. And with those

words, she did something he would not have expected—she reached out and placed her hand over his.

A jolt of awareness shot through him, slamming his heart against his chest. Her fingers were soft and warm, so delicate and gentle in their every movement. Staring down at them, he found himself transfixed. He couldn't move or speak. All he could do was save every aspect of the touch to memory and watch as her fingers curled around the sides of his much larger hand, holding it briefly—too briefly—before letting go.

Expelling the breath he'd been holding, he tried to gather his thoughts so he'd sound more coherent when next he spoke. But it was proving difficult when all he could do was feel his skin tingle right there where it had made contact with hers. It was as if every bit of awareness he owned had been pushed into his hand, leaving it bereft in the wake of such unexpected sweetness.

Flexing his fingers, he blinked before meeting her gaze once more. "I'm right?"

She chuckled lightly, easing the tension brought on by her touch. "This time."

That made him smile. "Just this time?"

She nodded, her eyes lit with a sudden hint of mischief. "It will be a shame if you get too conceited."

"I wasn't aware I was at risk of doing so," he said with a grin.

"You're not as long as I am here to ground you."

Her comment reminded him she might leave at any moment, as soon as the weather was more agreeable. Which was something he did not want to think of right now, so he settled himself more comfortably in his chair and said, "Tell me about your childhood, Eve, about your family and where you grew up."

Her startled expression confirmed she had not expected him to say that. "Why?"

He smiled and told her honestly, "Because physical attraction isn't enough. I would also like to get to know you properly."

☾

Fearing the next syllable to leave her mouth would make her sound like the befuddled nitwit she'd turned into, Eve pressed her lips together while staring up at the man whose face had become so dear in such a short time. She'd been ridiculously pleased when he'd opened the door, and she'd seen it was he who had come to see her. And when she'd taken courage and reached for his hand, it had been with every bit of emotion he'd begun to instill in her heart.

Hearing him speak of his physical attraction toward her, however, reminded her of their scandalous encounter in the library and of the provocative words he'd spoken both then and the following morning. With no more effort, he'd awakened a keen desire inside her, a desire compelling her to act without any consideration for her own safety. Her intention had been to preserve her sanity since the alternative would be surrender.

Except she was now confined to a bed without much chance of anything untoward happening.

And Ravenworth had just confessed an interest in getting to know her better. To say she wasn't thrilled by this was an understatement, because it meant she wasn't the only one hoping to forge a bond that transcended lust and desire.

"Eve?"

Blinking, she forced herself to gather her wits. "I, er, I grew up a few hours north of London, in the village of Dashford. My parents owned a decent-sized property, a five bedroom house my grandfather helped them acquire."

"That sounds like an exceedingly comfortable home."

"It was." She thought back to how she'd played in the garden there. Funny, her memories only included bright sunny days. "There was a tall oak tree behind the house that my sisters and I used to climb. It had a swing attached to it. One of those with really long ropes that can make your belly soar."

"I wish I could have seen you on that swing," he murmured. "Judging from your smile right now, I imagine you found great joy in it."

"I did." Focusing, she said, "I also enjoyed picking berries. Mama was especially fond of raspberries and blueberries, so we had several bushes. And there were always flowers too. Bright displays for us to pick and carry inside. The lilacs were probably my favorite."

"Is that why you choose to use lilac perfume?"

Stunned by the intimacy of the question, she quietly nodded. "You've noticed."

His eyes seemed to darken slightly. The air grew thicker. "Not doing so is impossible."

"Just as impossible as it is for me not to smell the scent of sandalwood and pine you seem to favor?"

"Yes," he murmured. "Just as impossible as that."

Holding his gaze until she started to squirm with restless discomfort, Eve swallowed and quickly returned to the safety of what she'd been saying. "I was happy. *We* were happy. As a family."

"So what changed?"

His voice was quiet and tender, and yet she could hear the urgency behind it, telling her the answer mattered to him. That, alone, was enough for her to share what she'd never shared with anyone besides her sisters.

"Mama got sick and Papa began to lose focus. He worried about her so much, it affected his work. He wasn't particularly skilled at it to begin with, but at least he'd made the necessary effort." Closing her eyes, Eve allowed herself to remember a past she rarely chose to revisit. "As Mama got progressively worse and it became clear she would not survive, Papa took solace in drink. His brandy became his best friend, more so after she died. He gave up on work and on himself. We lost the house in Dashford and were eventually forced to sell our Mayfair townhouse too."

"I'm so sorry," he whispered, and this time it was he who placed his hand over hers, startling her with his touch so, her eyes sprang open. He was leaning toward her, his expression grave and full of compassion.

"Me too," she said. "My oldest sister, Josephine, managed to procure another home for us. It's not in as affluent a part of town as Mayfair, but it's still respectable enough. She has done so much to help us all through this change of circumstance. So has Louise. Both are working in an effort to give me a proper Season. Their greatest hope for me is to make a respectable match, to marry well so I might restore our place in society to some extent."

Ravenworth's hand tightened around hers, and for reasons she couldn't explain, Eve sensed he was finding it hard to speak. Eventually, he nodded and said, "Then that is what you must do."

It was a reasonable statement. She couldn't understand why it made her heart feel as though it were breaking. But it did. Perhaps because the words sounded so final, as if he would not be a part of this process. He'd take her to Margaret when doing so became possible. Her acquaintance with him would come to an end. He was an earl, after all, and she'd given him every reason to avoid any kind of attachment to her. With this in mind, she drew her hand away from his, unwilling to let herself hope for something that would not come to pass.

"We all have our duty. I'm sure you have yours too."

"I used to think so," he said, "but that was before…" Looking away, he held himself completely still for a moment. When his eyes met hers once more, the penetrating depth of it left her breathless. "My reputation is not what it once was."

"How so?"

She could see he was clenching his jaw. Whatever it was he was trying to say, getting it out was proving difficult. In the end, he chose not to answer, asking instead, "Would you throw away your chance to make a respectable match on a man who's been shunned by his own family? On a man who will never again be invited to dinner parties or balls?"

The notion he might be guilty of something awful enough to warrant such harsh condemnation was startling. "What happened?"

Wincing, he stood and shook his head. "Your answer is in your eyes, Eve. What happened no longer matters."

Speechless, she watched him take his leave. The door closed, and the hot sting of tears surprised her. Their connection had been severed. He'd avoided expanding upon the truth, which meant it had to be terrible. Especially if his own family had cut all ties to him on account of his actions.

Still, after everything she'd shared about her own past and her current situation, she would have appreciated blunt openness. Instead, she'd been given innuendo. He'd denied her the chance to make an unbiased decision by avoiding the facts. And as she reflected more on it, the evasiveness with which he'd spoken, she decided she was not going to let him hide behind the fear of what she might think of him when he told her the truth. Because that was what this had to be about. In light of his question, she could think of no other reason.

What happened no longer matters.

How wrong he was.

If he was beginning to feel for her a fraction of what she felt for him, what happened was possibly all that mattered. It would either convince her to fight for him, or to let him go.

But when he returned that afternoon and she tried to raise the subject again, he asked her to leave it alone. His voice was firm and unyielding, informing her that pleading with him would give no results. Which meant she might have to ask someone else. So she tried her maid in the evening, asking the woman a few leading questions. None resulted in satisfying responses, however. The maid's loyalty to Ravenworth was unfortunately impressively apparent. So was Radcliff's and that of every other servant with whom she attempted to speak for the next three days.

Ravenworth himself stayed on his best behavior, entertaining her with cards and the occasional game of chess. He read from the book she'd found in the library when all she'd been wearing had been her nightgown. But as he did so, he kept his distance, remaining detached in a way she found thoroughly vexing. It felt like he was preparing himself for her departure, like he'd come to terms with the prospect of saying good bye and would not allow further emotional attachment to form between them.

"I think the road will be clear by this afternoon," he said while he stared out of the window one morning. He'd been standing there for a long moment with his back turned toward her. "I will send a note to the Havishams letting them know you plan on joining them tonight."

"So soon?" It was impossible for her not to sound disappointed.

Smiling wryly, he turned to face her. "Not soon

enough, I expect, if you ask them. They will no doubt be pleased to have you in their midst and to know you are safe."

"They'll know I was here for a week if you do as you suggest."

"Yes, but the plan I had of returning you to the main road and pointing you in the right direction so they might think your carriage was simply delayed went out the window when you sprained your ankle. I cannot in good conscience allow you to walk alone, even if you are feeling better."

"So then…"

"You will simply have to tell your friend what happened. And if she fails to believe I made no attempt to seduce you, my servants have promised to inform her that you and I were never alone behind closed doors."

"I suppose that is technically true." Even if she hadn't been properly dressed on one of those occasions. "In any case, Mrs. Havisham and I have known each other since we were little girls. I'm sure she would have no reason not to believe my account of the events that have taken place since my arrival."

Giving her a blunt look that made her want to shake some hint of desire out of him, he crossed to the door and said, "On the contrary, she has every reason to suspect the worst."

He was gone before she could question his comment, which prompted her to punch the mattress. "Ugh!" The man had developed an infuriating habit of saying something dramatic whenever he made his exit. And, once again, it made her wonder what he could have done to invite condemnation, because she'd seen no hint of the scoundrel he claimed to be. Not when he hadn't even attempted to kiss her.

☾

Seated behind his desk in his study, Bryce signed the missive he'd written and blotted the ink. He folded it and added his seal before taking it through to Radcliff. "Please have someone deliver this to Mrs. Havisham immediately."

"Are you sure?" Radcliff asked. He stared down at the crisp paper Bryce held toward him.

"Yes. Miss Potter leaves today. I've already told her to pack."

"What if—"

"There is no what if, Radcliff."

He thrust the letter forward, forcing his butler to take it. Eve's purpose was clear. She meant to marry a man who might return her and her sisters to their rightful positions within society. He was not that man and never would be. Love was not enough, and God help him, he did love her. He'd suspected it ever since he'd found her lying in the snow and a piece of his heart had shattered. He'd struggled against it since then, dreading the moment when she would leave him. But with each passing moment, his love for her had increased. Which was why he would do what was in her best interest and let her go.

"She is destined for better things than what I have to offer."

The dubious look in Radcliff's eyes said he did not believe an ounce of that. But it didn't matter. The important thing was Bryce did what was right for Eve and gave her the chance to have the life she'd been dreaming of when fate had landed her on his doorstep. Which was why he flinched when the knocker rapped loudly against the front door. His heart almost ceased beating when Radcliff opened it to reveal the displeased expressions of Mr. and Mrs. Havisham, who'd apparently come looking for their guest.

Chapter Five

"**W**HERE IS SHE?" THE PETITE woman who stood beside her much taller husband wore a militant look of determination. It forced Bryce to take a step back, allowing her to enter the foyer. She looked around, peering into every corner before returning her sharp glare to Bryce. "What have you done with Miss Potter?"

"Mrs. Havisham," Bryce began, "Welcome to—"

"I know she must be here somewhere," Mrs. Havisham insisted. "This past week we believed her coach might have been delayed on account of the weather, but then…" She leaned toward him, forcing him back another step. Bryce gave her husband a wary glance but found no help there since the woman continued to say, "My head groom, whom I'd sent out this afternoon to watch for an approaching coach, halted the exact same one my good friend, Miss Potter, apparently arrived on seven days ago. SEVEN days ago!" Her voice had risen to a screech.

Bryce took a deep breath and stiffened his spine before doing the one thing Mrs. Havisham probably did not expect him to do. He confessed with a succinct, "Yes. Miss Potter did indeed arrive here a week ago. By accident."

Mrs. Havisham's eyes went wide. "Accident?" she scoffed, while jutting her chin out. "I will have to listen to Miss Potter's account before taking your word on that."

It was a well-aimed volley, one which made Bryce bite his tongue in an effort to remain civil. He turned to Radcliff, whose solemn expression conveyed no hint of what he might be thinking about this turn of events. "Perhaps you can show Mr. Havisham through to the parlor and ask a maid to bring up some tea." To Mrs. Havisham, he said, "In the meantime, allow me to show you to the guestroom where Miss Potter has been staying." But before heading off, Bryce paused to consider Mr. Havisham, who still hadn't uttered a word and added, "Feel free to partake of my liquor if you prefer stronger stuff than tea."

Mr. Havisham's lips twitched. "Thank you, my lord. I dare say I'll take you up on that offer."

Bryce turned toward the stairs and waited for Mrs. Havisham to follow before starting up them. They reached the landing in silence, continuing down the corridor to the room in which Eve had been staying. Bryce knocked.

"Come in," came Eve's reply.

Bryce reached for the handle, but Mrs. Havisham stepped in front of him, blocking his path. "I believe I can manage from here," she said. "Miss Potter and I will see you downstairs in the parlor when we are ready."

Briefly, Bryce was tempted to argue, but gave

up. Mrs. Havisham had every right to want him gone from the vicinity of Eve's bedchamber. She probably thought the worst already because of how quickly he'd reached the room. He hadn't bothered to pretend to doubt which one it was. So he dipped his head in acquiescence and retreated to the stairs, descending them with the full intention of joining Mr. Havisham for a much needed brandy.

☾

The door opened, and Eve was surprised to see Margaret coming toward her, her face transforming from hard lines of determination into fragile concern. Eve rose to greet her as best as she could and was suddenly wrapped in her friend's embrace. "I have been so terribly worried about you," Margaret confessed. She hugged Eve tightly.

"I'm sorry." Eve pulled out of her arms so she could speak with her friend properly. "I took the wrong road on the day I arrived and ended up here instead."

"If only you would have waited." Margaret's eyes filled with regret. "Our coachman was sent to fetch you. He told me he waited until the roads grew icy, and he began to suspect you must have been delayed."

Pressing her lips together, Eve didn't quite know what to say except, "Ravenworth was kind enough to let me warm myself by his fire."

"Of course he was," Margaret said. "You're a beautiful young woman, Eve. I'm sure he was quite eager to get his hands on you."

Eve's mouth fell open. She stared at Margaret. A ferocious expression had settled upon her face while her hands had balled themselves into tight fists.

"He could have turned me away," Eve said. "But he didn't. Instead, he offered me something to eat and asked his groom to prepare the carriage. But then the roads froze, and it became too hazardous for us to venture out."

"So he offered you a bed instead."

Eve started getting annoyed. It had been a couple of years since she'd seen Margaret last. She'd been so full of laughter and mischief. Not at all the stern stickler for propriety she was proving to be at the moment. Which made Eve wonder if marriage might not agree with Margaret, or if there was some other reason for her to leap to the worst conclusions. "I don't believe I like what you are implying," Eve said, matching Margaret's blunt tone.

Margaret stared at Eve for a long moment as if considering something, then said, "If you were in my shoes you would not be so flip about this. That man…" Her voice began to shake, and it struck Eve how deeply this situation affected her. "He is the worst sort of scoundrel, a reprobate of the first order, Eve! If word of your sojourn here gets out, you will be ruined! No respectable gentleman will want to marry you. Do you understand that?"

Eve tilted her head and contemplated the warning. "Ravenworth made that point perfectly clear," she mused.

My reputation is not what it once was.

Would you throw away your chance to make a respectable match on a man who's been shunned by his own family?

"Did he really?" The sarcastic edge with which Margaret spoke wasn't lost on Eve.

"Yes," she said. "But he didn't tell me why that is."

Margaret snorted and rolled her eyes. "That is hardly surprising."

"I would like for you to do so right now, however," Eve pressed. She'd been trying to make sense of the whole situation for several days without success. But Margaret was loyal to her, not to Ravenworth, and Eve meant to take advantage of this.

"It is not for an innocent's ears," Margaret said. She sank down onto the same chair Ravenworth had made use of when he'd come to check on Eve for the past few days.

Eve wondered if her friend might leap straight back out of it if she knew. Which made her lips twitch in response to the funny image such an idea posed. She forced back her momentary amusement and said, "Be that as it may, I am not leaving this room until you tell me what he has been accused of."

Margaret stared at her and suddenly frowned. Her eyes narrowed, and she tilted her chin so she could look Eve straight in the eye. "Have you done something stupid like fall in love with him?"

Eve dropped onto the edge of the bed with a sigh. "Don't be ridiculous. I barely know the man."

A second passed, followed by another. Eve held

her breath, and then Margaret suddenly said, "Goodness gracious me, you have!"

"Just tell me why Ravenworth doesn't deserve my affection. All things considered, I believe I ought to know."

"He seduced a young gentlewoman. Miss Edwina Jenkins, is her name. She's the daughter of a local landowner."

Eve tried to wrap her mind around that bit of information. She shook her head. "No."

"Ravenworth reportedly bedded her and refused to take her to wife. Her father called Ravenworth out. The two fought a duel with pistols, resulting in Mr. Jenkins getting shot in the shoulder. He missed Ravenworth, who claimed victory, but after what happened, Ravenworth never showed his face in polite society again. Nobody invited him. His own family, from what I hear, refuses to have anything to do with him anymore." Margaret winced. "He even had a fiancée at the time. Naturally, the lady called off the engagement and chose to marry someone else."

"And Miss Edwina Jenkins?" Eve asked. "What happened to her?"

"She moved away. From what I gather, her father was able to get her married to a widower who wasn't too picky about her lack of innocence."

Eve frowned. "Was Ravenworth actually caught in a compromising position with her?"

"It is my understanding," Margaret slowly told her, "that he was found in the middle of the act."

Eve's back went rigid. "Are you certain of this?"

Her friend leveled her with a frank stare. "It is what people say."

People had also said Eve's father was prone to violence after he'd yelled at a woman who'd chosen to comment on his lack of responsibility toward his children. As rude as the woman had been, her statement had been apt, though she'd been wrong to start spreading falsehoods simply because she didn't like how Papa had reacted. He'd never struck another person in his life, and yet word suddenly had it he probably beat his daughters on a regular basis. The pitying looks Eve and her sisters began to receive had been disheartening. Worst of all, nobody had believed them when they'd insisted their father would never take out his anger on them.

"People say a lot of things, Margaret. Only half of it is true, if that."

"You don't believe me?"

Smiling, Eve reached out and squeezed Margaret's hand in a gesture of reassurance. "I believe you think you know the facts. What I don't believe is the verity of these facts." She shook her head gently. "Ravenworth didn't bed Miss. Edwina Jenkins. I'm not sure what might have happened to make people think he did, but they're wrong. He has been falsely accused." She knew this in her heart as easily as she knew her own name.

Margaret stared at her as if she were mad. "How can you be so blind, Eve?"

"How can *you*?"

Margaret sat back in her seat. She drew her hand away from Eve's. "Very well. Explain your reasoning to me. Tell me why I'm wrong to think he did such a thing."

Eve considered the man she'd come to know, of

how generous he'd been and how well he'd treated her, even when he'd admitted to his desire for her. "Because he has had every opportunity to seduce me during my stay here, and yet he refrained. He didn't even attempt to kiss me. Not for lack of wanting to, for I have no doubt in my mind he did, but because he refused to compromise me any more than I already was by remaining under his roof."

"Are you saying he never made any advances?"

Eve nodded. "He said a few things he probably shouldn't have said, but he kept himself under control. Which is just as well, since I fear I would not have been able to resist him if he had tried to lure me into his bed."

"Eve!"

Margaret's expression suggested she was thoroughly appalled, but Eve merely shrugged. "It is the truth. Besides, you are my dearest friend and a married woman to boot. Surely I can confide such things in you?"

"Well, yes, I suppose so," Margaret said a little grudgingly. She bit her lip. "It is merely surprising to hear you talk so candidly on such a taboo subject."

Eve smiled. "I don't think I would have done so five days ago, but after meeting Ravenworth and getting to know him… Do you realize he strode through snow and freezing rain to save me after I tried to make my own way to you? I sprained my ankle in the process, and he carried me back here, ensured my every need was met and—"

"Not every need, I suspect," Margaret murmured, prompting a bit of sputtered laughter on

Eve's part. She slapped Margaret's shoulder, and for a moment, the two of them shared an amused bit of amicable silence.

"The point is, I think he has been misjudged."

"And if he hasn't?"

Expelling a breath, Eve pondered her friend's question. She didn't believe it was possible for a second, but if it were... "Then he is not the man I believe him to be. In which case I'll never see him again. But first, I intend to speak with him. Not once did he share the details of his unpopularity with me. He simply concluded I would not choose a man whom Society would not welcome and determined, therefore, that the past didn't matter."

Margaret shook her head. "Men can be so thick sometimes." She puffed out a breath. "They think they know best and deny us the chance to make an informed decision."

Suspecting her friend might be speaking from experience, Eve made a mental note to ask her to elaborate on that point later. For now, however, she had a difficult earl to contend with. "I love him though. So if I'm right and he never did ruin Miss Edwina Jenkins, he'd better prepare himself for a few choice words and a hard fight on my part."

"You hope to marry him, don't you?"

"I think it goes without saying. If he'll have me, that is." She didn't even dare suppose he wouldn't.

"He'd be a fool not to," Margaret told her loyally. "But Society's opinion about him is highly unlikely to change, which means, even if he is innocent, you will still become the face of scandal as soon as word of your engagement gets around. Have you considered how this will impact not only you but your sisters?"

Squaring her shoulders, Eve quietly nodded. "It is not what they would have wanted, but on the other hand, their greatest wish is for me to be happy and well taken care of. And perhaps, since I would not be requiring a Season, their financial concerns would be eased a little. Plus, I'm sure Ravenworth would help Josephine keep the house in London. And regarding our social position, it might be time for us to accept that our lives will never be what they once were. What matters is we have each other and friends like you, who would never turn their back on us no matter what."

"I could never do so," Margaret whispered. "I will back whatever decision you make for yourself, Eve."

"Then let us go downstairs." Eve rose with resolve. "It's time for me to confront Ravenworth."

☙

Bryce had just poured himself his third glass of brandy when Mrs. Havisham entered the parlor with a much more approachable demeanor than she'd exuded earlier. She offered her husband a fleeting glance before directing her attention at Bryce. "Miss Potter would like to have a word with you," she said. "She is waiting in the library."

This, he had not expected. "In the library?" When Mrs. Havisham nodded, Bryce set down his glass. He considered Mr. Havisham, with whom he'd actually been enjoying a political debate during the absence of female company.

The man now frowned. "Are you sure that would be proper?" he asked his wife.

"Not entirely," Mrs. Havisham said, "but I do think we ought to allow it."

Mr. Havisham hesitated briefly, then addressed Bryce. "I must confess, you're different from what I expected, so I'll concede to Miss Potter's wishes if you agree to leave the door wide open."

"Of course."

Bryce left the room with a quick stride which brought him to the library in a matter of seconds. Stepping inside, he drew to a halt when he spotted Eve. She was sitting in one of the armchairs next to the fire, with her foot propped up on a cushioned stool. Bryce drank in her profile—the smooth curve of her cheek and the careful sweep of her nose. Her golden hair came alive in the glow from the crackling flames, tempting him to cross the floor with haste so he might touch it.

Instead, he held himself perfectly still. Inside his chest, his heart ached with the knowledge that once this conversation was over, she would leave Ravenworth Manor together with the Havishams. She would leave *him*. And upon this realization, he felt his entire world begin to crumble, the facets of his life disassembling to the point where he would be left a raw and tortured mess.

She must have sensed his presence, for she turned her head to look at him, her expression so firm and serious his insides quaked a little with apprehension.

Nevertheless, he took a step forward. "Mrs. Havisham said you wished to see me."

"I do." Her eyes, a darker shade of blue than usual, locked onto his. "Come join me."

He went toward her on leaden feet. For reasons he couldn't explain, he felt like a young lad about to be chastised as he'd once been for painting the floor with marmalade. Reaching her side, he lowered himself into the adjacent chair and gestured toward her foot. "How is it feeling?"

"It's more tolerable than it was before. I made it down the stairs without too much trouble, though it did begin to ache a bit by the time I arrived here. The warmth from the fire seems to help."

"I'm glad to hear it." Even if it would make her walk away from him faster. He drew a labored breath and pushed it back out past the tightness in his throat. "Are you ready to go to Amberly then?"

She pinched her lips together and frowned. For a second, his heart went utterly still and he began to imagine her telling him she'd never be ready to do so, that she would stay here with him and face whatever consequences were bound to arise.

Instead she gestured with her hand and said, "Come closer."

Eyeing her, he wondered at her curious request and her tone. "Why?"

"Because I am asking you to."

Hesitating briefly, he finally acquiesced and leaned forward slightly. So did she, and for one delightful moment, he expected her to breach the rest of the distance and kiss him. Instead her fist made contact with his shoulder in an unexpectedly hard punch for a woman of her size, and he instinctively pulled back. "What the he—" He clamped his mouth shut around the rest of the expletive. "You hit me. Again."

"And I may do so once more if you continue to be so impossible to deal with." Her eyes narrowed to a pair of reproachful slits, while a few stray strands of hair fell over her brow, curling beside her ear.

Bryce's heart beat faster. His muscles flexed, and his body grew tight while desire surged through him. Christ, he'd not imagined he'd ever be so aroused by a woman's high temper, but the fact was his blood was running hot, and damn it all, he was tempted in ways that would not be easy to explain if he succumbed to impulse. So he did his best to focus on what she was saying, except her lips were proving to be an inconvenient distraction. They continued to shape her words with the most enticing movements.

"Are you even listening?" she asked, adding a glare.

"Hmm?"

She rolled her eyes. "How are we going to deal with this if you refuse to cooperate?"

He could think of several ways, all of which would indeed involve his full cooperation. "Forgive me," he murmured. "My mind began to wander."

Tilting her head, she gave him a curious look before settling back in her chair with a sigh. "I want you to explain to me why everyone thinks you stole Miss Edwina Jenkins' virginity."

Well. There was a sobering thought to draw him

out of his lust-induced state. Bryce steeled himself before saying, "Mrs. Havisham mentioned that, did she?" He'd expected her to, yet it still bothered him she had. He did not like Eve knowing about his dark and dirty secret.

"What I cannot comprehend is that you did not!"

And as she said it, he knew she wasn't merely angry with him for hiding this from her, but also thoroughly hurt. "Eve…" He scarcely knew what to say. So he reached out toward her. When she didn't retreat, he allowed his hand to settle over hers. "The days you and I have spent together have been incredible. It was as if you cracked open the tomb in which I'd been buried and brought me back to life. I didn't want you to treat me with the same contempt everyone else did, but to simply enjoy the brief time we had together without judgment or prejudice."

"You still should have told me," she said. Her gaze rose toward his.

Framed by long lashes, her eyes blinked away tears. Bryce felt his heart break for the pain he was causing. "How could I," he asked, without knowing precisely what to say or where this conversation would lead. His fingers closed more tightly around her hand. "Losing your respect was not a risk I was willing to take. I'm sorry, but it's the truth."

She bowed her head, and he imagined she might be looking at their entwined fingers. The fact she didn't retreat was a comfort. It made him feel more grounded somehow, as if he might not fly away in the storm of emotion assailing his world.

And then she raised her gaze to his, and he caught his breath as clarity brightened her eyes and eased the strain of her features. "Did it ever occur to you," she asked, "that I might believe your side of the story?"

Stunned, he shook his head. "No."

"Then let us start over. I want you to tell me exactly and very precisely what led to the inconceivable notion you might be capable of doing what you've been accused of."

He stared at her, and he could not seem to stop staring. "Why on earth..." He blinked, shook his head, and met her gaze once more. "Why on earth would you choose to ignore what everyone else is saying when even your friend, whom I assume you trust, believes I'm a no good scoundrel."

"Because I've gotten to know you these past few days, and because I believe I can say with confidence you would never force your attentions on an innocent woman, no matter how tempted you might be to do so." She gave him a frank look. "Not unless you were willing to marry her."

His breath hissed from his lungs, his entire body sagging beneath the weight of her meaningful words. "You're right. Keeping my hands off of you has been no simple task," he confessed, delighting in how easily she blushed in response. "But it would have been wrong of me not to do so."

"Then tell me the truth."

Surrendering to her will, he gave a quick nod and said, "Miss Edwina Jenkins set her sights on me about five years ago. Every time I would visit the village, she would fall into step beside me, and every time I attended a dance, she would present me with her dance card, leaving me with no choice but to partner with her."

"So she was determined."

"Exceedingly so." Swiping his palm across his jaw, he continued by saying, "I tried to show polite disinterest, but that didn't seem to dissuade her. And then I got engaged to Viscount Trenwick's daughter, Lady Rose." Seeing how Eve's mouth suddenly flattened into a firm line, he reached up to cup her cheek. "It would have been a practical arrangement with no emotional attachment. You mustn't think…I would hate for you to suppose my feelings for her were anything close to what they are for you."

Eve's lips edged slightly upward at one corner. "Go on."

Gathering his composure, Bryce did his best to tell the rest of the story. "Miss Jenkins became incredibly jealous. She wanted me for herself, but since I'd gotten engaged, there was no way to make that happen unless—"

"Unless you compromised her so thoroughly, you would have no choice in the matter."

"Precisely."

And now for the delicate part. There was really no tiptoeing around it if she truly wanted all the facts. Which he could tell she did. So he took a fortifying breath and proceeded.

"At the last assembly hall dance I attended, a servant brought me a note summoning me to one of the private supper rooms. It appeared to come from Lord Trenwick, with the insistence I join him for a discussion about my impending marriage to his daughter. But when I arrived at the designated meeting spot, the room was empty. No one seemed to be there until I turned around to leave and found Miss Jenkins blocking my path." He recalled the awful sense of foreboding that had snaked its way through his belly. "She closed the door, locked it, and slipped the key into her décolletage."

"Good lord," Eve murmured. "She was a predator."

If only the rest of the world had been as astute, Bryce mused. "Before I knew what was happening, she'd…" He looked away, unable to meet Eve's gaze while he said this next part. "She tore the front of her gown, flung herself onto the table, and hitched up her skirts, exposing herself completely." His voice strained to get the details out while rage and frustration crashed through him. "Someone came to the door and started knocking, at which point she started to make certain sounds."

Eve had gone completely still. Her eyes were wide and stricken with horror. "She pretended you were…that you were…" When he nodded, she slapped a hand over her mouth and produced an anguished groan. "I'm so sorry."

Nodding, he hastened to tell her the rest. "The door was forced open by Trenwick himself. He didn't seem to notice none of my own clothing was out of place. Instead, he punched me. I fell back onto Miss Jenkins, which is what Lady Rose witnessed when she arrived in the room. Naturally, I was encouraged to marry Miss Jenkins, but since I knew misery was unavoidable at that point, I chose to face it without her. Word spread, my friends and family took her side, and…well, here we are."

A long moment of silence followed Bryce's admission. He didn't know what else to say, though he tried to think of something. Eve had said she'd believe him. She'd seemed like she did while he'd given his account. But her inward contemplation unsettled him because he couldn't discern what she was thinking or if he'd actually managed to convince her of his innocence.

Finally, when he began to fear she would stand up and leave the room without saying another word, she pulled her foot down off the stool and lowered herself to her knees before him, taking his hands between her own. "Ravenworth." The look in her eyes was so incredibly tender. "Will you give me your Christian name?"

His chest squeeze around his expanding heart. "It's Bryce."

"Bryce." It whispered across her lips with aching sensuality. And then she said, "What Miss Jenkins did to you is unforgiveable. That you should have to suffer for it, more so. You're a good man though, a kind and generous man, the sort of man who deserves to be loved."

Swallowing, Bryce held himself in check and gazed down into her open expression. The truth was in her eyes, so overpowering he could scarcely credit it. Yet he needed to hear her say it before allowing himself to hope. "What are you telling me, Eve?"

"That I know you did nothing wrong and that I love you."

Her declaration was perfect in its simplicity. It was also the one thing capable of weakening the tightly held control he'd been maintaining since the moment she'd entered this room for the very first time.

"I love you too, Eve."

He wasn't sure if she rose up toward him or if he dipped his head toward her. Perhaps it was a mutual coming together, but all that mattered was that his lips were finally pressed over hers and that he was kissing her with every bit of his heart.

Her arms came up and around his neck, and he was suddenly lifting her onto his lap, loving the feel of her warmth when she angled around and her chest pressed into his. A whimper stole its way past her lips, and he swallowed it on a groan, deepening the kiss, pulling her tighter and holding her close so she'd know he'd never let go.

Although... Reluctantly, he eased back a little and made an effort to think. Which was no easy task, all things considered. "What of your sisters and the duty you have toward them?" Although he hated reminding her of it, of giving her a reason to leave, he could not in good conscience ignore it.

"I think they will understand. And if you're willing to marry me..."

"Of course I plan to marry you, Eve! What sort of man do you take me for?"

She smiled in response to his teasing tone. "Well, if you'll help my sister Josephine cover the cost of her townhouse—"

"Done," he told her sincerely. "I'll even buy her a new one in Mayfair if she so desires."

"Really?"

"Absolutely." Upon which he kissed her again, savoring the taste of her and all the delightful little noises she made.

A loud cough broke the spell, drawing Bryce's attention toward the doorway where Mrs. Havisham had materialized. "You were taking too long," she announced. Crossing her arms, she gave them a steely look. "I can now see why."

"Er..."

Eve didn't sound as though she knew what so say, so Bryce interceded. "Miss Potter and I will be getting married."

"Really?" Mrs. Havisham smiled at Eve. "Well, it is what you wanted, so how can I be anything but thrilled?"

Carefully, Bryce eased Eve off his lap and helped her back into the chair. "And since you've caught us in a rather compromising position, I would like to propose a special marriage license and forego the reading of banns." He turned to look at Eve, adding, "Unless, of course, you would rather plan a proper wedding so your sisters can attend." He'd likely expire from pent-up desire by the time such a ceremony took place, but he'd suffer through it if it was what Eve wanted.

A blush darkened her skin to a pretty pink hue, and she shyly whispered, "I doubt I can wait so long. A special license sounds perfect."

"Then it's settled," Bryce said. "I'll take care of the arrangements straight away."

"And in the meantime," Mrs. Havisham told him, "Miss Potter will come with me. She and I were supposed to enjoy two weeks together, and now I'll be lucky if I manage to get one day."

It was a fair point, however reluctant Bryce was to let Eve out of his sight. But he would be busy too, not only visiting the Archbishop of Canterbury in London, but also procuring a ring. "I will call at Amberly Hall once everything has been taken care of," he promised, mostly to Eve, who did not look the least bit eager to leave his company. And as he watched the Havisham carriage roll away a half hour later with her inside it, he knew what it meant to feel like he was losing the most precious part of himself.

So he turned about swiftly and called for Radcliff to have a groom saddle his horse. The faster he completed his tasks, the sooner Eve would be his.

CHAPTER SIX

WOOLGATHERING, EVE DIDN'T REALIZE MARGARET had been talking until she jabbed her in the shoulder. "Yes?" Eve blinked. She raised her gaze from the garment resting in her lap, her needle and thread poised in preparation for the next stitch.

Margaret's lips stretched to form a wide smile, her eyes laughing with unabashed amusement. "Dare I ask you about your ponderings?"

Eve sank back against the sofa and sighed. "It has been three whole days."

"And thank goodness for that." Margaret poured a cup of tea and placed it in front of Eve. "If Ravenworth had arrived any sooner, your gown would not have been ready."

"I suppose that's true."

The moment Eve had arrived at Amberly Hall, Margaret had insisted on finding an appropriate gown for her to wear on her wedding day. She'd riffled through her wardrobe while Eve had watched, amazed by the rich collection of fabrics, until her friend had produced a stunning creation of light blue silk. It had required a few alterations to the bodice and hem, which had kept Eve busy during the following days.

Still…

"He hasn't even sent a note though, which makes me wonder if—"

"What? He might have reconsidered?" Margaret shook her head. "The man is clearly enamored with you."

"Do you truly think so?"

"I know so, Eve. The archbishop is getting on in years. I've been told he likes to take his time with things. So it wouldn't surprise me if he is dawdling over the marriage license."

Unsatisfied with the answer, Eve puffed out a breath and completed the final stitches. "There. All done." She rose and laid the gown across the back of a nearby chair so she could enjoy her tea. "I'm also eager to tell him what Mr. Havisham has discovered."

"It's possible Ravenworth already knows. Gossip travels faster than forest fires, Eve."

A knock at the door brought Margaret's butler into the room. "The Earl of Ravenworth is here to see you. May I show him in?"

Eve's breath caught, suspended until her friend answered in the affirmative. It then whooshed from her lungs, matching the speed of her racing heart while she hurried back to her seat, claiming it seconds before the door opened again to admit the most dashing man in the world– the only man Eve cared about–Ravenworth – Bryce.

His gaze swept across the room, honing in on Eve with a predatory gleam. It pulled at her belly, and a surge of awareness swept through her.

Dressed in a dark blue jacket with breeches to match, he cut an impressive figure--broad-shouldered and tall, his dark hair windblown and with his jaw bearing signs of day-old stubble. Bowing, he greeted Eve and Margaret in turn, his voice sounding gruff and perhaps a little fatigued as well.

"Eve has been awaiting your arrival with great anxiety," Margaret said. She stood and went toward him.

Blushing, Eve began to look away, but Bryce caught her gaze and held it, the darkness therein conveying intense degrees of longing. "Procuring the license took time. Longer than I had anticipated." He glanced at Margaret. "Will you grant Miss Potter and me a moment of privacy? Please."

Margaret dipped her head in an elegant nod. "Of course." She went to the door, paused to gaze across the distance at Eve, and gave her a secretive smile. "Take your time." And then she was gone, the door clicking shut behind her.

Eve's skin pricked with awareness. She was alone with Bryce for the first time in three days, and he was coming toward her now at a slow prowl. Her lungs tightened and so did her stomach. Calming her heart had long since become impossible. It was racing away, producing a tremble that spread from the tips of her fingers all the way down to her toes.

"You look…" His voice was softer than before, his throat working as if struggling with the ability to speak. "As lovely as I remember–lovelier even, if such a thing is possible."

The heat of his gaze made her cheeks warm.

She knew she was blushing. "Thank you, my lord." His increasing nearness afforded her speech with a breathless tone. There was more to be said, however. "Mr. Havisham says Miss Edwina Jenkins's husband has left her. He overhead a group of people talking about it in the village yesterday."

Bryce stilled. "Really?"

"Word is she's been unfaithful on countless occasions, that the child she carries belongs to another." She held out her hand, encouraging Bryce to come closer. "The incident has cast doubt on what really happened between you two. So chances are your reputation will be restored."

Reaching her, he lowered himself to the vacant spot on the sofa and quietly murmured her name. "Eve." There was anguish and hope and passionate need all rolled up in one simple utterance.

"Yes." One word to encompass so much. *Yes, I want you; yes, I need you; yes, I will be yours forever; yes and yes and yes, a thousand times yes.*

His hand found hers, cradling it gently against his own. A pause followed, and he cleared his throat before proceeding in a firmer voice than he'd used before. "I hope that will be the case. For your sake more than for mine." When she started protesting, he hastened to say, "Everything happened so quickly before, I never managed to make a proper proposal. So please allow me to do so now, to offer you what you truly deserve."

Reaching inside his jacket pocket, he produced a small box and flipped open the lid to reveal the prettiest ring Eve had ever seen: a simple gold band adorned with a gilded forget me not. He'd made it himself, and this alone made it the most precious gift she would ever receive.

"My life was an empty void before you arrived to give it meaning," Bryce said. He picked the ring up and held it between his fingers. "I cannot think of living without you, of us not sharing every lasting moment together. My heart is yours, my love for you as infinite as the stars in the sky. Please accept this ring with the promise that I will make you the happiest woman in the world. Marry me, Eve."

"Yes." Her hand reached around his neck to draw him close for a kiss. "Yes." His lips met hers while the ring slid into place on her finger. "I was yours the moment we met." She kissed him again. "And I will be yours until death do us part."

☾

The ceremony took place the following day with the Havishams in attendance. It was swift, completed much faster than Eve had expected, but every bit as romantic as she could have hoped. Snow drifted over them like white winter blossoms when they exited the church as husband and wife. A joyous gathering followed at the nearest inn, before Bryce and Eve set their course for home.

Home.

Snuggling into Bryce's embrace during their carriage-ride back to Ravenworth Manor, Eve couldn't help but marvel at the idea. She'd already dispatched letters to Josephine and Louise and now wondered how they would respond to her hasty decision to marry. She hoped they were going to be happy for her and not too displeased with her reluctance to wait.

"What are you thinking about?" Bryce asked against the top of her head.

She turned in his arms and gazed up into his stunning dark eyes. "That I am so incredibly lucky and that I cannot wait to introduce you to my sisters."

A touch of seriousness flattened his mouth. "Do you think they will like me?"

The fact he might be concerned they wouldn't made Eve's heart swell. "Without a doubt," she assured him, kissing him for good measure. She continued to do so until the carriage swayed to a halt, alerting her to their arrival at Ravenworth Manor.

Bryce opened the carriage door and helped her alight. His hand firmly at her back, he guided her up the front steps and into the foyer. Silently, he helped her remove her pelisse and her bonnet before leading her toward the stairs. Eve's stomach tightened around a knot. It seemed to squeeze her insides together. Her heart fluttered against her ribs, her breath growing increasingly labored with every step she took.

Reaching the top of the landing, he stopped to face her and offered his hand. "Come." One word, luring her with the promise of pleasure, impossible to resist when accompanied by the hungry look in his eyes. She placed her palm upon his, watching his fingers close around hers. With deliberate steps, he drew her toward a door at the end of the hallway, opened it, and ushered her into the bedroom beyond.

Draped in burgundy and gold, the four-poster bed which stood at the center like a lavish enabler of sexual craving, reminded Eve of what would transpire. A shock of anxiety shot up her spine, until she felt Bryce's hands behind her, firm upon her shoulders. His mouth sought the curve of her neck and pressed a trail of kisses there, scattering her concerns so only her need for him remained.

"Mine." His voice heated her skin, calling on her awareness while his fingers plucked the pins from her hair and allowed them to scatter across the floor.

Leaning into him, she sighed as her hair tumbled down her back, then again while his fingers worked on the fastenings of her gown. The sleeves slipped over her shoulders, down over her arms, until the gown vanished completely – forgotten somewhere at her feet. Her stays and chemise followed, and she was naked in his arms, save for the fine silk stockings tied with light blue satin ribbons around her thighs. A kiss was pressed to the nape of her neck and a hand slid over her waist, circling her with a lazy caress that threatened to be her undoing.

"Bryce." She breathed his name.

"Finally," he murmured.

Another kiss touched her shoulder, followed by the gentle scrape of his teeth raking over her skin. It produced a flurry of heightened sensations in other parts of her body. He stepped away, allowing cool air to cascade over her back as he moved to stand before her. With darkened eyes, he allowed his gaze to travel the length of her body, so slowly she was certain she'd expire from anticipation.

"Ever since the night in the library, my mind has been filled with the vision of you, the hint of your naked body beneath your nightgown. The things it did to me, the ache it stirred, and the need." Reaching out, he trailed his fingers down over her breasts, forging a reverent path to her belly. "My wildest imaginings failed to do you justice, Eve. You are so much more glorious and so much more tempting than anything my mind was able to conjure."

Unable to speak in response to his forthright declaration, her body clamoring for more of his touch, Eve stared as her husband began to undress. He did so with torturous slowness, dragging out the process until she feared she would scream. Finally, after divesting himself of cravat, jacket, waistcoat, and socks, he pulled his shirt over his head, and his trousers and smalls joined the increasing pile of clothes on the floor. He stood before her, magnificent in his nudity, his muscles rippling across his torso in a way that demanded exploration.

"You are..." She tried to think of the perfect word. "Absolutely glorious."

Two swift strides brought him right up against her, his mouth meeting hers in a feverish kiss. He wrapped his arms around her, surrounding her with his masculine strength. Without breaking the kiss, he picked her up and carried her straight to the bed and laid her down so her head could rest on a soft pile of pillows. His gleaming gaze roamed the length of her body. She squirmed with restless desire.

"I've pictured this too," he confessed, the sensual lilt of his voice inviting sparks to dance across her skin. "You, spread out like this on my bed, waiting for my touch." His eyes captured hers while he trailed one finger along the length of her leg, over her hip, and up the center of her chest.

"Yes." Her back arched of its own volition.

"Yes?" A teasing edge to his question matched the mischievous smirk he gave her.

"I need you… Please, Bryce…I need…"

"As do I," he said. He came to join her, kissing her softly at first and then with increasing fervor, his hands stealing over her flesh and teasing her lightly until she was ready, until she begged for him to join his body with hers.

He did so gently, accompanying their union with loving words of assurance. She welcomed the new sensations and savored the closeness she felt to this man. It was awe-inspiring and sweet, inviting a promise of something greater between them, of a pleasure unlike any other she'd ever experienced before. He carried her toward it, urging her to capture it for herself, to revel in every last dazzling second of this new wonder. And then it tore its way through her, shattering every bit of remaining control in a spellbinding thrill that bordered on madness. It was more than she'd ever imagined it would be, a sacred pact binding their souls.

For long moments after, no sound filled the room besides their deep breathing. Reluctant to move, Eve enjoyed the press of her husband's chest against her own. But he suddenly stirred, rising above her once again so he could look down into her eyes. "You're incredible, Eve."

Heat rose in her cheeks as self-awareness swept through her. "So are you," she said, hoping to match his candor.

A wicked smile touched his lips. "You can't imagine how pleased I am to hear you say that." His hand trailed down her thigh, re-igniting her need for him in a heartbeat. "There are so many ways in which I want to love you."

And he proceeded to show her each of them until she lost count and the only words remaining between them were, "Love. My love. Forever."

THE DUKE
WHO
CAME TO TOWN

CHAPTER ONE

JOSEPHINE WAITED UNTIL THE COACH carrying her youngest sister, Eve, out to the Great West Road had turned a corner, disappearing from sight. She then wrapped her shawl tighter around her shoulders and started making her way back toward the townhouse they'd shared with their other sister, Louise, until yesterday. The place would be empty now with both sisters away. Eve had been invited to visit with a friend for the holidays, while Louise had gone to Whitehaven in the northern part of the country to become a governess to three young children.

Some extra income would certainly be welcome. Josephine wasn't sure how much longer she would be able to cover their expenses on her own. The townhouse, alone, took most of her wages, while food and clothing swallowed the rest. It was a struggle, but to accept defeat and relocate to humbler lodgings was out of the question. Already, they'd had to give up the status their Mayfair home and country estate had once afforded them. As the great-granddaughters of an earl, they'd enjoyed a comfortable position in society—until their father had squandered it all in a downward spiral of drink and depression.

Pushing the unpleasant memories as far back as they would go, Josephine determined to focus on the future. The townhouse wasn't the only thing at stake. There were also Eve's prospects and their reputations. While Josephine and Louise had resigned themselves to working for a living, they both hoped Eve might still be able to enjoy the Season they'd been denied, that she might marry well, and that her life might be a little easier and happier than what they faced. There would be no large dowry, only the meager sum Josephine had managed to put aside during the last year since their father's death: a few wages here, a bit of pawned jewelry there.

Turning onto Vine Street, Josephine bowed her head against the gust of wind sweeping toward her. She'd used the last firewood that morning and would have to see about buying more —yet another cost eating away at her income. But this was England, and they were only in December. It would be several months before she'd be able to forego heating. Unless she wished to get sick and not only risk losing her job but also having to pay the exorbitant fee of seeing a doctor. To do so was not an option, so when she spotted a woman with firewood strapped to her back, Josephine crossed the street and made her approach. "How much for three pieces?" It was all she could carry.

"Thirty pence, love."

Swallowing the bitterness of surrendering the sum, Josephine exchanged the coins for the wood and resumed walking, pushing through the wind as it whipped her skirts around her legs.

She was almost at her door before she noticed the carriage parked at the side of the road. The two black horses hitched to the front of it silently watched her progress. Giving them a wary glance, Josephine balanced the firewood in one arm so she could retrieve her key from her pelisse pocket.

Her face burned with cold and she took a step forward, prepared to seek refuge indoors, when the carriage door opened and a tall, broad-shouldered figure stepped down onto the pavement. His hair was black beneath his beaver hat, his features matching the harsh winter climate. Eyes as dark as night caught hers, and his jaw immediately set with distinct determination.

"Miss Potter?" He shoved the carriage door shut and strode toward her. The wind caught the hem of his somber greatcoat, forcing it out behind him in jerky movements.

Josephine raised her chin. "Who wants to know?"

Halting his approach, he told her frankly, "The Duke of Snowdon." He dipped his head and touched the brim of his hat. "At your service."

☾

The woman standing before Devon stared at him with incomprehension. Her lilac eyes, set against an oval face, had widened to the size of saucers, her rosy lips parted with undeniable shock. He wasn't sure what he'd expected the Potter sisters' appearances to be, but this one was certainly prettier than he had imagined. Cautious, too, judging from her response to his presence.

"Your guardian," he said, deciding to put her mind at ease, "has asked me to look in on you and your sisters."

Knitting her brow, she pressed her lips together and moved a bit closer to the door. "The Earl of Priorsbridge?"

"Precisely."

Her expression turned increasingly wary. "Forgive me for saying this, but I don't believe you."

Devon tried not to be affronted by the insult, but he couldn't resist asking, "Are you calling me a liar?"

She seemed to consider the question but chose not to answer it in the end, saying instead, "He has never showed any interest in us before." Her gaze slid toward the door and the welcome warmth no doubt waiting for her beyond.

"Perhaps you're thinking of his father."

"His father?" Confusion seemed to bring interest with it.

Which surprised Devon. "Have you not heard of his recent passing?"

She shook her head. "No. I do not read the papers very often."

"Then allow me to inform you that he died last month. It is his son who has asked me to make sure you're well and in no dire straits." Retrieving his calling card from his pocket, Devon handed it to her so she could confirm his identity. Her fingers trembled, the firewood pressed against her chest like a barrier of sorts. Devon drew a breath and expelled it in a ghostly mist. "Might I suggest we continue this conversation indoors?"

Her hesitance could not have been more obvious if she had actually told him she did not want him in her house. But the chill air must have banished the thought, for she quickly nodded and handed him the firewood. "If you will please hold this."

She unlocked the door and led the way through to a tiny foyer with barely enough space for the two of them to stand. Devon shut the door behind him to block the cold.

"In here." Miss Potter spoke briskly as she opened the door to a modest parlor and led the way through.

He followed her inside, noting it was only marginally warmer in there than it had been in the foyer or even outdoors, with the fire in the grate reduced to embers. Crossing the floor, he considered the orange sparks glowing amidst the ashes. He hadn't lit a fire in years, not since his father had taught him how when he'd been a lad. A lesson in practicality, his father had called it. As heir to a dukedom, Devon would probably never need the skill, but his father had insisted upon him knowing it all the same. It was being put to good use now, he decided, as he crouched down and set the logs on the floor. He reached for the fireplace spade and broom.

"What are you doing?" Miss Potter asked from somewhere behind him. She sounded slightly appalled.

Devon started to clean out the ash. "What does it look like?" She probably wasn't accustomed to dukes stopping by and ensuring comfort.

There was a pause—a very distinct one—and then, "But you cannot possibly...I mean, I can easily do this, Your…er…ah…Grace."

It was curious really, but there was something charming about her perplexity. Something amusing too. Devon glanced at her over his shoulder and instantly sucked in his breath. While he'd been busying himself with the fireplace, she'd removed the bonnet she'd been wearing to reveal the fairest hair he'd ever seen. Wisps of it curled against her cheeks with untidy abandon, tempting him to stand and approach her so he could examine it in greater detail.

Instead, he returned his attention to his task, blocking her from his view. "It's no trouble." His voice was slightly gruffer than before. "I am more than happy to help."

Especially since he'd promised Priorsbridge – Edward – he would ensure the Misses Potter were well taken care of until he was able to do so himself. Some might call it a tall order, given its inconvenience, but Devon owed Edward, and the time had come for him to pay his debt.

"I see."

She said nothing further while he continued to clean out the ash and proceeded to build the fire. He lit it using the tinderbox sitting on the mantle and stoked it with the bellows. "That ought to do it," he eventually said, unable to hide the pleasure he found in the task. "Come warm your hands, Miss Potter."

Carefully, as if she feared he might bite, she moved toward the welcoming heat with a gentle tread. Devon stepped to one side, allowing more space to fall between them, but not enough to prevent him from seeing the shades of blue unfurling around her irises. Her eyes were stunning, remarkable in their transformation of color. And her hair… It wasn't white, and it wasn't blonde. Rather, it was something in between, something he could not adequately describe, though it held him riveted with its uniqueness.

Stretching out her fingers, now free from the gloves she'd been wearing, she allowed a sigh of distinct pleasure. Devon followed her example, but it wasn't the fire that held his interest. It was her – the rosy glow brightening her cheeks, the dark lashes feathering across her skin, the soft curve of her nose, and the plush fullness of her lower lip. He considered each feature discreetly, all the while pretending he needed warmth too, when the truth was, he hadn't felt cold since catching his first glimpse of her without her bonnet.

He shrugged aside the distraction and glanced around the room. For a house inhabited by three women, it was unusually silent. "Where are your sisters, Miss Potter? Priorsbridge wrote there ought to be three of you living here."

"And so there were until recently." After flexing her fingers as if hoping the action would force the heat to penetrate further, she lowered her hands and turned slightly toward him. Her eyes were now entirely blue, a deeper shade quite similar to the one found at sea on a hot afternoon. "Louise left for Whitehaven the day before yesterday in order to accept a position as governess to the Earl and Countess of Channing's children."

Devon felt his jaw tighten with displeasure. "But she is gentry, the Earl of Priorsbridge's cousin and ward. Allowing her to work for a living is highly irregular—unacceptable in so many ways—and likely to suggest Priorsbridge has failed to do his duty by you."

Her eyebrows rose. "You speak as though you imagine we had a choice, as though we could afford to continue living in this house without seeking employment."

Briefly, Devon considered their humble surroundings, the worn-out velvet upholstery covering the nearby sofa and chairs, the lack of rugs and display pieces. The tables and sideboard were bare. Not a single vase or ornamental figurine could be seen. And then the manner in which she'd spoken hit him. His eyes found hers, lost for a moment in the clarity of her gaze. "*We?*"

A shrug shifted her shoulders. "I work as an accountant, Your Grace."

"I beg your pardon?" He'd never heard of a female accountant before, and was so surprised to be faced with one now, he tactlessly followed his question with, "But you're a woman!"

"Yes."

The clip of her tone suggested she wasn't the least bit pleased with what he said. Still… "That is even worse than being a governess, Miss Potter. The scandal you might cause. Why, it is—"

"I don't see how my position would cause an ounce of scandal for anyone."

Blinking, he stared down at her upturned face. "You are doing a man's job, which might not have been too bad if you had been born into the working class. But you were not. Your status, most particularly as it relates to Priorsbridge, demands a certain…" He waved his hand, unsure of how to finish his sentence, especially since she was glaring at him now with distinct hostility. "The point is, your actions reflect upon him."

"What would you have had me do instead, Your Grace? Starve? Lose my home? Allow my sisters to do so?" She jabbed a finger at his chest, the blunt point of contact scolding him as effectively as her words. "I did what was necessary in order to survive after Priorsbridge proved to have no intention of helping us in any way."

"I will agree the former earl was lax in his duties toward you, but his son means to right that wrong. He intends to do what his father did not. It is why he asked me to come here personally and check on you."

She gave a snort. "It must be nice to have a duke at your beck and call."

Gritting his teeth, Devon leaned toward her. "He helped me when my father passed and I was out of the country. He saw to the funeral arrangements and ensured my mother and sister were well taken care of. Since he is otherwise occupied at the moment with the details surrounding his new inheritance, he asked if I could return the favor and handle this particular matter on his behalf." Drawing a breath, he forced calmness into his voice before saying, "So you will hand in your notice at wherever it is you work, and then you will write to your sister and ask her to do the same. Immediately."

☾

For a long moment, Josephine could do nothing but stare at the duke. The aloof manner in which he'd just spoken made it abundantly clear he was accustomed to getting his way. And in case his voice did not accomplish this goal, he wore a stern expression indicative of his strength and power, an expression intended to intimidate and defeat a weaker individual. Josephine knew there were men and women who would swiftly surrender to his demands when faced with the hint of his impending wrath, but she wasn't one of them. Not when she'd faced much worse.

So she straightened her spine and squared her shoulders, addressing him with more honesty than a man of his rank had likely ever been subjected to before and said, "Your arrogance is astounding." His jaw went slack, fuelling her resolve. "The fact you would presume to have the right to tell me what to do is preposterous. How dare you come into my home and play the entitled lord? How dare you behave as though I am subservient to you, as though I must bow to your will?"

She fairly shook with anger, the cold she'd felt consuming her body a moment ago, completely forgotten. "You..." She pointed a finger at him, and he actually took a step back. "You pompous ass!"

Her breaths were shallow, her chest heaving beneath the weight of each inhalation while she struggled to calm herself to some degree. She'd never been the sort of person to raise her voice to anyone or to throw insults around. That she did so now with a duke was testament to how deeply his overbearing manner had offended her.

"Are you quite finished?" Irritation had banished all signs of the shock he'd portrayed in response to her outburst. Instead, he now encompassed more fierceness than ever. She chose to hold her tongue this time, allowing him to have his say. "Considering I've been tasked with ensuring your welfare and quarrelling is unlikely to be productive, I will pretend you did not insult me in such direct terms."

"Would you rather I did it in indirect terms?" The words were out before she could stop them. Inwardly, she cringed at her childish inability to resist the jab, while managing to maintain an outward appearance of stubborn defiance. Thank God.

His teeth ground together, nostrils flaring while his hard stare drove boldly into her. "If you think coming here is enjoyable to me, think again, Miss Potter, for I can assure you I would rather be elsewhere. However, I have made a promise to Priorsbridge, and being a man of my word, I intend to do precisely what he has asked, however undeserving I think you are of anyone's good graces at the moment."

He drew a deep breath as if gathering his strength. Affording her with the most patronizing stare she'd ever borne witness to in her life, he said, "So you and your sisters will receive a monthly stipend of seventy-five pounds, and in exchange, you will do everything in your power to ensure your actions do not reflect negatively on Priorsbridge."

"In other words, you are bribing me."

Muttering something beneath his breath—a curse, no doubt—he closed his eyes for a second, squeezing them tight before opening them again with frustration. "What woman in her right mind would rather toil away her days than accept a relative's generosity?"

She knew it seemed ridiculous, especially to a man like Snowdon who'd never been shunned by his peers or faced the threat of destitution. But for her, the idea of taking money from a man she'd never even met was no different than stealing. "I do not wish to be a charity cause, nor do I want to take advantage. What I desire is to prove myself capable of self-sufficiency." She would prove to the world and, more importantly, to herself she did not require anyone's help. Two men had failed her already—her father and her uncle—and she would be damned if she was going to allow herself to rely on a third.

"Why?" He studied her as though he considered her utterly hopeless. "Isn't life difficult enough? Why complicate it further by insisting on making it more so?"

"Because nothing worth having is easily won," she muttered, casting a glance toward the crackling flames. A log snapped, sending up a flurry of sparks.

His sigh, long and laborious, filled the air between them. "I suppose I can relate to that."

Snorting, she crossed her arms. "Really?" She didn't believe him for a second. He was a duke after all, the sort of man for whom roads were paved with gold and doors were flung wide open.

He glanced toward the fire. "The day I turned eighteen, my father came to inform me it was time for me to prove my worth. Turns out, he'd purchased a small cottage in Cornwall where he expected me to live for the duration of a year without relying upon the conveniences to which I'd been accustomed."

It was Josephine's turn to be shocked. "You cannot be serious."

"Indeed, I am quite so. For you see, my father believed such an experience would allow me to relate to my tenants and servants, while giving me a true appreciation for what I have. He felt forcing me to lead a life of hardship for a year would make me a better duke in the end, and I suspect he was right."

"You never accepted any help from him during this time?"

"No. I made my way by selling fish and wood carvings at the market. The last thing I wanted was to fail, to have to return home and admit defeat."

Amazed by his confession, she studied him for a long moment. "So you understand why I cannot give up my position or accept a stipend from Priorsbridge."

"I do." A hint of sympathy warmed his eyes, and for a second Josephine believed she'd won. Until he said, "But your situation is different from what mine was. For one thing, great care was taken to ensure my identity would not be discovered. Can you honestly tell me nobody knows you're related to Priorsbridge?"

She thought of lying, then decided against it. "No." The gossip columns had written extensive articles on her father's pitiable downfall and on his daughters' struggle to survive in the wake of his death. Their family history had been used as an example of how far one could fall when gripped by vice. And when Josephine and her sisters had been forced to sell their Mayfair home, whispers had followed in their wake, assuring them they would not easily be forgotten.

"Then consider this, Miss Potter. It is no longer your reputation alone that's at risk, but his as well. If word gets out he failed to support you, that you were forced to make your own way in the world, he will be painted a heartless man."

Josephine frowned. "Nothing of the sort has been said of his father. What makes you think anyone will care about Priorsbridge's actions now?"

"Because having acquired the title no more than a month ago, he will be scrutinized in every imaginable way. So please, show some consideration and help him avoid criticism."

When put like that, it was difficult for Josephine to maintain her determination. Still, she could not allow two men—one whom she'd never met and the other to whom she was not related —to guide her future. "While I sympathize, I cannot accept Priorsbridge's support. I am sorry."

"You are, without a doubt, the most stubborn woman I have ever met." He said it as though it were an affliction, his hand raking furiously through his hair, ruffling it in a way Josephine found disturbingly charming under the circumstances. "The stipend is not the only item on the table. I've also been asked to help ease your way back into society. I have family and friends on whom I can call, contacts who can help you regain your position. Surely this must be desirable in some way or other, if not for you, then for your sisters." Her hesitance must have shown, for he pounced on it like a lion catching its prey. "What of your youngest sister? You've made no mention of her seeking employment, but if you're what— " He was suddenly giving her a critical assessment. "Seven and twenty?"

"Six and twenty," she corrected, doing her best to ignore the blush threatening to burn her cheeks.

"Then your youngest sister must be of marriageable age. Correct?"

Josephine nodded. "Eve set out for Amberly Hall near Bournemouth yesterday morning. Her friend, Mrs. Havisham, has offered to introduce her to her social circle. If doing so yields no result, there is still the coming Season. I have been saving what I can with the intention of giving Eve the debut she deserves."

He went completely still, his eyes fixed on her face with pensiveness, twisting her stomach and making her heart beat a little bit faster. It unnerved her, and she had no choice but to remove her gaze from his. So she considered the lackluster floorboards beneath her feet instead, until he said, "As confounding as you are, I must confess my admiration for your stalwart perseverance."

Instinctively, her gaze latched onto his. A pause followed, one in which all of her problems, her future, her sisters' happiness, and Priorsbridge's interference with all of it remained suspended. The only two people in the world at the moment were her and Snowdon, caught in a most peculiar web from which escape seemed increasingly difficult.

It didn't help that he looked like sin and seduction or that she was old enough to consider herself a spinster, a woman who might enjoy a man's kiss without the threat of marriage. Was it wrong for her to feel desire? To secretly long for some shred of passion before she became too old to gain a man's attention? She had no prospects, had inherited nothing but shame, and yet here she was, attracted to an aggravating aristocrat whom she didn't much care for, if for no other reason than principal.

It was a wretched notion, and it brought her promptly out of her reverie. "Thank you," she managed to say with a steadier voice than she'd ever imagined possible. A bit of awkward silence passed between them while she gathered her composure. "If that is all, I believe I must ask you to leave. Your presence here is far from appropriate, and your carriage the sort bound to gain attention from those with nothing better to do than observe the lives of others. Whatever my reputation may be, it will suffer even more the longer you stay. Especially once my neighbors discover my sisters are no longer here, and I invited you into my home without chaperone."

A frown pinched his brow. "Forgive me. I should have excused myself the moment I discovered you were alone, though you ought to have conveyed such information sooner rather than later."

"Duly noted." He was right, but she'd been freezing with cold outside, and he'd obviously had a great deal to say. *You didn't mind having a handsome man's attention to yourself for a while.*

She was ashamed to acknowledge the fact, but

her life had lacked excitement for so long. It had revolved around her mother's death, her father's decline, his death, financial loss, and a dire future from which she'd struggled to protect her sisters. With Louise, she'd failed, but there was still hope for Eve. *More so if you simply surrender and take the money Priorsbridge is offering.*

Her pride, however, would not allow it. Not when she stood to succeed on her own. It would be harder, the sacrifices greater, but in the end, she wouldn't owe anyone a thing. Her life would be her own. It would not belong to another man. She would have the freedom to make her own choices without interference or criticism or any other kind of involvement from anyone.

Snowdon strode toward the door and paused, his hand on the handle. "I expect you to take my advice seriously, Miss Potter." There it was again, the blasted arrogance grating on her nerves. "Priorsbridge is my friend, so while I sympathize with your situation and admire your effort to survive without anyone's assistance, I will not allow you to tarnish his name in any way. Is that clear?"

"Perfectly, Your Grace."

His eyes narrowed, no doubt in response to her tart tone. It couldn't be helped. Not when he meant to strip her of her freedom.

A curt nod followed. "Good," he said. "I shall expect a missive from you no later than tomorrow afternoon, informing me your position has been terminated. Then we shall see about taking you out in Society. I've a sister who likes the occasional project. She'll no doubt be thrilled to make your acquaintance."

He tipped his hat and made his exit, leaving Josephine to wonder if he knew how offensive he was being, or if he simply didn't care.

CHAPTER TWO

ARRIVING AT THE HOTEL HE'D acquired two years earlier, Devon entered the manager's office after a quick rap on the door. He'd bought the building shortly after inheriting his title, when he'd realized the true cost of running his estates. Fearing the day would come when his descendants would not be able to afford the expense, he'd done what most would consider unusual, perhaps even unacceptable, for a duke. He'd gone into trade, albeit in a classy sort of way and with complete discretion.

"Mr. Roth," he said, greeting the middle-aged gentleman to whom he entrusted the daily running of his business, "I would like to discuss the letter you sent me."

Mr. Roth rose from behind his desk and extended his hand. "Your Grace. I am much relieved by your presence." Devon shook his hand and lowered himself to a vacant chair. Mr. Roth sat too. "Your opinion of my suggestions to aid the business is most welcome."

"From what I gather, the Park View isn't doing as well as we'd hoped."

Flattening his mouth, Mr. Roth drummed his fingers against his armrests before saying, "Income has been steadily declining since the hotel opened. This year, we stand to make half of what we made last year."

Devon frowned. As far as investments went, this was proving to be a catastrophe. "Any idea why this might be?"

Mr. Roth nodded. "Few clients return for a second visit. They seem to favor the High Tower. The rooms there are significantly cheaper."

"So you advise a price reduction?"

"And the dismissal of twenty employees." When Devon raised his eyebrows, Mr. Roth added, "We have to cut cost somewhere, Your Grace. This is the most obvious approach."

"It will also hurt a lot of good people."

"Yes, but keeping them on would be detrimental. Unless you plan on putting more money into the business, which rather defeats the purpose of your investment."

"Of course." Devon leaned back in his chair and considered the problem at hand. "What I need is for it to sustain itself and grow without additional funds being added."

Nodding, Mr. Roth looked him squarely in the eye. "Then allow me to make the necessary adjustments, Your Grace."

Devon hated the idea of referring to the discharge of employees as a necessary adjustment, but he could see Mr. Roth's point. Still…"I expect each of these people to receive some compensation, thirty pounds at least, along with a decent letter of recommendation."

Mr. Roth inclined his head. "Of course, Your Grace. You may rest assured no one will feel the least bit slighted."

Devon grunted his response since he believed the opposite would be true. They were discussing people's livelihoods, after all—more specifically, the snatching away of them. Resentment would be inevitable. But to say as much would serve no purpose. Rising, Devon made to take his leave. "I trust you to keep the best employees and to dismiss only those whose work has been found lacking."

If it wouldn't have been exceedingly rude of him to do so, Devon imagined, Mr. Roth would have rolled his eyes. Instead, he gave a tight smile. "Naturally, that goes without saying."

Devon asked the manager to keep him apprised of the progress, before leaving the Park View's future in Mr. Roth's capable hands. Devon had other pressing matters to attend to, like convincing Miss Potter to do what he asked. He'd written his sister the previous afternoon, immediately after returning home from his visit with Miss Potter, and asked her to come to Town post haste.

Rowena would not be thrilled. There was little to do in London this time of year. Most families chose to rusticate in their grand estates for the winter. But at least Miss Potter would not be alone. *With him.* He winced at the prospect while his driver set a course for Piccadilly, where he intended to do some necessary shopping.

She was attractive. No doubt about it. And he...hell, there had been a moment—several, in fact—where he'd been inclined to be anything but proper. Like when she'd called him a pompous ass. There had been something about the fiery look in her eyes as she'd stood there, stiff and commanding. It had roused his senses.

No one had ever put him in his place with such exemplary efficiency before. The effect had been not only humbling but thoroughly arousing. It had tempted him with thoughts—wild and wicked—of what her chastising mouth might taste like and how she'd respond to his touch. Would she apply an equal measure of passion to lovemaking? Would she be equally free and honest in her demand for pleasure?

Most assuredly, he reckoned. And as this idea began to take root, he found himself wanting to explore the possibility, to take her in his arms and show her what it meant to stir a man's blood.

Christ!

He'd clearly gone too long without a bed partner. Perhaps a visit to Madame Lizette would be in order. Having sordid ponderings about Miss Potter was definitely not the right approach. It had to stop. Immediately. So he set his mind to the items he needed to purchase and did his best not to think of Miss Potter. Having an affair with her would lead to a whole new set of problems, which was something he wanted to do without.

C

Two days had passed since the duke had made his demands. Arriving home earlier than usual, Josephine entered her parlor on wooden feet and slumped down into the nearest armchair. Her job, the one she'd depended so thoroughly on, had been taken from her no more than an hour earlier. She could scarcely credit it, could not even feel the cold on account of her numbness. Somewhere deep in her chest, she felt her heart beat—a dull thud of failure. Her breath came raggedly, pushing its way in and out of her lungs as if forcing life into her disheartened body.

She'd no idea how long she'd been sitting there before a loud knock broke the silence. It came not from the front door but from the back, and with increasing incessancy. Rising, she hastened toward the sound.

"What?" she demanded, not caring who it might be as she tore the door open.

The Duke of Snowdon stood before her, his expression immediately hinting at caution. "Is this a bad time, Miss Potter?"

She closed her eyes, willed herself to be calm, then said, "I thought you told me to write."

"And you've not done so, which is why I decided it would be best to look in and ensure all is well."

His charm was enough to make her scream at the moment. She did not want him to be nice or polite. She wanted someone deserving of the anger in need of release. "As you can see," she bit out, "I am here and in perfect health. No need to worry."

"And your job? Have you managed to—"

"You got your wish." She almost spat the words on a wave of resentment rolling through her. "I was discharged this afternoon."

His eyes widened a bit, and then he said the most astonishing thing. "You're clearly distressed.

Perhaps you would like me to make you a cup of tea?"

Laughter rushed up her throat and out through her nose in the form of a sputtering snort. When he remained serious and she realized he hadn't been jesting, she clasped the doorframe and tried to find purchase in this odd turn of events.

"Thank you for your kindness, Your Grace, but we've already talked about how your presence in my home might be construed."

"Which is why I chose to arrive at the back door. There is no view of this entry from the neighboring houses. I already checked."

"Really?" She couldn't hide her surprise. Uneasily, she peered toward the gate at the end of her walkway. Walls rose from both sides, tall enough to ensure they couldn't be seen.

"So please step aside and allow me to enter before we freeze to death on your doorstep."

Against her better judgment, Josephine did what he asked. Not because she had any interest in keeping company with a man as attractive as he or because she liked the attention he gave her. It certainly wasn't because she hoped to experience another moment of physical awareness with him or because she wished he might do something more improper than keep her company in the privacy of her home. No. It was only because he was cold, and it would be rude to turn him away.

"I brought a few things for you too," he said, passing her in the entryway. His arm and shoulder brushed against her so smoothly she gasped. He turned about swiftly, facing her in the tiny space and crowding her with his much larger size. "Are you all right?"

Unable to speak, she managed a nod.

He frowned as if he didn't believe her. But whether he did or not, he chose to drop the subject, for which she was immensely grateful. "I imagine the kitchen must be through here?" he asked, gesturing toward a door on the right.

She nodded again, though he couldn't see since he'd turned his back.

"There's some ham and cheese, a couple of oranges, and three tomatoes in here," he said, setting a bag on the kitchen table.

Josephine felt her throat close around the words she wanted to say. He was being so nice—too nice—and she'd treated him abominably. "I'm sorry I snapped at you earlier," she tried, hating how raw the words sounded and what they revealed.

"You lost your employment, which must have pained you." He'd found the kettle and was busy filling it with water from a jug.

Swallowing, she turned away, just enough to hide the tears welling in her eyes. "I wasn't going to do what you asked. I intended to keep my position. But now…" A burst of uneasy laughter slipped past her lips. "Apparently I am redundant and too costly considering my sex. My employer told me so right after he suggested he might want to keep me on if I was willing to…to…." Lord help her, she could not say it.

"If you were willing to what?" When she failed to answer, Snowdon's voice spoke more firmly. "Miss Potter, did your employer ask you to do certain things in order to keep your position?"

She spun toward him, hands clenched by her sides as anger returned, hot and quick. "I told him to go hang himself." Tension strained her body to the point of snapping, and yet she managed to keep herself still and to stop the tears from falling.

The duke's face had hardened, each line drawn tight to reveal his fury. "Miss Potter—"

"You must forgive me." An exhalation of breath calmed her nerves to some degree. "I'm not sure why I'm sharing all of this with you, except I usually have my sisters in whom to confide. Without them here, you are the only person I can talk to."

He held her gaze as if searching for more information. Then, breaking eye contact, he lit a fire in the hearth and hung the kettle over it. "You will tell me who did this to you, Miss Potter." His voice was low, his words carefully spoken while he busied himself with finding a tray, a teapot, and some cups and saucers.

Befuddled, Josephine watched for a long, silent moment. He retrieved some tealeaves and a strainer. "Why? I said my piece to the man and left. There is no need for you to go and defend my honor or whatever it is you are planning to do."

"Perhaps not," he agreed. "You did the right thing, but will it be enough to stop this man from mistreating other women in the future? How can we be certain he will not prey on someone too weak to deny him?"

Josephine felt her throat tighten at the prospect of such a thing happening. The possibility had not occurred to her, though she knew it should have. But she'd been too caught up in her own feelings of shame and anger to consider the consequence of such a man going unpunished.

"Very well. His name is Mr. Roth." The duke's expression hardened even further. "He is the manager of the Park View Hotel."

For a second, it seemed as though Snowdon might hit something, perhaps even her if she happened to be in his way. So she took a step back, disliking the hostile atmosphere swamping the small space.

"Are you sure?" His voice had grown taut, as though it required great effort for him to keep the words steady.

She nodded. "Of course I'm sure. I have worked there for almost a year."

"Did he make other advances on you in that time?"

Offended, she glared at him. "In light of what happened today, do you honestly think I would have remained in his employ if he had?"

Nostrils flaring, Snowdon gave a swift shake of his head. "No. I don't believe you would." His brow creased with deep grooves and he dropped his gaze to the tray. He drew a deep breath, then expelled it, his hands clenching and unclenching by his sides as though he struggled with some inner turmoil.

"Your Grace?"

He did not answer immediately. A few seconds passed before he finally glanced at her, the stormy display of emotion held in the depths of his eyes effectively sending a shiver along her spine. "I am so sorry this happened to you, Miss Potter."

"Thank you. I appreciate your saying so, considering our differing opinions on the matter of my employment."

"You don't understand."

Something about his manner, some great sense of regret, gave Josephine pause.

And then he said, "I am to blame for this. Mr. Roth is in my employ, and while I can assure you of his impending punishment, I wish it had never happened in the first place."

She gaped at him, aware her lips had parted with absolute disbelief, her eyes no doubt wider than the ocean, while she stared at him, unable to think of what to say next except, "What do you mean?"

Swallowing, he told her plainly, "I own the Park View Hotel."

Clarity whipped through her with terrifying precision. "Dear God." She took a retreating step back. "You must have known I worked there."

It was his turn to look confused. "Nonsense. I only found out about it right now, during the course of this conversation."

"Really? So it is a coincidence that you demanded I stop working, and I lost my job two days later?" She could feel the anger returning, more violently than before, the notion of betrayal cutting deep.

"Yes." His eyes were wild now as he moved toward her with startling swiftness to close the door at her back, effectively halting her progress. He leaned in, his hand on the handle behind her, his chest so close she could feel his heat suffusing her body like a welcome balm.

It was tempting to sigh with pleasure, to tilt her head back, and to wish for a kiss. But not when there was a chance he'd caused the misery she endured, the helplessness losing her job had stirred. So she stood up tall, as rigidly as she could manage, pretending a wall existed between them, a wall through which he was not permitted to pass.

As if sensing her standoffishness, he pushed back onto his heels, allowing more space to come between them. "The truth is, the business is struggling. Mr. Roth suggested cutting costs by relieving a few employees of their positions. I had no idea you would be among them, and indeed, I am sorry to hear you are."

She took a moment to study his features, a moment in which to gauge if he was being sincere. Deciding he was, she allowed herself to relax as much as one could relax when one had lost one's livelihood and faced a man who did curious things to one's body. So she said the first thing that came to mind. "I think the water is boiling." Something safe and mundane.

Without hesitation, he grabbed the kettle and poured the steaming water through the strainer in the teapot. "I will have him discharged without reference."

She nodded, even though he wouldn't see. "You know, the trouble was never with the employees. In fact, I think letting them go will prove to be a mistake."

"How so?" He began tidying away a few things, extinguished the fire, and picked up the tray.

Josephine opened the door and led the way through to the parlor. She instantly groaned in response to the cold greeting them there. "I am sorry," she said, cringing at her ineptness at playing hostess. "I was so upset when I got home, I forgot to start the fire, and then you arrived and—"

"Do not trouble yourself." He set the tray down on the table and went to select one of the two remaining logs, allowing her to place the cups and saucers on the table and pour the tea.

"You must not forget I worked in accounting. I saw the hotel books. And it is my belief the financial problem stems from increasingly inferior quality. I can tell you, for instance, the cost of ingredients being purchased for the kitchen decreased by more than thirty percent in the past year. Now, I don't know much about the price of duck, but I do not expect it to cost the same as a chicken."

Crouched before the fireplace, the duke turned to stare at her. "Mr. Roth served mediocre food to our guests and passed it off as high-class cuisine?"

Josephine nodded. "I believe so. How long has it been since you ate in the restaurant or checked on the bedrooms?"

He blinked. "I have not done so since the place opened. Mr. Roth appeared capable enough, and I had other matters to attend to—my estates, parliament, family matters." Turning away, he muttered a curse while stoking the newly lit fire. When he finally stood, Josephine noted the slump of his shoulders and how his head hung while he stared down into the flames. "I should have been more involved."

"It is not too late to start."

Shifting his stance, he tilted his head in her direction. The edge of his mouth drew up in a slant not entirely unlike a smile. "Perhaps not."

"And I can help, if you wish. As long as you let me return to work."

All traces of a smile faded. "Absolutely not."

"But—"

"It was bad enough when I thought you were working for someone else, but if Priorsbridge discovers I allowed you to work in my employ, he will have my head, and rightly so." He strode toward the sofa and took a seat opposite her. "I am sorry, Miss Potter, but your days as an accountant are officially at an end."

Gnashing her teeth with frustrated ire, Josephine wondered how he might respond to having the contents of the teapot dumped over his arrogant head. "And so I remain in the hands of men, my life and future irrevocably tied to their desire."

"Careful, Miss Potter." His eyes darkened, his teacup suspended a fraction of an inch beneath his lower lip. He was watching her—assessing her—in a way that produced a wave of heat beneath the surface of her skin. And then, so low she barely heard him at all, he murmured, "You are putting ideas in my head."

She stared at him, at how his lips parted over the rim of his cup, the satisfied gleam in his eyes while he drank, and the secretive smile he gave while returning his cup to its saucer. All of it combined to form a yearning deep in the pit of her belly. Her mouth went dry as he continued to hold her gaze. His casual ease, coupled with a predatory undertone, quickened her pulse. She felt her stays grow tight, and she suddenly saw what he saw—what he'd spoken of seconds earlier—the idea she'd put in his head when she'd mentioned desire.

It barreled toward her, fast and furious, the wickedness of his imaginings blatantly clear in the depths of his eyes, now hooded and knowing – aware of the vision they shared – one in which she was wrapped in his arms while he...he...

Dear God, she dared not take the fantasy further, and yet she could not stop from seeing more. An unwilling groan forced its way up her throat. He hadn't touched her, only looked, and yet she felt like she'd been caught up in scandalous pleasure while doing nothing less proper than drinking tea. And she'd groaned! Heaven help her, she could not stop the furious blush or the embarrassment wrapping its way around her.

Snowdon chuckled, equal parts sin and amusement.

"You're awful," she managed to say.

"At least now I know what I only suspected before."

"And what would that be?" Stupid question. She should have known better than to let him goad her.

He leaned forward. "You're an incredibly passionate woman, Miss Potter."

A thrill of something forbidden snaked through her. "Nonsense." She had to find a way back to solid ground before she allowed him to seduce her. That would certainly not bode well for her reputation, a reputation she'd soon be unable to salvage if he continued to stop by like this. So when he prepared to say more, she deliberately cut him off. "I want nothing to do with passion. All I want is for you to let me go back to work."

His sigh sounded tortured. "This again?"

Her nod was firm. "Yes."

"I've already told you, letting you do so will be impossible. However..." He seemed to consider something with a great degree of pensiveness. "If you accept the stipend Priorsbridge is offering, I might agree to let you advise me on how to improve my business."

It wasn't the worst suggestion in the world. It wouldn't put her mathematical skills to good use, but it was certainly something she could take some pride in. She would also feel as though she were getting a salary, rather than taking money from a man she did not know without doing anything in return.

So she squared her shoulders and told him firmly, "Very well, Your Grace. You have yourself a deal."

Whatever he believed of her willingness to agree, he showed no sign of it. Instead, he got up. "I should take my leave now, Miss Potter." His eyes scanned the space around them. "Will you be all right here by yourself?"

"Certainly, Your Grace."

He gave a quick nod. "I expect my sister to arrive tomorrow. When she does, I will ask her to invite you to stay with us at Snowdon House for the holidays."

Whatever he might have said, this was quite possibly the most unexpected. "Thank you, Your Grace, but I couldn't possibly accept such an offer." Least of all after the moment they'd shared.

"I insist. Remaining here, alone, isn't safe. Suppose you fall and hurt yourself or someone comes to threaten you? You're vulnerable without your sisters, not to mention cold and uncomfortable."

"Your Grace—"

"At Snowdon House you will be given a comfortable room of your own with a blazing fireplace and plenty of tasty food to eat. You will also have excellent company." He waggled his eyebrows, and she could not for the life of her stop from laughing. "Say yes, Miss Potter. My sister will appreciate some female company."

"Then by all means, I shall do it for her."

Because she was absolutely not doing it for herself or for him. To acknowledge as much would be terribly dangerous indeed.

CHAPTER THREE

WHEN MISS POTTER ARRIVED AT his home two days later, Devon could scarcely contain his excitement. Which was why he chose to let Rowena greet her, while he secluded himself in the library. Honestly, he had to get himself under control. The fact he'd asked her to stay beneath his roof proved his weak resolve to do the right thing. Instead, he was allowing his lust for her to guide him—to bring her closer, into a bedroom where he would be able to visit if he chose to do so.

He would not be quite such a scoundrel, of course. But the possibility of it alone stirred his blood. Christ, it had taken every bit of restraint he possessed not to climb across the table in her parlor the other day and take her into his arms. Or in the kitchen earlier, when he'd been the cause of her anger. He'd stepped close enough to smell the perfume of roses upon her skin and had barely resisted the urge to push her up against the door and kiss her until she grew breathless.

Bloody hell!

He'd wanted to do a lot more than kissing. Especially when he'd allowed himself a moment of wicked imagining. Desire had washed over her face as if their minds had been linked, and she'd seen the pictures he'd painted of her, of her head thrown pack while he pushed up her skirts and tore open her bodice. And then, God help him, she'd groaned, as if he'd actually done it, as if he'd actually placed his mouth against her breasts and allowed his hand to slide over her thigh.

Frustrated, Devon went to refill the empty glass of brandy sitting before him. He'd gone to visit Madame Lizette as planned, but after selecting a girl who shared Miss Potter's appearance as much as possible, he'd been too disgusted with himself to do anything with her. Especially since the girl in question had been sultrier than Miss Potter and lacked the feistiness he found so incredibly arousing in her.

But now she was here, invited to stay until her youngest sister returned. Devon took a long sip of his brandy. His sister had been appalled by the idea, because she'd seen right through him. His dissembling excuses and explanations had not been able to convince her of anything but an ulterior motive.

"You never want to have guests," she'd said. "So what is this really about, Devon?"

He'd muttered something about Priorsbridge, while walking away and shutting a door in Rowena's face. When they'd crossed paths later, she'd wagged a disapproving finger at him. "If you seduce this woman, I'll never speak to you again. Do you hear? You'll be just as awful as all the other reprobates out there."

He'd hated the word, hated the fact his sister

knew of the weakness he felt when faced with Miss Potter. So he'd locked himself away, plagued by guilt and need and something so desperate, he feared it might easily consume him. He decided to only come out for meals. And to escort Miss Potter over to the Park View. His sister would chaperone, so there was no risk of him behaving as anything other than the perfect gentleman.

But in his heart he wanted, more fervently than he'd ever wanted before. Which had made him consider all manner of solutions. He could, for instance, return to the country and send a letter to Priorsbridge informing him he'd done his duty, and Miss Potter was well. Which she would be, now she'd agreed to the stipend.

He could also try to convince her to be his mistress. Now there was a satisfying option, though he had to admit such a position would be rather demeaning for her. She was, after all, a gentlewoman, even if she had fallen on hard times, and her father had sullied their name. To actually ask her to be one step above a whore would likely lead to a tongue lashing the likes of which humanity had never seen.

Which left one final possibility.

He hardly dared contemplate it. Because the more he did, the more sense it made. Which only led to him wanting it more and, consequently, to the fear of failure. After all, their mutual attraction aside, he knew he and Miss Potter had had their differences. Also, their acquaintance was fairly new. They'd met no more than four days ago. Which meant they did not know each other particularly well. Except he felt like he knew her, as though he was able to predict her response to any situation with certain accuracy.

She was stubborn and proud, unwilling to bend to any man's will, and by God, he wanted her by his side and in his bed, even if that meant marrying her.

There. He'd actually allowed the entire idea to form in his head. Taking another sip of his drink, he savored the calm settling deep in his bones now he'd found the right path. Whether she would agree to be his wife or not had yet to be determined. But he was a duke, damn it, and he knew she wanted him as much as he wanted her. Surely he'd manage to convince her of the benefits to their union.

With this in mind, he set his glass down and strode to the door, determined to begin his courtship as promptly as possible—before he did something foolish like toss her over his shoulder and carry her off to be ravished. Which was definitely the most tempting course of action, even if it wasn't the wisest.

☾

Seated at the long dining room table that evening, Josephine wondered at Snowdon's attentiveness. Not that he hadn't been kind before when he'd made the fire in her parlor, brought her food, and prepared her tea, but it seemed like he was going out of his way to prove himself tonight. In a way, she found it endearing, but it did not diminish her suspicions. He was obviously up to something, the only question was what?

"So tell me, Miss Potter," Lady Rowena began, "what prompted you to seek a position as an accountant?"

Josephine glanced across at Snowdon, who promptly stuck a piece of meat in his mouth and shrugged. She couldn't decide if she liked the idea of him discussing her with his sister or not, especially since this was an aspect of her he did not approve of.

Returning her attention to Lady Rowena, she said, "I have always been fond of mathematics."

The duke suddenly coughed. "Really?"

"Why do people find such a thing so surprising?" It had always confounded her, ever since she'd been a girl and she'd favored equations over embroidery.

"I suppose it is rare, that is all," the duke muttered, following his statement with a hasty sip of wine.

Josephine fought not to roll her eyes. "My mother always insisted on putting education first for all of her daughters. She believed knowledge would give us the power to survive even if everything else went pear-shaped. Which it did. But thanks to her determination to have us tutored in mathematics, science, literature, French, and Latin, my sister Louise and I were both able to land respectable positions." She glanced across at the duke before adding, "Even if you disapprove of our doing so."

"I believe my brother is of the opinion women exist so men can have something pleasing to look at," Lady Rowena murmured. "And because it would be deuced difficult for them to produce an heir on their own."

Stunned by the blunt sense of humor, Josephine found herself laughing more openly than she'd done in some time. It felt good. Liberating. As though she was truly keeping company with friends. Lady Rowena laughed too, then added something equally amusing about the duke having said so to a dowager countess once. But when Josephine swept her gaze toward him to gauge his reaction, she didn't find him laughing. Not because he appeared annoyed by his sister's jabbing, but because he watched Josephine closely, pensively even, and with more consideration than she felt comfortable with.

After dinner, he excused himself quickly, allowing Josephine to enjoy a sherry with his sister in the parlor. "Might I ask you a personal question, Miss Potter?" Lady Rowena asked, when they'd said all there was to say about their favorite books and their fondest childhood memories.

"Of course." Josephine wasn't sure if she wanted Lady Rowena to do so, but it was one of those situations where saying so would have been rude.

"What do you think of my brother?"

Of all the questions in the universe, why did it have to be that one?

"I, er, I hardly know him well enough to give my opinion."

Lady Rowena frowned with distinct dissatisfaction. "Come now, Miss Potter. He has invited you to visit with us, which he would not have done unless he considered you a friend. Please. I am curious to hear your opinion. And I promise not to be offended if you have something negative to say."

"In that case, I must confess I found him a bit too…dukely, when first we met."

Lady Rowena snorted. "You mean arrogant. He does tend to come across as such whenever he's playing the highborn aristocrat."

"I gathered as much after seeing him be less so. In fact, I preferred him when he was simply being…" She waved her hand, unable to find a better word than, "Normal."

"When he wasn't trying to tell you how to live your life?"

"Yes! Precisely. I rather liked him then, when no considerations had to be made about what would be proper or scandalous, or how my behavior might influence someone I've never even met."

"Hmm. I suspect it must be difficult for him, however." Lady Rowena met Josephine's gaze. "He is, after all, a man with a title, not simply a man. Never that."

Except when he built the fire, crouched on the floor without a care for the soot that would stain his knees after.

Josephine nodded. "Life has handed him a role, just as it has made you the lady in need of a perfect match and me the woman whose future was ruined by her father's weakness." She wished she could have avoided the bitterness, but the truth was, her life was as tarnished as a piece of oxidized silver. Making her chance of marrying a duke as unlikely as traveling to the stars.

Gasping in response to such an idea, Josephine bowed her head, her eyes fixed on her lap. Where on earth had such a ridiculous idea come from?

She hardly knew the man, and now she was thinking of marrying him? A hysterical bit of laughter burst past her lips, prompting her to do what she could to explain it away by saying, "Fate can be such a tragic thing, my lady."

Lady Rowena's hand settled smoothly over hers, drawing her gaze back to hers. "Yes, it can, but I want you to know I would never judge you on anything other than your own actions. I hope we can be friends, Miss Potter, which is why I should like it a great deal if you would call me Rowena."

"Only if you will call me Josephine."

Rowena smiled softly and nodded. "Agreed."

⁌

Courting a woman was no simple task. One had to determine what pleased her, or more importantly, what impressed her. Devon had been contemplating this since dinner the previous evening. He'd enjoyed their amicable conversation and had found himself enthralled by Miss Potter's beauty when she'd laughed. Recalling the sparkle in her eyes and the joyous sound escaping her mouth, it had been as though the heavens opened and angels started singing. But he couldn't for the life of him figure out how to take his relationship with her one step further without being too obvious or seeming too eager. Neither of which were likely to encourage a *tendre* on her part.

Flowers and jewelry were simply too easy. Anyone with money could give a woman such things without much effort. And if there was one thing he suspected, it was that Miss Potter would greatly appreciate something suitable to her interests. Which meant he would have to get to know her better. So he'd suggested they visit the Park View for luncheon, in order to try the food there before taking a look at the rooms. If they finished up quickly, he would propose they go skating on the Serpentine and enjoy some hot chocolate afterward at one of the nearby bakeries. Spending time together was paramount. The more time the better, in fact.

A knock on the door brought his sister into the room. "You look awfully serious," she said. "Is something the matter?"

"No. Nothing at all." He stood and pulled at his sleeves. "I am simply thinking about something."

Rowena's lips twitched with amusement. "And do these thoughts of yours involve a certain Miss Potter by any chance?"

"Of course not." He deliberately frowned.

"I know her name, you know. Her *given* name. In case you're interested." She smiled at him with annoying degrees of mischief.

Devon tried to conceal his interest, but Rowena must have spotted the brief flash of curiosity he'd felt in response to her words, because she actually grinned with devious glee. "Shall I take pity on you?" she asked.

He shook his head. "No need. Whatever her name is, it does not signify." If there was one thing he would not be reduced to in all of this, it was a man dependent upon his sister's mercy. He'd rather feign indifference.

Rowena shrugged as though dismissing the matter. "Well, in that case, I am here to tell you

Miss Potter and I are ready to depart whenever you are."

"Excellent." He could do with a change of scenery and a bit more closeness to Miss Potter. "I'll ask for a carriage to be brought around." He went to the bell-pull.

Rowena remained in the doorway. Her eyes met his, and she suddenly said, "Her name is Josephine, and in case you're wondering, she likes you. Not the duke, Devon, simply the man."

"What the devil do you mean by that?"

The words were out before he could stop them, chasing his sister into the hallway beyond as she left his study without answering the question.

It certainly gave him something to think about during the ride over to the Park View. *Josephine*. The name haunted him while he watched her converse with his sister, as he helped her down from the carriage – their hands briefly touching, separated by gloves--when he led the way into his hotel, and while he guided both women about. She liked him but not as a duke, which presented him with a problem. He'd no idea how to separate one from the other or if such a thing were even possible.

It had to be, or Rowena wouldn't have suggested as much. Which meant Josephine must have seen something in him, something apart from his title and all the restrictions it carried with it, something more *him*. He scarcely noticed the food they were served in the hotel restaurant, he was so deep in thought. She liked him. Not the duke, simply the man. Going over every moment they'd shared and every conversation they'd had, he tried to make sense of.

The duke had responsibilities. He was bound by social rules and etiquette and would never attend to menial tasks. Devon considered this idea more thoroughly. Had she found his ability to light a fire or make a pot of tea appealing? Those were simple chores—a servant's chores—but perhaps the unexpectedness of a duke carrying them out, of him ensuring her comfort in such a basic way, had touched her somehow? Perhaps the lack of fanfare, the simple stripping away of social mores, had allowed her to see something in him others rarely witnessed.

She'd certainly seemed appreciative. More so than when his title had compelled him to take away something important to her, her employment. He popped a piece of something or other into his mouth. Of course she disliked the duke. The duke had demanded she bend to his will, while the man was humble and kind. Which meant in order to win her, he'd have to force the duke into the background and bring the man to the forefront.

The idea struck him at the exact same moment he realized the meat he chewed was not getting any smaller. "This is like eating a shoe," he muttered, staring down at his plate.

"I agree," Rowena told him. "And the vegetables are the soggiest I've ever had. Bland, too, in terms of flavor."

"What is your opinion, Miss Potter?" Devon asked, deliberately forcing her to speak, not only because he valued her thoughts but also for the pleasure of hearing her voice. It was the loveliest he'd ever heard.

"The food does not live up to the standard one might expect from a restaurant this expensive. It is also bound to have a negative effect on the hotel, because even if the rooms are comfortable, no guest will want to eat here more than once."

Devon nodded. "I agree." It did not escape his notice that she blushed or that she hastily averted her gaze the moment their eyes met. "Let us try a few more items from the menu before inspecting the rooms, shall we?"

They did so, only to be increasingly disappointed. "This is awful," Devon said, tossing his napkin aside after swallowing a bit of dry cake. He considered his wineglass and elected to drink some water instead.

"There is certainly room for improvement," Josephine said sympathetically.

Wincing, Devon pushed back his chair and stood. "Let's hope the rooms are better than the food."

Each bedchamber appeared to be presentable at first glance, but Josephine quickly ascertained the bed sheets were not the high quality cotton Devon had asked Mr. Roth to purchase. The price had certainly been high enough, however, as evidenced by the accounting books. After leaving the bedchambers, they'd stopped by the office so she could show them to him. "It appears Mr. Roth is not the man you thought him to be," she said, the hesitancy with which she spoke suggesting she wasn't quite sure of how he'd react to such news.

"Letting him go was the right thing to do. He

treated you abominably and took advantage of me," Devon leafed through other pages in the book. He would have to check all the wines too, because the one he'd had with his meal was not deserving of any cost listed in the account book. "I will call on my solicitor tomorrow and ask him if legal action can be taken. Mr. Roth is about to discover I won't accept thievery."

"Nor should you," Josephine murmured.

Her hand went to his arm in a gentle show of solidarity and comfort. One second and it was gone, returned to her side as she went to speak with his sister. But it had been enough, enough to expand his heart and enough to strengthen his resolve to win her. So he slammed the accounting book shut, determined to focus on a more enjoyable matter.

"I think we're done here," he said. "May I suggest an outing to Hyde Park? The air is crisp but at least the sun is finally shining."

"Oh yes, that sounds like a wonderful idea," Rowena said. She turned toward Josephine with a cheerful smile. "Do you not agree?"

"I cannot recall the last time I visited a park, so yes, by all means, the fresh air and exercise will be most welcome."

It was settled. Devon asked the remaining office clerk to pack up the account books so he could take them with him for further study. He then led the ladies back out to the carriage so they could set off for the park.

Try as she might, Josephine could not resist casting the occasional glance in the duke's direction. He was as handsome as ever, his black hair slightly tousled, his eyes looking inward as if he were lost in deep contemplation. There would be a lot for him to think of too, considering what he'd discovered today with regard to Mr. Roth's treachery. She did not envy the task the duke faced, of having to set everything to right, trying to win back the customers he'd lost, and the potential lawsuit he'd have to endure.

Unable to stop herself, she'd reached for him, hoping to offer some small piece of consolation. But it hadn't been proper, an overstepping of bounds so personal, she'd been forced to snatch her hand away for fear he might see the truth: that she was falling for him in every impossible way. So she tried not to look, and she tried not to think of how happy she was in this moment.

Because it was destined to end.

Eventually, her sister would return, and Snowdon would realize his responsibility toward her had come to a conclusion.

"Miss Potter?"

She flinched, alerted by the deep timbre of the voice now speaking from outside the carriage. Blinking, she realized they must have arrived at the park. The duke peered at her, and his hand reached toward her, ready to help her alight. Drawn by the light in his eyes, her gaze locked with his, narrowing space and time to a fine little point in which only the two of them remained. Catching her breath, she allowed her hand to settle firmly against his palm, allowed herself to revel in the feel of his fingers tightening over hers. And then she climbed out, descending onto the pavement and dreading the moment when he would release her.

He assisted her slowly, so slowly she felt his reluctance to let her go in the unhurried slide of his hand— palm against palm, fingers against fingers, then subtlety followed by nothing. Or perhaps she simply imagined it. Perhaps he wasn't as affected by her as she was by him, and she only saw and felt what she wished to. After all, he was a duke, a powerful man who could have any woman of his choosing. So what would he possibly want with her? Was it not more likely she lived in a fantasy of her own creation, a fantasy built on longing and broken dreams?

They set out along a wide path on which a few riders steered their horses along at a moderate pace and other pedestrians walked. "The snow is so pretty here," she found herself saying. "It looks like frosting on a cake, completely undisturbed by carriage wheels."

"There are the occasional prints from squirrels and birds. Some from children too," Snowdon said. "Like the ones over there. Looks like they're building a snowman."

Rowena chuckled. "Remember when we used to do that? We'd always come back inside with frozen fingers and toes."

"And Cook would have scones with clotted cream and jam waiting for us by the fire." Snowdon's manner of speech conveyed his fondness for the memory. "We'd eat while Mama played the piano and Papa smoked his pipe."

"She's not the best pianist in the world," Rowena said, "but the pleasure she finds in her music has always been palpable. It is a joy to watch her play."

Josephine hadn't known the woman still lived. The duke had made no mention of her before, which she found rather odd, all things considered. "Why didn't she come to Town with you?" she asked. "Surely she does not wish to spend Christmas alone in the country."

Snowdon dropped a look in her direction. "Mama has gone to Scotland for the holidays to visit her sister, who's married to the Laird of Glenmoore."

"She asked me to go with her," Rowena said, "but I chose to remain at Bevelstoke. Whenever our mother and Aunt Rose get together, they're like two young debutants, gossiping and giggling, sharing confidences. Frankly, I find it hard to stomach. And it turns out I made the right decision since I got to meet you instead."

"I am grateful to you for coming to London on such short notice, Rowena," Josephine said. "I realize it isn't much fun this time of year."

"It is hardly less entertaining than Bevelstoke. At least here I have the two of you to keep me company. I must say I have no complaints."

"I'm glad to hear it," Snowdon said as they came up over a small rise below which the Serpentine could be seen in full view. It snaked its way across the snowy landscape, providing skaters with a smooth surface on which to glide. "I've asked the servants to put up some pine and ribbons so the house can be more festive. We'll have a goose on Christmas Eve, with a chocolate and caramel tart for dessert. I hope that agrees with both of you. If not, you're welcome to make alterations."

Josephine liked his agreeability, but since she had no issue with his suggestions, she said, "I think it sounds wonderful. I haven't had goose in years."

"Then you must eat to your heart's content," he told her with sparkling eyes.

She wasn't entirely sure why it pleased him to know she approved of the menu he'd chosen, but it was obvious it did. In fact, there was something softer about him right now, something less serious, as though he was letting himself forget the responsibilities clinging to him at every moment of every day. She'd resented the duty because it made him insist she give up her employment, the strict adherence to protocol preventing her from continuing her work. Even now, after discovering she'd lost her job because of one of his employees, Snowdon refused to let her resume it. Indeed, she ought to be furious with him. More than anything, she ought to resist the ever-present attraction developing between them.

But she couldn't. Because the more she considered the situation as a whole, the more she understood him. And if there was one thing she could say with certainty, it was that understanding him undermined any wish she might have to disapprove of his actions. He was, after all, a duke, a principled gentleman who'd made a promise to a friend. If he broke that promise for her, he would no longer be the man she'd come to admire. So although she disliked the effect his promise had on her life, she appreciated his insistence to honor Priorsbridge's wishes.

CHAPTER FOUR

"Have you ever skated before?" Rowena asked as they approached the edge of the lake.

Glancing out over the smooth expanse, Josephine watched the men and women already out on the ice. "Yes, but it has been a while."

"You will remember how to do it quickly enough," Snowdon said. "I will see about some skates, shall I?"

Josephine watched him walk away with a sure stride. Heavens, he was handsome, even when seen from behind.

"You're staring," Rowena said, nudging her arm.

Josephine blinked. "What?"

"Am I mistaken to think you might be smitten with my brother?"

"Don't be silly. I am no such thing."

Taking a seat on a nearby bench, Rowena waited for Josephine to sit beside her. She then crossed her arms and tilted her chin. "You sound soooo convincing."

Swallowing, Josephine tried to hide her concern.

The last thing she wanted was for the duke to be made aware of her growing affections. It would never lead anywhere, which meant she would risk severe humiliation if he ever found out. So she told his sister more firmly, "Your brother and I have been at odds from the moment we met. To suggest I might be smitten with him is absolutely ridiculous considering how infuriating he can be. In fact, I dare say he's the last man on earth with whom I would ever imagine forming an attachment since—"

"You flatter me, Miss Potter."

"Oh God." Josephine squeezed her eyes shut before opening them again. "He's standing right behind me?" Rowena nodded with mischievous smugness. Josephine cringed. "Why didn't you tell me?"

Her friend actually grinned – devilish girl. "Where would the fun be in that?" And then to make matters worse, she got up from the bench and immediately yelped before sinking back down. "I think I've twisted my ankle."

Josephine frowned. "Really?" She wasn't sure how she might have done so.

"Yes…oh yes…ah…it hurts." Her face twisted into a pained expression. "I am sorry, but I'm afraid you will have to go skating without me."

"Or," Josephine said, convinced Rowena was trying to force her to spend some alone time with her brother, "we could go home, so you can get the rest you need."

"No." One word, spoken by the duke with accurate precision. "My sister can easily rest her ankle here while you and I go skating." Leaning over the bench so his head came close to her ear, he whispered, "That should give you ample opportunity to explain your infuriation with me. Or how I have come to be the last man on earth with whom you would ever consider an attachment."

Heat raced up her spine, and as he rounded the bench and crouched down before her to fasten the skates to her feet, she knew she had to be blushing, not only from embarrassment but also from his touch.

She sucked in a breath, holding it while his fingers worked the leather straps across her boots. One hand steadied her ankle, lingering there so briefly no one would notice the impropriety of it, but long enough for her to feel the careful scrape of his thumb sliding over her stocking. And Lord help her, it did something to her, strange and wonderful things, just as his gaze had done in her parlor. The promise it held, the hint of desire and want, was shamelessly evident in that one touch. It stoked a fire in her core and made her skin tingle in anticipation of more.

Fearing her legs were too weak to carry her weight, she remained where she was while he put on his skates, as well.

She focused on her breaths, deep inhalations to steady her racing heart. And the way she felt in other more intimate places…the curious ache he'd managed to stir with nothing more than the briefest of touches…was horribly distressing. So she sat, quietly listening to Rowena talking about the upcoming Season and how she would love to take Josephine to some balls.

And then the duke was before her once more. "Come," he said. His expression set in serious lines, he offered her his hand.

With eager reluctance, she allowed herself to accept his assistance. She would not dwell on how perfectly her hand fit into his or how lovely the contact felt. Nor would she ponder the way her body clamored for his attention, for more wicked glances and more discreet touches.

Heavens, she was turning into a veritable wanton, the sort of woman a man might lure into a dark corner and ravish. Most troubling of all, she didn't mind the prospect of such a thing happening. Not anymore, and certainly not with him.

"You must forgive me for overhearing you earlier," he began as he led her slowly across the ice. "What you said—"

"Was inexcusably rude. It is I who should be apologizing. The last thing I wish to do is to cause offense, but your sister suggested I might be developing a *tendre* for you, so I said what had to be said in order to dismiss such a notion."

"So you're saying she was wrong to presume such a thing?" His voice was gentle and somewhat curious.

"Of course!"

"Of course?" His hand tightened on hers and he led her around in a wide circle.

"Well, yes." She laughed, hoping to lighten the mood. Instead, she ended up sounding too nervous, so she aimed at leveling her voice instead. "You're you and I'm me. It would be an impossible match. Ridiculous even."

His eyes, all seriousness, met hers. "I do believe

you have offended me again."

Oh dear.

"Forgive me, but surely you must agree. It is a silly idea Rowena has created. I mean, we hardly know each other at all. Certainly not well enough for either of us to consider an attachment of any sort and…" Good God, she had to find a way to stop babbling. "While I appreciate your hospitality and, er, your friendship, I do hope you know I have no designs on you in that way."

He pulled her along with him. A bit of the tension in his face began to ease. "In what way?"

Flattening her mouth, she frowned at him while they skated back toward the opposite side of the lake. "Must you be deliberately obtuse?"

With a shrug, he allowed a quirk of his lips. "I find your discomfort amusing."

She shook her head. "I don't."

"Not now, perhaps, but I dare say you found it enticing earlier."

Her heartbeat quickened. "How do you mean?"

"When I helped you with your skates." He drew her closer, enough for his breath to waft across her cheek when he spoke once more. "Don't think I did not notice how well you responded to my touch or that I was not aware of how perfectly your wants and desires matched mine the other day in your parlor. We shared a moment there, you and I."

"What moment?" Her voice was but a gasp of air. "I have no idea as to—"

"When all that remained between us was need— when you were struck by a deeper awareness—so deep you began to understand what it means to want and be wanted in return. I could see it in every facet of your expression—the secret ache for intimate caresses, the carnal desire brightening your eyes."

She tugged on her arm and he set her free, allowing her to skate on her own before catching up to her again. Her breaths were coming fast and ragged, her fear of where all of this might lead overwhelming her senses.

"Why?" It was all she could think to ask as he came up beside her once more. "Why must you say these things?"

"Because I am tired of pretending there's no sexual attraction between us, Josephine."

Her name, spoken with thorough frustration, punctuated everything she felt. Slowing to a halt, she tried to make sense of what his motive might be for such unabashed honesty. Only one thing came to mind, and it was not in the least bit to her liking. "I will not be your mistress," she said. "I will not allow you to force such a role upon me."

He stared at her, bewildered. "I would never do so."

"And yet you did your best to make me hand in my notice at work and later to make me stay at your home. You have tried to get your way with me since the moment we met, but there is nothing you can say or do to make me lower myself to such a…a…disrespectful position."

"Josephine." He spoke her name as if it meant everything, as if it encompassed all he might say. "Forgive me. I have behaved poorly. What I said was unforgivable. It will not happen again, I assure you. My only intention was to inform you of how I feel and to make you acknowledge you are not as immune to me as you like to pretend."

She'd hurt his pride, that much was clear, but even so, she could not accept his reaction. There was no excuse for it. "I have obviously given you the same impression I gave Mr. Roth," she said, her anger growing with each passing second. "You seem to think I'm the sort of woman who can be lured into bed, either by threatening to discharge me or by offering me a comfortable place to stay."

Snowdon's eyes darkened and his features grew tight. "Don't ever compare me to that miscreant."

Ignoring his warning, she continued. "I should have known you had an ulterior motive when you invited me to visit your home. What man does such a thing unless he has designs on the woman in question?" She shook her head, acknowledging her own stupidity. "I should have seen it. Perhaps I did, and I chose to overlook it, the prospect of company, warmth, and delicious food too tempting to ignore." Turning away before he could answer, she started back toward the embankment.

"Josephine…" He came up beside her, denying her the chance to flee his company with dignity.

She quickened her pace. "I do not want more apologies or excuses. My only wish is to go home."

"But—"

"My house might not be as comfortable as yours, but it is my home—a home I've fought to keep—and at least there I will have whatever remains of my reputation."

"I wish you would stop speaking as though you're a fallen woman when you are anything but."

Skidding to a halt at the edge of the lake, Josephine steadied herself before facing him once again. "That is not what people will say if they see us together. If they discover I have moved into your house."

"As my sister's guest!"

The outrage with which he spoke only clarified their situation. He wanted her close, and while she secretly wanted the same, she did not trust herself to resist him indefinitely. Eventually, their desire would prompt them to do something foolish, and while he had the power to walk away from such indiscretion without any affect to his reputation, she did not.

"I am sorry," was all she could think to say, after which she made her way back to the bench and proceeded to take off her skates.

☙

"What did you tell her?"

Having entered his study seconds earlier, Rowena now stood with her hands on her hips and a disconcerting glower. Devon shifted in his seat, uncomfortable with the idea of where this conversation might lead.

"Who?" he asked, trying to think of how best to answer her question.

His sister marched toward him. "Don't pretend ignorance, Devon. Josephine was furious after the two of you went skating. She is presently preparing to leave our home and refuses to tell me why."

"Suffice it to say we had a disagreement." He still felt rotten about his faux pas. If only there were a way for him to take back everything he'd told her.

"A disagreement?"

Sighing, Devon acknowledged Rowena would not let the matter rest without receiving a reasonable explanation. "I told her I like her."

"And?"

He looked her straight in the eye. "I told her I like her *a lot*."

Rowena frowned as she lowered herself to the chair opposite Devon's. "That doesn't seem like the sort of thing to cause offense."

Since she wasn't getting his subtlety, he told her more directly "It led her to believe I might want to make her my mistress."

"Good heavens!"

He grimaced. "I never did have a flair for tact."

"And you clearly don't have respect for my warnings, either. Did I not tell you to stay on your best behavior? Josephine is a guest in our home, Devon. To proposition her, or whatever it is you did, is utterly disgraceful."

"You sound like Mama right now."

"Only because you've behaved like the worst sort of reprobate."

Wincing, he did what he could to turn the conversation around by saying, "You are the one who ensured I would be alone with her on the ice with that ridiculous lie of yours."

Rowena gave him a chastising glare. "So you could form a closer attachment to her if you wished to do so. It never occurred to me you might muck it up with vulgar insinuations."

Hating himself for what he'd done, Devon stood

and went to pour himself a brandy. "Would you care for some port?"

"No thank you. What I want is for you to fix this."

He blew out a deep breath. "I already tried to apologize."

"And?"

"I think doing so made her angrier."

"Hmm." Devon waited for Rowena to continue speaking while taking a sip of his drink. She eventually said, "That must mean she didn't believe you were being sincere."

"Honestly, I feel terrible about the whole thing. But my pride was wounded when I overheard her telling you I'm the last man on earth with whom she would ever consider an attachment. I wanted to prove her wrong." And in doing so, he'd betrayed the gentlemanly code of conduct with which he'd been raised. "Mama would be horrified if she found out. Promise me you'll keep this between the two of us?"

"Of course." Rowena leaned back in her seat with a sigh and contemplated Devon. "You need to figure out what Josephine wants, and I don't mean flowers or a trip to the opera, because that is too easy. Any man with a moderate income can give her those things."

"I am well aware, Rowena." As if he hadn't drawn the same conclusion days earlier.

"Then...?"

"I need to leave for a few days." It was the first thing that came to mind.

Rowena sat up straight. "What?"

"If I go to the hotel, you'll be able to convince

her to stay. She will feel more comfortable doing so—obliged, even, since you'll be alone otherwise—while I'll have the distance required to think more clearly on how to proceed."

"But—"

"I'm right about this," he said, convinced he was doing what was best for Josephine and any potential future he might have with her. "Does absence not make the heart grow fonder?"

"Maybe?"

"Then it is settled. You may inform her of the change in plan." In the meantime, he would set his mind to romancing the woman from a distance, since staying close to her was clearly not helping.

☾

Josephine accepted the letter the butler brought her and carefully sliced it open. It had been three days since the duke had gone away and she'd agreed to stay on at Snowdon House. Three days without having to argue with him.

She ought to be relieved. She ought to be glad it was only her and Rowena now, without him there to cause her unease. She ought not to miss him. Especially since she and Rowena had been occupied with outings. They had gone to visit one of Rowena's friends, the Countess of Riply, who'd elected to stay in London with her husband for the winter. The couple was in the process of setting up a charitable foundation for orphans and hoped to finish by March, so they would be ready to encourage donations as soon as the rest of the *ton* returned.

After this visit, Rowena had taken Josephine to the British Museum, where they had spent hours strolling between magnificent marble statues and admiring stunning paintings. Her mind should have been occupied—enough for her to stop dreaming of Snowdon.

And yet, in spite of her better judgment, she could not steer her contemplations away from him. She missed his handsome face, his reluctant smiles, and the warmth with which he watched her. She missed their conversations, even if they didn't always agree. And she missed the way she felt whenever he was near: appreciated, desired, beautiful.

So she read the letter, savoring every second of the experience, from the unfolding of the paper to her perusal of the elegant script.

My dearest Josephine,
I hope this letter finds you happy and in good health.

In good health yes, but happy? Not really.

Please know you are in my thoughts, every second of every day. If there were a way for me to go back – to reverse the hands of time – and avoid offending you as grievously as I did, I would do so. But I cannot, which leaves me with only one hope: to one day earn your forgiveness.
Some might think it unreasonable for me to be so enamored with you after only a brief acquaintance.

Josephine blinked. He was enamored?

But the truth is, I long to hear your laughter again and to see you blush when I subject you to my attention. I even miss your set downs, the fire in your eyes when you are angry. Most of all, however, I wish I had the opportunity to get to know you better and perhaps then realize the dream steadily building within my heart since the moment we met.

Until I see you again, I remain affectionately yours,
Devon

Josephine's heart fluttered in response to his given name, boldly penned across the bottom. *The dream steadily building within my heart.* It sounded so utterly romantic, she feared she might melt right there on the sofa. But what did it mean? To what dream was he referring? She dared not allow herself to hope, but he had written that he remained affectionately hers. Who would do such a thing unless there was an emotional investment surpassing the bounds of friendship?

Puzzled, she refolded the letter and wondered what the duke might be playing at. Which was how Rowena found her several minutes later when she entered the room. "I've a note from my brother," she said as she went to the bell pull and rang for a maid. "He asked if we would join him for dinner tomorrow evening at the hotel."

"He made no mention of it in the letter he sent me."

Rowena's gaze shifted to the neatly folded paper in Josephine's lap. Her eyebrows went up. "He wrote you?"

"I suppose it is rather surprising."

Something curious lit behind Rowena's eyes.

"How many lines?"

Confused, Josephine frowned. "What?"

"How many lines?" Rowena repeated.

"Why do you ask?"

"Because my brother is famous for dispatching one sentence notes. Here is what I received, in case you doubt me." She handed Josephine a piece of paper with one short sentence: *Dinner at the Park View tomorrow evening? Devon.* "What he will *not* do is write a letter with words filling an entire page. So if you received one, Josephine, it has to be because he cares for you a great deal."

She'd suspected it from his phrasing alone, but it had never occurred to her that receiving a letter from the duke was such a rare thing, she might be the only woman in the world to ever have done so. The thought of it made her heart swell and her entire body warm with appreciation. Because it wasn't just a question of him caring for her. It was a question of him showing her the extent to which he did so. And while she'd been hurt by the prospect of him wanting only seduction, she was starting to realize his physical need might be intrinsically tied to his growing fondness for her as a person. And if that were the case…

"May we accept the invitation?"

"By all means." A maid arrived, and Rowena asked for some tea to be brought up, before addressing Josephine once more. "But I was of the impression you did not wish to share Devon's company."

"I didn't."

"Past tense. How fascinating."

Josephine raised her eyes to the ceiling and

sighed. "Very well, I will admit I might have changed my mind."

Rowena snorted and came to join her on the sofa. "That must have been quite the letter he wrote."

It was, written by quite the man, a man whom Josephine now looked forward to seeing with great anticipation. If only to let him know she felt exactly the same way as he.

CHAPTER FIVE

WHEN JOSEPHINE AND ROWENA ARRIVED at the hotel the following evening, they found Devon waiting for them in the foyer. "Ladies," he said, his eyes settling first on Rowena before sliding across to Josephine, where his gaze lingered. "You look lovelier than when I last saw you."

"You don't look so bad yourself, Duke," Josephine teased.

Truth was, he looked incredible, dressed in all black evening attire, his hair neatly combed, save for a few unruly strands insisting on falling across his brow.

The edge of his mouth drew up in that roguish smile she'd come to adore. "I made a particular effort this evening." With a wink, he made her stomach flip over, then asked, "Are you ready to try the cuisine here again?"

Rowena visibly shuddered. "Do we dare?"

Devon laughed more openly than Josephine had ever seen him do before. He seemed so relaxed tonight, so at ease, and so undeniably comfortable. It certainly added to his attractiveness and made her want to be nearer to him so she could bask in his positive energy.

"I think you will be pleased with the way things have changed around here since your last visit." He guided them through to the dining room where other guests were already enjoying their meals.

Josephine stared as she took in the scene. "It's almost full!" She followed him over to a vacant table and waited for him to pull out her chair while a waiter helped Rowena into her seat. "How on earth did you manage it?"

"All it took was a new chef, some proper ingredients, and an article placed in the Mayfair Chronicle yesterday morning."

"I hardly know what to say. The speed with which you turned this around is so utterly impressive. " Josephine shook her head, befuddled by his ability to make such a drastic improvement in so little time.

"Just wait until you try the food," he said. "I do believe it may be the best you've ever had."

"Now you're boasting," Rowena muttered, following the comment with a sip of the wine a waiter had poured. "Although if the food is as good as this, you may be right."

"I doubt it will be better than what your cook is capable of producing," Josephine said. "I find her meals extraordinarily tasty."

And yet the smoked trout with seafood mousse, lemon and dill, followed by oxtail stew served on a bed of sautéed root vegetables, was so divine, Josephine feared she might overeat. For dessert they had ice cream served in the peel of an orange and garnished with chocolate shavings and mint leaves.

"You were right," she confessed, when she set her spoon aside. "This is the best food I have ever had."

"And it is all thanks to you," Snowdon said, sipping his Muscat. "Had you not made me aware of the issues the hotel was having, it could very well have failed before I had a chance to save it."

"Thank you, but I'm sure you would have realized what was wrong with the business eventually. Especially once you discovered dismissing people is not going to help, which would have become clear within a few weeks."

Devon studied her a moment, then grinned. "Even when I'm trying to compliment you, you find a way to argue."

Josephine frowned. "I wasn't—"

"There you go again," Rowena said.

Eyeing the siblings, Josephine flattened her mouth and sat back in her seat. "You're right," she acquiesced, "and I'm sorry. I am not very good at being flattered."

"As long as you recognize the errors of your ways," Devon said, a twinkle in his eyes, "there's hope for you yet, Miss Potter."

☾

Seeing Josephine dressed in a deep blue evening gown his sister had no doubt loaned her had almost made Devon's heart stop beating. She was simply stunning with her blonde hair piled high in an intricate coiffure, a few long strands curling against her cheeks. The vision of her encased in fine silk, her bodice so snug against her breasts he now assessed them to be more perfectly shaped than he'd ever imagined, had almost undone him. But he'd held himself in check by some miraculous force of will, hiding the overwhelming effect she had on him with easy banter and laughter.

He'd avoided moving too close to her, afraid her scent might prompt him to do something stupid and ruin the progress he hoped he was making. He knew his climb toward mercy was steep, but he was committed to making the effort if the prize to be won in the end was her heart.

So he chatted and smiled, allowing the occasional glance of appreciation to settle upon her more fully while banking the lust and the need that were bound to scare her away. And when he walked her and his sister out to their carriage later, he politely bid them good night before handing them up into the conveyance. The door closed and the driver whipped the reins, directing the horses toward the end of the street.

Look at me.

Turn around and look at me.

A second passed, then another. The carriage moved onward, almost turning the corner when she finally did what Devon wished. And it took every bit of restraint he possessed not to jump and shout with joy.

She cared. More than a little. Which was without a doubt a victory to be savored, one of far greater importance than her appreciation for the hotel cuisine.

The only question now was how to proceed

from here. He puzzled over the problem as he returned inside and made his way upstairs to his room. Perhaps a dance. Although he'd never cared much for dancing, he knew he'd enjoy it with her. And although no balls were being hosted in London this time of year, there were a few assembly halls on the outskirts of the city where they might be able to enjoy a festive evening. So he penned a note to his sister. *Let us go dancing*, it read. *I will pick you up tomorrow at seven.*

Satisfied, he settled in for a good night's rest and sent his missive out in the morning. His sister wrote she and Josephine would be pleased to accompany him to the assembly hall the following evening. So with this in mind, Devon happily busied himself with hotel improvements, while looking forward to seeing Josephine again. But when he woke the next day, it was to discover a disagreeable piece of gossip making the headline.

Damn!

He crumpled the newspaper between his hands and tossed it aside. This was exactly what Josephine had been afraid of, to have people wonder about their connection. Thankfully, her friendship with his sister had prevented any mention of the word mistress, but implications had been made. It was suggested there was more between him and Miss Potter than met the eye, and everyone knew what *that* meant.

Christ!

He had to act quickly to snuff out the fire before it could spread. Which meant only one option remained if he was to save her reputation at this point, and he bloody well hoped she agreed.

So when he arrived at his house in the evening, intent on escorting her and his sister out, he met Josephine in the parlor with nerves on edge, his entire body trembling with the prospect of her refusal. It shouldn't have been this hasty. He'd wanted more time. But there was nothing like the threat of scandal to demand action be taken, which was why he did his best to ignore the rapid beat of his heart as he took a step toward her.

With a swift glance directed at his sister, he got her to leave the room before giving all his attention to the woman he meant to marry. "Have you seen today's newspaper, Josephine?"

She shook her head, eyes widening with apprehension. "No."

His butler had no doubt been considerate enough to ensure it went missing, for which Devon was immensely grateful. "It is suggested you and I are having an affair." He would not repeat the title of the article which had read, *Snowdon's Seductive Spinster.*

Gasping, Josephine covered her mouth with her gloved hand. "But we're not," she murmured.

He couldn't ignore the terrified look in her eyes. It tore at his soul and filled him with guilt. "This is my fault. I shouldn't have stayed in this house while you were here, and I shouldn't have said what I did when we were out on the lake." She blushed, no doubt recalling his words. "I am convinced a journalist saw us arguing and drew his own conclusions. Most of what the gossip columnists say is rubbish. They can turn enemies into lovers simply by questioning the implication of certain things."

She allowed her hand to fall away. "Is that how you see us? As enemies?"

"No. Of course not. I was merely making a point. Because when it comes to you…" He reached for her hand, relief sweeping through him when she did not pull away. "I never intended for it to be like this, rushed by circumstance. My plan was to court you much longer, a month or two at the very least since this is what I believe you deserve. "

"Court me?"

"Has it not occurred to you that this is what I've been trying to do these past four days?"

"No. I mean, maybe. Your letter was rather telling, I suppose, but I never dared hope for more than friendship from you. Not after I made it clear that being your mistress was not going to happen."

Raising his hand to her cheek, he smoothed it over her skin. "I told you I would never ask you to do such a thing. The only position I would ever want you to fill is that of my wife and duchess. Marry me, Josephine, fill my life with challenge and excitement and make me the happiest man there is."

She hesitated, and in the following seconds, he knew what he offered wasn't enough. She might take it all the same, but it would not satisfy the cravings of her heart, so he took a step closer and shared the contents of his own. "I have fallen in love with you, with your stubbornness and pride, with your kindness and your undeniable sense of morality. We started out on uneven footing, I will grant you that, and I have cost you something you held dear, I will accept that too. But as my wife and joint owner of the Park View Hotel, you will be able to do the accounts to your heart's content, if that is what you wish."

Staring up at him, her eyes began to shimmer. "Truly?"

"You won't be an employee, and that makes all the difference."

"But…" She still wasn't saying yes. "I would surrender my independence to you."

He'd known she would struggle with such a prospect. After all, she'd been so determined to hold on to what was hers—to her employment, to the house she struggled to keep, to her dignity. "We will draw up a satisfactory contract before we say our vows, one which gives you as much freedom as you may wish."

"It will be unprecedented."

He nodded, moving closer still, so close he could smell the fragrance of roses wafting off her skin. "Yes, but the thing of it is, all I want is you, Josephine. I have no desire to rule your life or force my will upon you. Though I would like to know your answer."

"My answer is yes, Devon. It has always been yes."

"Even when we fought?"

"Even then."

Which was all he needed to hear before dipping his head and claiming her lips with his. The tiniest sound escaped her, part sigh, part whimper, so thrillingly tempting in the innocence it conveyed. Gently, as if uncertain, she wound her arms around his neck and leaned into his embrace. His palm settled against her back, pressing her close, so close their chests touched, so close he could feel her heart beating in time with his.

"Josephine." He leaned his forehead against hers, allowing their breaths to mingle across the short distance.

"Devon."

His name, a whisper of sweetness upon her lips, filled him with hope for the future. Miraculously, she would be his, and nothing in the world had ever felt more right or more glorious.

☾

Gazing up into Devon's dark eyes, Josephine trembled with love and emotion. He was her fiancé now, her soon-to-be husband. "Is this really happening?" It seemed like a dream. A marvelously wonderful dream from which she never wanted to wake.

"Yes." He kissed her again with languorous affection. "Now you've agreed to marry me, I'm never letting you go."

As if to ensure she knew he was serious, he tightened his hold and kissed her harder—until she was breathless—until she could think of nothing but him and what spending the rest of their lives together would be like. An incredible journey, she imagined. One she looked forward to with increasing excitement bubbling through her veins.

"Can we tell your sister now?"

"I hoped to have a few more minutes alone with you," he murmured against her lips.

And since she could not complain about his reasoning, she tilted her head back and welcomed more heady kisses. They weakened her knees, imbuing her with delicious pleasure and the all-encompassing knowledge of being loved.

"We probably should inform my sister now," Devon said a while later, his breaths coming just as rapidly as hers. "Before I lose my finely held control and do something improper." He drew back, eyes gleaming with deep emotion entwined with desire. "Besides, it is pretty rude of us to keep her waiting in the hallway when we're supposed to be heading out to the assembly hall."

Josephine gasped. "I quite forgot." Which rewarded her with a roguish grin from Devon. "Oh dear. How utterly thoughtless of us." She drew out of his embrace, just enough to regain some measure of her composure. "We should go and join her immediately."

"I agree." His reluctance showed in the slowness with which he stepped away from her and moved toward the door. There he paused a second, his eyes locked with Josephine's as he quietly said, "This moment right here is, without a doubt, the happiest of my life."

"Mine too."

They shared a smile before he opened the door and called for his sister to join them.

☾

The assembly hall was brightly lit by hundreds of candles, the music played by three violinists a cheerful collection of notes to match the good moods of those who'd come to enjoy an evening out. Resting their feet by one of the windows while Devon spoke to a gentleman friend some short distance away, Josephine and Rowena watched the country dance underway.

"Have I told you how pleased I am with your engagement to my brother?" Rowena asked.

Josephine smiled. "I believe you said it immediately after we told you, then twice on the way here, and three times since."

"I've always wanted a sister, and now I shall finally have one."

"Not only one but three if you count Eve and Louise."

"Oh yes!" Rowena's eager eyes met Josephine's. "We must write Lady Channing and ask her to let Louise come down for the wedding."

"Do you suppose she'll allow it?"

"I cannot imagine her denying a duke. Don't forget my brother is one of the most powerful men in England."

It was so easy to forget, secluded as they'd been from the rest of society this past week. But that would change. Already, she'd been given a taste of how it would be as whispers had swept through the assembly hall upon their arrival. Devon was not the sort of man who could go out in public without getting noticed. His attention was sought from men and women alike, and once it became known he would marry, the news of it would likely sweep through England like a blazing fire. Especially when everyone discovered the identity of the woman whom he intended to take to wife.

Fleetingly, Josephine wondered if he would ever

regret the choice he'd made. After all, he could have any lady he wished for. Most would happily walk barefoot through burning coals for a chance to wed him. And yet he'd picked her, a woman who would bring scandal to his name. It was an unwelcome thought, albeit a realistic one. It made Josephine wonder if she'd made a mistake by accepting his proposal. She'd been so overwhelmed by happiness, she'd ignored the implications of the match.

A knot began to form in her chest. It tightened around her heart, squeezing it until she grew short of breath. And then he was coming toward her, parting the crowd with his certain stride until he remained but an arm's length away. "Forgive me for staying away from your side so long," he murmured. "Will you do me the honor of partnering me for the next dance?"

Josephine hesitated one second longer than what was expected, long enough for him to raise a questioning eyebrow. She excused herself to Rowena, while placing her hand in Devon's and letting him lead her onto the dance floor. She said nothing as the music started to play a cotillion, her mind in turmoil over the magnitude of the path they'd embarked on that evening. Perhaps it was selfish of her to accept his proposal. If she truly loved him, should she not encourage him to make a better choice for himself?

"Are you all right?"

The question was spoken close to her ear, forcing her away from her troubling thoughts. Swallowing, she allowed herself to meet his inquisitive gaze while he guided her through the dance steps.

She did not want to ruin their evening, nor did she wish to dismiss her concerns with a lie. "Are you sure you wish to marry me, Devon?" Her voice was low, so low only he would hear.

Rather than answer, he posed a question of his own. "Where is this coming from?"

"I only want to be sure you've considered the implications."

"You mean how your father turning into a drunk and leaving you and your sisters impoverished will affect my reputation by association?"

As direct as the words were, she knew they were not unkindly meant. "People talk."

"They always do."

"But—"

"I have no second thoughts or regrets, Josephine." He turned her about, his hand cupping her elbow to send a spark of heat shooting straight up her arm. Leaning in, he added, "But perhaps you do?"

Her head swung sideways, forcing her gaze to collide with his. "No. I simply want to ensure your happiness."

"And so you shall, as long as you don't break off our engagement with some foolhardy attempt at saving me from critical gossip and social shunning." They moved between two other couples, stepping apart before coming together once more. "My title will always make me a subject of conversation, regardless of whom I marry. There will invariably be those who wish to discuss the minutest details of my life, right down to what I was seen eating at a particular luncheon or how I chose to order a jacket from a different tailor than usual."

"Surely you exaggerate."

"I wish I did, but last season, for instance, a piece was published regarding my preference for Chaucer rather than Shakespeare. Truth is, I don't care for either, but someone must have seen me purchase a copy of *The Canterbury Tales* without stopping to wonder if it was for me or for someone else." He shook his head, his expression portraying severe aggravation. "The book was a gift for my mother."

"Oh, dear."

"As for my reputation, you underestimate the power I wield if you think it is going to suffer. And even if it were likely to do so, I would gladly accept such an outcome in exchange for a life spent with you."

His words went straight to her heart. And yet… "But what of your sister? Will our match not affect her chance of marrying well?"

"I doubt it. Priorsbridge has had his eye on her for years, and he is not the sort of man to change his mind based on whom *I* choose to marry." The dance drew to an end, so he bowed while she curtseyed before leaving the dance floor together. Once they'd gone a few paces, he tugged on her arm and drew her into a private alcove. "Your experience has made you cynical. That much is clear. What I ask, however, above all else, is for you to give us the credit we both deserve. Because if you love me as much as I love you, we'll brave whatever obstacles come our way."

"Of course I love you, Devon. I love you so much it hurts."

His hand rose to tuck a loose strand of her hair behind her ear. "Then you should also know how unacceptable it would be for us to live our lives apart."

He was right. To do so would destroy her. "I only want to ensure you're making the best decision for yourself and your family."

"I am making the best decision for *us*, Josephine, and from this day forward, I will continue to do so, which is why we ought to discuss our wedding. It is important your sisters attend, so we will have to put off the service until they are both able to do so."

"Are you sure? It might take more than a month for Louise to get away from Whitehaven."

He looked her squarely in the eye with such serious resolve, she could feel her heart quicken with nervous anticipation. "These past few years you have nursed your mother in sickness, cared for your ailing father, struggled to hold on to your home while setting aside what little you could for Eve's future. Family matters to you. You've proven this with every sacrifice you've made."

"I only did what was necessary."

"The point being, your sisters matter to you more than anyone else in the world, more than me even, I suspect."

"Devon—"

"It would be odd if they didn't, considering you've been together with them your entire life while you've only known me a week. I might be the man you want to marry—the man fortunate enough to have won your heart—but the connection you share with your sisters is profound, built on years of shared experiences. So while I do hope to be of greater importance to you one day, I would be a fool not to recognize how much their presence at our wedding would mean to you."

"Oh, Devon." She could feel moisture forming at the corners of her eyes, pooling against her lashes in response to his insightful kindness. "Marrying you will be the greatest honor."

"Then your concerns are dispelled, and we are once again in agreement?"

Nodding, she said the only thing she could say, one word spoken with deep conviction. "Yes."

His expression eased, banishing all severity on a long exhalation of breath. "You cannot imagine how relieved I am to hear it." And with that, he caught her hand in his and raised it to his lips, kissing her knuckles in a gesture of intimate affection. It weakened her knees and quickened her pulse while making her think of only one thing. "You must write Lady Channing tomorrow. The sooner Louise arrives, the better."

He answered her with gleaming eyes and a wide grin. "My dear, I could not agree with you more."

Chapter Six

Snowdon House, five weeks later.

"I still cannot fathom that we are all married," Josephine said as she glanced at each of her sisters in turn. They were seated at the dining room table, enjoying the wedding cake she and Devon had cut a few minutes earlier. Her mother-in-law, the dowager duchess of Snowdon, was also in attendance, along with Rowena and Priorsbridge. "It certainly wasn't what I expected might happen when the two of you set off for Whitehaven and Bournemouth."

"Apparently a lengthy carriage ride can alter one's course in the best way possible," Louise said, a secretive smile directed at her husband, Lord Alistair.

"So can a snowstorm," Eve murmured, exchanging a heated glance with her husband, the Earl of Ravenworth.

Josephine found herself blushing profusely when Devon leaned closer and whispered next to her ear, "Apparently staying in Town can be quite exciting too." He addressed Lord Alistair. "I hear you will be investing in Eastern European wines?"

"Yes." Lord Alistair reached for Louise's hand and pressed a kiss to her knuckles. "My wife discovered the opportunity. It will compliment my investment in The Ace."

"The new club on Oxford Street?" Ravenworth asked.

Lord Alistair nodded. "Yes. I believe it will be a great success since its doors will be open to men and women alike."

"Oh!" Eve clapped her hands together. "How exciting. Can we apply for membership there?"

"I don't see why not," Ravenworth murmured. "With my reputation fully restored, I find myself eager to venture out into society again. Especially if it means showing off my lovely new bride."

"You have all made excellent matches for yourselves," the dowager duchess observed. As apprehensive as Josephine had been about meeting her future mother-in-law, she'd taken an instant liking to the older woman, whose frankness was quite on par with her own. "It is a pity you were denied the Seasons you should have had, though it all turned out well in the end. Your triumphs are certainly exemplary, my dears, and with your husbands' support, I've no doubt you will be welcomed back into Society quicker than you can imagine."

While Josephine had initially had her doubts, she'd begun to believe this might be true. Especially after seeing how many people had filled the church that morning, not only to gawk at her as she'd feared but to wish her and the duke a long and happy union filled with good health and prosperity.

"I am already looking forward to our first ball together in the spring," she said, catching a flicker of adoration from her husband's steady regard. He'd made the suggestion earlier in the week, claiming such an event would be the perfect way to earn her favor amidst the aristocracy.

"Please let me know if you need help planning it," the dowager duchess said. "I would be more than happy to do so."

"As would I," Rowena said. "Now that I've finished my matchmaking efforts and helped you with your wedding arrangements, I find myself in need of a new project."

Josephine set down her spoon after taking a bite of cake. "Matchmaking efforts?"

"Had it not been for my pretend sprained ankle, I doubt the two of you would have gotten engaged as quickly as you did."

"Trust me," Devon murmured. "We would have managed." For Josephine's ears alone, he whispered, "Though I dare say our subsequent argument did inspire a great deal of passion."

In spite of the heat he stirred in the pit of her belly, Josephine turned to face him with a frown. "Really?"

His eyes darkened, the edge of his mouth lifting in the wickedest smile she'd ever seen. "Did I not mention the effect your temper has on me?"

Her heart thudded against her chest. She cast a hasty glance at her guests to ensure none of them were paying attention to their exchange. Satisfied they were talking among themselves, she shook her head. "No."

"Well, suffice it to say, the incident might have played out differently than it did had we been alone behind closed doors." The casual ease with which he reached for his wine and took a sip belied the sizzling timbre infusing his voice. "I'm glad I managed to show some restraint, however. It will make our wedding night so much more special."

Unable to speak on account of the flustered state she was now in, Josephine did her best to focus on what her guests were discussing in the hope she would not reveal how much her husband's scandalous words affected her. The desire he stirred in her was intense, so much so she could hardly wait for the two of them to be alone in the suite they'd be occupying at the Park View for the next week. She began tapping her foot, as if doing so would move the meal along at a faster rate.

And then it was finally over, and their family and friends were wishing them well as they climbed back into their carriage and started making their way toward the hotel. A comfortable silence settled, during which Josephine reflected on all the events that had taken place in the previous month and a half. It really was incredible. She was thrilled on behalf of her sisters and for herself, as well. Her hand clutched Devon's, holding on to his comforting strength.

It wasn't until they were truly alone, standing in the large bedchamber they would be sharing and with the door closed and locked to the outside world, the magnitude of what would soon transpire began to sink in.

"I don't know what to do," she said.

The warmth of his smile soothed her nerves.

"You have nothing to worry about." He shrugged out of his jacket and started unknotting his cravat. Taking a seat in a nearby chair, he removed his shoes and socks and told her to take off her slippers. He then rolled up his sleeves and came toward her, crossing the distance with a careful tread. "Remember the kisses we've shared until now?"

There had been several in the weeks following his proposal, whenever they'd managed to escape his mother and sister. "Yes."

He placed his hand against her cheek, infusing her with his warmth. "It came naturally to you, did it not?"

She could only nod this time, her words stolen from her by the force of his nearness when he stepped closer still.

"This will be no different. All you have to do is give yourself up to passion."

Her eyes met his, the intensity of his gaze reminding her how much she wanted this man in the most elemental way possible. Surrendering to this awareness, she allowed herself to be bold, to lift her hand and run her fingertips down the side of his neck. Curiously, she watched his tendons there work, listened to his shuddering breath as her thumb smoothed over his collarbone.

"Josephine." Her name hissed past his clenched teeth.

"Hmm?"

She tugged at his shirt, and he caught her wrist. A pause followed—one long hesitant moment in which her anticipation grew—and then his mouth captured hers, kissing her feverishly and dragging her to him until their bodies were molded together in one singular form. His hands slid up her back, his fingers working the buttons of her gown and then the ties of her stays until both were eased away from her body, leaving her only in her chemise.

And since she had no intention of being the only one left in a state of complete dishabille, she tugged Devon's shirt free from his trousers and pulled it up over his head. The garment sailed through the air in a flurry of white, banished from Josephine's mind. All she could do at present was admire her husband's stunning physique. Stilling, he allowed her perusal. Nor did he move to stop her when she hesitantly set her palm to his abdomen, marveling at the rows of muscle and how they flexed in response to her touch. Unable to resist, she leaned in and pressed a reverent kiss to his chest.

But when she ran her hands toward the waistband of his trousers and dipped her fingers inside, he moved with incredible speed, clasping at her chemise and drawing it over her head before she could manage a breath. She was suddenly in his arms, her mouth subject to his exploration as he carried her to the bed. Gently, he laid her on the mattress, sinking down with her while deepening the kiss in a sensual exploration of taste and touch.

His hands forged sensuous paths along the length of her body, sliding across the curve of her waist and trailing over the length of her thighs. When she reached for his waistband again, he made no attempt to stop her, helping her instead in her effort to divest him of his remaining clothing.

And then they were both perfectly naked, their bodies touching in all the right places, heightening her need until she cried out with indescribable pleasure. "Devon!"

He planted a series of kisses upon her neck, sparking a deeper desire – an unfamiliar yearning for increased contact. "I love you," he whispered against her ear as he joined his body with hers. "You're everything to me—" He moved in closer, commencing an age-old rhythm of uninhibited craving. "My entire world."

Amazed by every sensation he wrung from her body, Josephine stared up into his hooded gaze. "I love you too. With all that I am." Nothing had ever felt truer than this, no experience more perfect and no future brighter. He was what she'd been looking for all of her life—the missing part of her soul.

EPILOGUE

SEATED IN THE PEW BESIDE her husband, Josephine clasped his hand as they watched Priorsbridge place a ring upon Rowena's finger. "With this ring, I thee wed; with my body, I thee worship; and with all my worldly goods, I thee endow: In the Name of the Father, and of the Son, and of the Holy Ghost. Amen."

The priest led the congregation in prayer afterward and added his blessing. Psalms were sung and a sermon read before everyone rose to follow the newly wedded couple out into the brilliant sunshine.

"Can you imagine, your sister will have a niece or nephew waiting for her when she returns from her wedding trip," Josephine said as she placed her hand upon her belly.

Devon smiled at her with complete adoration. "I can hardly wait."

"Neither can I." She glanced across at where her sisters stood with their husbands. Both looked equally pregnant. "It will be fun watching all of our children grow up together."

"We will take them fishing in the summer and

build snowmen with them in the winter."

They waved as Rowena and Priorsbridge's landau left, then Josephine linked her arm with Devon's and allowed him to escort her toward their own carriage. "We will meet you at Snowdon House," she told her sisters, who were presently being helped up into their own conveyances by their husbands.

"Never in a million years would I have imagined my life would change so much and so quickly when Priorsbridge asked me come to London and check on you," Devon said when the two of them set off for home.

Josephine smiled. "No regrets, I hope?"

"None at all. Quite the contrary." Reaching around her, he pulled her close for a loving kiss. "All is as it should be," he murmured. "Perfect in every way."

ACKNOWLEDGMENTS

I would like to thank the Killion Group for their incredible help with the cover art and edits. And to my wonderful beta-readers, Carol Bisig and Barbara Rogers, thank you for your insight and advice. You made this story shine!

ABOUT THE AUTHOR

Born in Denmark, Sophie has spent her youth traveling with her parents to wonderful places around the world. She's lived in five different countries, on three different continents, has studied design in Paris and New York, and has a bachelor's degree from Parson's School of design. But most impressive of all - she's been married to the same man three times, in three different countries and in three different dresses. While living in Africa, Sophie turned to her lifelong passion - writing. When she's not busy dreaming up her next romance novel, Sophie enjoys spending time with her family, swimming, cooking, gardening, watching romantic comedies and, of course, reading. She currently lives on the East Coast.

You can contact her through her website at www.sophiebarnes.com

Or stay in touch with her on Facebook, Twitter, Goodreads, Pinterest, Instagram.

For newrelease updates, please follow her on Amazon and Bookbub.

And please consider leaving a review for this book.

Every review is greatly appreciated!